Praise for the nove

"Yates brings her signature heat and vivid western details to another appealing story in the excellent Gold Valley series…. Fans of Kate Pearce should enjoy this."
—*Booklist* on *Rodeo Christmas at Evergreen Ranch*

"Yates's outstanding eighth Gold Valley contemporary… will delight newcomers and fans alike…. This charming and very sensual contemporary is a must for fans of passion."
—*Publishers Weekly* on *Cowboy Christmas Redemption* (starred review)

"Fast-paced and intensely emotional…. This is one of the most heartfelt installments in this series, and Yates's fans will love it."
—*Publishers Weekly* on *Cowboy to the Core* (starred review)

"Multidimensional and genuine characters are the highlight of this alluring novel, and sensual love scenes complete it. Yates's fans…will savor this delectable story."
—*Publishers Weekly* on *Unbroken Cowboy* (starred review)

"Yates' new Gold Valley series begins with a sassy, romantic and sexy story about two characters whose chemistry is off the charts."
—*RT Book Reviews* on *Smooth-Talking Cowboy* (Top Pick)

Also by Maisey Yates

Secrets from a Happy Marriage
Confessions from the Quilting Circle
The Lost and Found Girl

Four Corners Ranch

Unbridled Cowboy
Merry Christmas Cowboy
Cowboy Wild

Gold Valley

Smooth-Talking Cowboy
Untamed Cowboy
Good Time Cowboy
A Tall, Dark Cowboy Christmas
Unbroken Cowboy
Cowboy to the Core
Lone Wolf Cowboy
Cowboy Christmas Redemption
The Bad Boy of Redemption Ranch
The Hero of Hope Springs
The Last Christmas Cowboy
The Heartbreaker of Echo Pass
Rodeo Christmas at Evergreen Ranch
The True Cowboy of Sunset Ridge

For more books by Maisey Yates,
visit www.maiseyyates.com.

MAISEY YATES

The Rough Rider

CANARY STREET PRESS

CANARY
STREET
PRESS™

Recycling programs
for this product may
not exist in your area.

ISBN-13: 978-1-335-60098-1

The Rough Rider

Copyright © 2023 by Maisey Yates

For questions and comments about the quality of this book, please contact us at CustomerService@Harlequin.com.

Canary Street Press
22 Adelaide St. West, 41st Floor
Toronto, Ontario M5H 4E3, Canada
CanaryStPress.com

Printed in Lithuania

MIX
Paper | Supporting
responsible forestry
FSC® C021394

To the heroes, in fiction and real life,
who show up when we need them the most.

The Rough Rider

CHAPTER ONE

ALAINA SULLIVAN ALWAYS landed on her feet.

It was the thing she was most proud of. Her ability to pivot when things went wrong. Dad cheats and abandons the family and ranch? Pivot. Learn new skills and work the land as best she could, until Fia had decided renting the ranch land out was more profitable for them. Mom leaves, no problem. Lean in harder to whatever her sisters were doing.

But the reality was, she didn't want to garden. That had been Fia's solution to keeping Sullivan's Point open. Gardening and farming. Alaina was a *rancher*. And that was what she wanted. Fia had plans, and when Fia had plans…well, no one could deviate from them. She had a prescribed place she wanted everyone in and it came from a very good place.

When Alaina was twelve, her dad left. And Fia had held the broken pieces of their family together. When Alaina, the baby of the family, had turned eighteen their mom had moved away too, and Fia had clung tighter to the remnant of all they were, and with the force of her love she'd kept them going.

It made it hard for Alaina to say what she wanted, because she didn't want to step on her sister's heart.

And the farm and garden stuff was totally her sister's heart. But Alaina hadn't gotten mad about it; she'd just started planning.

It had gone hand in hand with her plan to grow up, get some experience and stop being treated like a kid.

But that ill-conceived plan had landed her where she was now. In this situation where she couldn't figure out how to pivot at all.

This was life-changing *bad*. Two-pink-lines *bad*.

The-jackass-ran-off *bad*.

The jackass she had convinced herself she had feelings for because…

And this was the problem with her feelings. With the way she was always trying to rush in and fix everything *right this second*. Because she hated being uncomfortable. Because she hated being sad.

Because she hated living in a world where she couldn't control the things happening around her and the minute something happened that…the minute something hurt she did everything she possibly could to make that go away.

She was gritty-eyed, because she couldn't cry. *Wouldn't* cry. In Alaina's world it was all the same.

This was all because of Elsie. Her best friend.

Okay, maybe it wasn't fair to blame it all on Elsie. It was a series of complicated missteps. They hadn't *seemed* like missteps at the time, though. That was the problem.

It had all started with Alaina's ridiculous crush on Hunter McCloud. Or maybe it had started with Elsie's crush on Travis, which had turned into Hunter trying

to help Elsie figure out how to get Travis, which had
resulted in Hunter giving Elsie flirting lessons, which
had…

Well, when Alaina had discovered Hunter and Elsie
were sleeping together she hadn't been all that thrilled.

But Elsie wasn't just sleeping with Hunter. She was
in love with him.

It had hurt, but really, what could Alaina do in the
face of love? She'd *liked* Hunter a lot. She'd had a whole
lot of fantasies about him being her introduction to sex.
But she hadn't wanted to marry him or anything.

It wasn't Elsie and Hunter getting together that had
hurt, not so much. It was that Elsie had lied to her.

It was the feeling that—yet again—Alaina had had
absolutely no idea what was happening in her own life.
It had reminded her of the world blowing apart when
her dad had walked out. She hadn't seen it coming. And
it had devastated everything.

She'd imagined Hunter and Elsie laughing about her.
About her futile crush on Hunter, and she knew Elsie
wouldn't do that to her except…

It had put her right back into that dark space she'd
been in at twelve when she'd found out life wasn't perfect after all. And she couldn't stand being unhappy like
that. Couldn't stand being uncomfortable.

And then she'd started scrambling, to figure out how
to land on her feet. To figure out how to make it okay.

And Travis had been the solution.

She didn't *want* to be hurt by Elsie. She didn't *want*
to be hurt by Hunter. She didn't want to be hurt by anything. So she'd just decided…

Travis was cute and he was just as good as Hunter. She'd invited him out to Sullivan's Lake and she'd watched him and another one of the hands show off and she'd decided he really was very cute, so why not?

They'd all gone to the bar later, and partway through the night she'd followed Travis out to his truck, then he'd driven around the back of the bar and they'd done it in the cab of the truck. It was fast and it wasn't so good for her. It had hurt.

You a virgin?

Oh, sorry. Yeah. I was.

And he'd looked so smug about it that it had made her feel like she mattered at least a little.

When they were done he'd gotten a text from the friend that had come with them.

Better head back to the bar.

But she hadn't wanted to. She didn't want to go face people.

I'll...be in soon.

But instead she'd sat in the parking lot feeling upset and miserable. A big knot in her throat, tears that she couldn't cry.

Then *he'd* shown up.

You look in need of a ride home, mite.

It had been the lifeline she'd needed.

Yeah, sure.

So she'd texted Travis she was leaving, then taken the ride back home.

She'd had a hard time connecting with Travis after that. He'd been busy working, and then he'd taken another job at a sheep farm in Salem. And Alaina had felt...

She didn't love Travis.

Heartbreak wasn't the problem. But she hadn't expected to have sex for the first time and have it be just one fifteen-minute escapade that hadn't even resulted in an orgasm.

She'd been under the impression losing her virginity would be transformative in some way and instead she'd felt weird and depressed and not at all more enlightened.

And still very lonely.

Four weeks after her impulsive act, it had become clear to her that if she was bummed about the lack of transformation she'd experienced, her body had a big old consolation prize for her.

And she'd panicked.

She'd texted Travis about it.

Fuck, honey, can't someone give you a ride to a clinic?

She hadn't texted him back after that.

The thing was, it was her mess. Her consequence.

She had jumped into…the truck with Travis because she was so desperate to make her hard feelings go away, but this…

This had felt different.

She'd decided to shelve it all until she had to deal with it. She'd hidden her sickness, her listlessness, from her sisters. She'd hidden it from Elsie. She'd plastered a smile on her face and hand waved Travis's defection.

I didn't love him anyway, she told Elsie, her tone light, *he was just a roll in the hay.*

And so now here she was, eight weeks in and her

morning sickness was actually worse and she needed a doctor and she…

She had no clue what landing on her feet looked like here.

Alaina Sullivan had reached the end of her certainty and it was a terror she had no idea how to confront.

Of course, she had no idea what she was going to do. What she hated most of all was how ashamed she felt. Because it wasn't like she could stand by the events that had led up to this. She'd been an idiot. Oh well, if there was one thing she was good at, it was standing stubborn in who she was. Digging in. Justifying the choices she'd made in those rushed, heady moments when she was trying to fix her world.

It was about all she was good at.

And with those thoughts still swirling in her head, she put her truck in Park in front of the barn. Tonight was a town hall. Unfortunately, not at Sullivan's Point. Rather, over at McCloud's Landing, the exact *place* she would like to avoid, full of all the *people* she would like to avoid. Garretts, McClouds…

Truth be told, she wouldn't mind avoiding the Sullivans right now.

She was on the edge of a precipice and she felt wretched about it.

But you couldn't avoid people at Four Corners. It wasn't really possible.

The four families that made up the massive joint ranching spread were constantly in each other's pockets. And while each family had quite a bit of autonomy running their individual operations, they were also relatively dependent on each other. There were also certain agreements that needed to be made as one. Certain things that had to be decided as a group.

And that was why they had town hall meetings once a month, joining the families and all the workers from the different ranches together, and normally she enjoyed it. But then…

How much life had changed in the last few months. Before this, she had loved it. She had gotten a thrill out of seeing Hunter McCloud. She couldn't say exactly when she had started to have *feelings* for him. It was just something that had…happened. But the problem with living on Four Corners was you kind of knew everybody. And she had known everybody all of her life.

The boys her age hadn't really interested her.

But there was Hunter. He was older. He was beautiful. Unquestionably. She had developed a serious fascination with him. She'd kept a lot of it to herself, because she'd found it embarrassing. The only person she'd confided in had been her best friend, Elsie.

The whole betrayal had hooked into so many of her issues, past and present, that it had thrown her into a tailspin.

She was reckless. She had always known that about herself. All the fire inside of her had been so close to the surface since her father had left. Then her mother had moved away. And Alaina was the youngest. Of all the Sullivan sisters, she had barely been grown when her mother had gone.

She'd never slowed down to let herself feel bad about it. If she couldn't fix it she ignored it.

Sort of like you've been trying to do with the pregnancy?

She gripped the steering wheel tight for a moment and took a deep breath then blew it out, loudly. Her sisters were already there, fluttering around in floral dresses with pies and fruits and cakes.

The Sullivan sisters.

And Alaina.

Alaina had always been the horse girl. Alaina had always been her dad's girl.

For all the good it had done. And now what? Whose girl was she now?

Maybe still her dad's. He'd screwed everything up too. Ruined his good life here at Four Corners and destroyed their family and abandoned her.

So great, she had all his bad traits and none of his presence or support anymore. Fantastic.

Daddy's girl for all the fucking good it did.

How was she going to tell her sisters?

Fia would try to aggressively make everything fine. Another burden she would take on and try to apply her relentless, unyielding, terrifying optimism to. Fia wasn't a cheerful optimist. She was a warrior for the glass half full, and she'd damn well make it all the way full with her elbow grease if she had to. Rory—who was soft and hopeful, a romantic who read too many books and believed in good even when the universe had proven it was only doling out bullshit. And Quinn—who Alaina understood much better—would respond with violence. She'd go on a rampage trying to hunt Travis down.

Travis was in Salem. She should probably text him

and tell him she had taken care of it. So that he wouldn't come back ever. She would do that at some point.

Just to keep it clean. Just to make sure he never wondered about the girl he'd left pregnant and abandoned in Pyrite Falls, Oregon.

He won't wonder about you. He doesn't care.

Just like your parents.

"There you are," Fia said, handing her a basket full of goodies.

"Here I am," she said.

Fia looked at her, far too closely. "Alaina, are you okay?"

Fia had become the parental figure when their family had fallen apart, and she took it upon herself to make all of her sisters' business her business.

Of course, when it came to her own business, Fia was like a steel trap, but Alaina knew better than to call her out.

It wouldn't lead anywhere.

"I'm good," she said, forcing a smile.

"You're a liar," Fia said, looking both suspicious and worried.

She swallowed hard and wondered if she looked as miserable as she felt. Why was she falling apart now?

Eventually, everyone will literally see the evidence of it and you won't be able to hide it anymore.

"Then why did you ask, Fia?" she shot back.

When the meeting started she made sure to take a seat in the back and as far to the right as possible. Far away from the Garrett clan. Far away from the McClouds.

She could go to the Kings' section.

Arizona King wasn't as unpleasant as she used to be, now that Micah Stone had come back to Four Corners and married her, giving her an instant family with a teenage stepson, but that didn't make Arizona warm and cuddly. The truth was, the Kings were kind of a breed apart. They closed ranks with each other when need be, and they also seemed to have plenty of conflict within the group.

One did not just go sit with the Kings. Sullivans most especially didn't.

Though, half the problem with the Sullivans and the Kings was whatever had transpired between Fia and Landry. Fia never talked about it, so none of them knew the details. But Alaina wasn't an idiot. She assumed her sister had slept with him. And that he'd done what men did.

Except, rather than run off to another ranch he'd stayed next door. Which must suck.

Alaina had new sympathy for how that must feel.

Though, Alaina couldn't see being mad about sex for all those years. Particularly when it didn't get you pregnant. If she could set aside her anger for a minute, the abandonment and pregnancy aside, she could sit in the disappointment that sex was just...not all that fun.

What a letdown. What a truly tragic thing to learn that there wasn't much fuss about it at all.

Sure, there had been contributing factors. Like it being a spur-of-the-moment thing. She hadn't had a whole lot of fantasies stored up about Travis to boost the moment. But Travis was a good-looking guy. And by all accounts he was a total playboy. He had... He'd done *stuff.* Made some moves. Touched her certain ways. But it just hadn't…hadn't *thrilled* her. And the main event had been uncomfortable. And that was it.

She wouldn't be rushing out to do it again anytime soon.

A hilarious thought, since she was so *obviously* not having sex again any time soon.

She realized that she'd been spacing out for the whole first part of the meeting. But it didn't matter. She wasn't high enough on the totem pole to be called upon to give much of an opinion. She and her sisters did work on their own ranch, and Fia was the acting head of Sullivan's Point.

Fia had grand plans for their parcel of land, but that didn't involve Alaina.

The McClouds had been making changes around Four Corners, and the Garretts had been working with them. But they'd always been the coziest of the four families.

Right now, though, listening to any of them talk felt like torture. And she just ignored them.

Finally, it was bonfire time, and she figured she would cut out as quickly as possible. She didn't have any patience for this nonsense. She didn't feel like being social. Not tonight.

But then Fia shoved a piece of pie into her hand and dragged her toward the fire.

"Dammit, Alaina, at least don't let them see you looking this sulky. You have to have more pride than that."

"What?" she asked, confused.

"You're upset. About Elsie and Hunter."

Oh, dear Lord if only. *If only!* She longed for the simplicity of being pissy that her friend had hooked up with Hunter. It would be vastly less *impossible* than a pregnancy.

But hey, if it would offer her a reprieve with her sister, she'd play that game.

"Why?" Alaina asked. "Like you and Landry?"

"This isn't about me and Landry."

"You're the only one that's allowed to be bitter and heartbroken for years, Fia?"

"I don't want to talk about that."

"You never do. It's been years, you slept with him, or whatever, and you're mad about it."

Fia scowled. "You don't know what you're talking about."

"Maybe I don't. But it's because you won't tell anybody. And that's your own fault, Fia. If you feel isolated it's because you won't talk to anyone."

And the irony was galling, because she currently had quite the secret. But she didn't care.

She wasn't in the mood to be fair. She wanted to be left alone.

She had eaten half the piece of pie when Sawyer Garrett held up his red solo cup and hit the side of it with his fork.

His wife was standing beside him, laughing. Evelyn was from the city, and the fact that she got along so well with any of the rednecks around here always amazed Alaina.

"We have a bit of good news to share," he said.

"The first bit is that Evelyn is expecting a baby."

A cheer went up from the crowd. Alaina felt the pie turn to sawdust in her mouth.

"The second bit of news is that Hunter and Elsie are getting married."

Married.

Elsie was getting married.

Evelyn was expecting *a baby.*

So was Alaina.

And Alaina was…having a baby.

A baby.

She'd thought of words like *pregnant* and *pregnancy* this whole time and she had never once thought the word…

Baby.

Then her stomach turned and what she already had swallowed started to come right back up.

She threw the plate down on the nearest chair and she ran. Ran away from the group and hoped that nobody noticed. Ran into the darkness, to the edge of the trees, and cast up her accounts in the bushes.

She fell to her knees, sweat and tears on her face.

And then she heard heavy footsteps behind her.

"Alaina?"

She turned around. It was dark, but she knew who it was.

Gus McCloud.

The savior she'd never asked for, but who was always there when she needed him. Even if it drove her nuts.

Gus McCloud, who was as ugly as his brothers were beautiful.

Maybe that wasn't fair. Gus had probably been as

beautiful as Hunter and the others at one time, but she didn't remember it. Because she didn't remember his face before it had been burned. Scarred up by an accident he never talked about.

People whispered it was something his father had done to him.

The father it was also rumored he'd killed.

But she didn't believe *that*.

Gus was a lot of things. She didn't think he was a killer.

Gus was big, broad and imposing. An inch or so taller than Hunter, and a lot thicker.

He was solid. He reminded her of the big bulls that grazed in the pastures on Four Corners. Thick. Solid. Mean-tempered.

Protective.

One of her indelible childhood memories was the time when she and Elsie had been up to no good and had ended up in the pond. Elsie had gotten out and Alaina had been bogged down by water lilies and pond scum, hollering like a cat.

Until Gus had plucked her out. Just like the kitten she was, practically by the scruff, and carried her to dry land. Then he'd wrapped her in a flannel and given her a scolding.

She'd been afraid of him. Of that rough face and his mean eyes. She'd never seen anyone with scars like his.

She'd also never felt quite so protected.

She shook the memory off.

Why the hell had he followed her out here?

Why was he always showing up to the hour of her disgrace?

"What do you want?" she asked, miserable.

"To know what the hell is up."

She scowled down at the ground. "I'm sorry, why do you care, Gus?"

"I'm not an idiot. Contrary to popular belief. What did my brother do to you?" She could feel his gaze burning hot in the darkness.

"Nothing," she said, rejecting that immediately.

She didn't know if she should be irritated, relieved or horrified that people still thought her mood was about Hunter and Elsie. She'd hung out with Elsie since. Maybe not a ton because her friend was busy being loved up and Alaina was busy hiding morning sickness, but they were clearly speaking to each other.

"Good. Because if he was messing with you…"

"He didn't." Then she tilted her chin up. "I wanted to but he never…he never liked me that way."

There, let him sit with that truth.

"I see." He shook his head. "And he's marrying your friend. And you're heartbroken enough that it made you throw up."

That made her sound weak and she couldn't deal with that. Not with Gus looking at her like that. Because there was something about Gus that always made her want to prove herself. Maybe it was staring in the face of his hardness, of his resilience. She didn't know.

She just knew she couldn't bear for him to think of her as weak.

Everyone would know anyway. Soon enough.

He might as well be the first.

"I threw up because I'm pregnant, you dumbass," she said, from her miserable position on the ground.

Oh, there. She'd said it.

It made her want to throw up again.

He crouched down next to her, and she could see his dark eyes glittering, even in the dimness.

Well. Shit. She hadn't planned to confess it now. But she didn't want to think she was a wimp. She wasn't a wimp. She wasn't throwing up because she was hurt. She was throwing up because her stomach was weird.

And because there was going to be a *baby*.

Gus grabbed her arm, his hold bruising. She hadn't been this close to him since she was a tiny child he'd fished out of the pond. The intensity in his eyes was like a black, blank hole. It made her shiver. "You said he didn't touch you."

"*He* didn't," she said, jerking away from him.

His expression closed off. "Who did?"

"It doesn't matter," she said. "It just doesn't matter, Gus. It is what it is. It's my problem. I've gotta deal with it."

"So, he's not around?"

"No."

He paused for a moment, and she could see right when it all clicked into place for him. "It was Travis, wasn't it?"

"Maybe." She hated this. She hated being this transparent. To Gus McCloud of all people. He wasn't sensitive. He wasn't nice.

He was kind of terrifying, actually.

"This is what I walked into at the tavern, isn't it? That's why you were so poorly."

She craned her neck, trying to look haughty, from her position on the ground where she'd just been sick. "I was not *poorly*. I am *never* poorly."

The bastard chuckled. "You are pretty damn poorly, sweetheart." She wanted to take a swipe at him, but instead she just sat there, fulminating. "So, he's not coming back?"

"No," she said. "I don't need him to." The words sat between them, and he didn't say anything, which pissed her off. It was just silent and she hated the silence. "It's just humiliating," she added. "Because everyone's going to know. Everyone."

"So, you had sex. Big deal."

The way he said it made her want to believe that's how people would think.

"You know it isn't like that," she said, feeling miserable. "People even judged Sawyer. Didn't he and Wolf have to get married?"

"The Kings won't judge you."

She laughed. Hollow. "That doesn't comfort me, Gus."

"Comforting isn't really in my wheelhouse, it may shock you to learn."

And in spite of herself, she laughed. "Yeah, I am… just wholly shocked to hear that." The air seemed to shrink around them. "My baby's not going to have a father. Just like me."

"You have a father. He's just a dick who left."

"Well, same as my baby's dad. Except, this one won't

even know their dad at all. Because I was a dumb… I guess I was kind of a slut."

"Stop that. That's bullshit." The ferocity in his voice shocked her. That he was taking time over this at all shocked her. "You don't need to do that to yourself on top of everything else."

"That's what everyone's going to think."

And the scrutiny would be unbearable. Them all wondering who she'd been with, what had happened.

It had been like that when her dad had left. Everyone had been curious—caring, sure—but it was hard enough managing a crisis without everyone being involved in it, worrying about, trying to give advice and…

She couldn't bear it.

She could feel her throat getting tight with tears.

He grabbed her chin and his eyes blazed into hers. And she felt her stomach bottom out. "Who the hell cares what everybody thinks?"

Then he released her, straightening and letting out a harsh breath.

He didn't. She knew he didn't. He never had. He was Angus McCloud, and people already thought the worst of him. Not that anyone blamed him; that was the thing. His father had been the meanest man in all of creation and everyone knew it.

And one day, he'd gone.

She stared at him. At his ruined face, barely visible in the dark. And she wondered if he'd done it.

"I don't know how not to care," she whispered.

She was going to look like exactly what she was. An

immature idiot. Who had been running away from her pain and had run right into trouble.

"You want the baby?" he asked.

"I'm having the…baby." It wasn't the same as wanting it.

He grunted. "Right. So, what's the problem?"

For the first time in her memory, she didn't have answers somewhere deep inside herself. For the first time in her memory, all her worries poured out of her.

"*Everything*. I don't want to be a single mother. I don't want the baby to not have a dad. I don't want everyone knowing I slept with Travis or…"

"Or that you were in love with Hunter?"

Her eyes were scratchy. "Whatever. Gus, let's just go back to the bonfire."

He lifted her up from the ground as he stood, his hands rough, his hold strong. Her heart thundered hard, her eyes still burning.

But he propelled her back toward the bonfire and her misery felt managed, if only for a moment.

When they emerged from the shadows and into the firelight, Fia was there, her arms crossed. "Where have you been?"

"I was…"

"You threw up, didn't you?"

Shame burned her cheeks. "Oh… Fia, I…"

"Tell me honestly," she said, her eyes flicking from Gus, then back to Alaina. "I found… I found a pregnancy test in the bathroom, Alaina. And no one ever said anything so I didn't either. I was waiting. Was it yours?"

Alaina felt like the ground had tilted onto its side. "Fia, I... I can explain. I can..."

"Yes," Gus said. "It was. But don't worry. I'm going to marry her."

ANGUS EVANDER McCLOUD was an immovable object once his mind was made up. And his mind was made up.

Alaina was miserable. And he knew that she wasn't up to the scrutiny that would come from doing this alone. And she was alone.

The dude had fucked right off, and he had no patience for that shit.

None at all.

Gus was nobody's savior. He'd also never planned to marry and have kids, so in a weird way that made it work even better. He wasn't losing any fantasies about the future.

He had a big house. Plenty of money.

Most of all, she could be married. She and the child wouldn't face stigma. No one on the ranch needed to know her business.

You think saving her will make up for everything else you've done?

No. It wouldn't.

But what the hell was the point of going on if he didn't try?

"Gus..." Fia's voice was a study in horror and Gus might have been offended...if he had the capacity to be.

He and Fia had known each other for years, and he respected the hell out of her tenacity and spirit, the way she'd taken the ranch and turned things around after her dad had left. The way she held her family together. He related to her as much as he did anyone, really.

He respected her. Her obvious desire to step in and protect her sister.

But really, she should know he might be an asshole but he had honor.

Fia looked ready to skin him alive.

"Got a problem?" he asked.

Fury emanated from her gaze. "Yes, several."

"Just stop, Fia," Alaina said. "Can I talk to you?" She directed that at him.

"Have at."

"Not here."

He shrugged and she took his arm this time, dragging him away from the fire. Not that little Alaina could drag him if he didn't want to go.

Once they were a good distance away, she rounded on him. "Are you out of your damn mind?"

She was furious, but then Alaina always was. The girl was a powder keg and it was only a matter of time before she exploded. This, he imagined, was it.

The explosion.

She'd always been like that. A wild, fierce little creature full of so many feelings. She was determined to bend the world to her will, and she hadn't seemed to notice the world didn't much care what anyone wanted.

What he kept in the deepest parts of his soul, she wore for all the world to see.

It fascinated him.

It terrified him. For *her*. He'd always been worried she'd be hurt, pretty much exactly like she was now.

"Why did you do that?" she asked.

He shrugged. "Why not?"

"*We…we don't… I'm…you're old.*"

He laughed. Because the little termagant was so fierce she wouldn't back down even when she was being helped. "I'm thirty-five."

"I'm *not*."

That sweet little, *angry* little, sharp little thing. "I'm aware."

"Why…"

"It doesn't have to have anything to do with *us*, Alaina. You want to save face, you want your baby to have a father, I can give you those things. I can do it with a marriage license. That solves all your problems."

"Except the ones where I'm having a baby and we're married."

"You said you were having the baby."

She looked enraged he'd pointed that out.

"Remember when you were five and you fell in the pond?" he asked.

Dark fury mottled her cheeks. "I don't see what…"

"I fished you out. And you hissed and spit like a mean little ferret the whole time. You said you didn't need help." He looked at her profile. Proud, angry. Familiar. "You needed help, mite. You need help now."

"I don't *want* to need help."

"I know. You never do." He sighed. "You gonna accept it or not? The people who know you best won't talk. They'll protect you. And hell, maybe they won't *know*. Or won't be able to be sure. If it's mine or his."

"People are going to…have a lot of questions. And I don't think my sisters are going to be very happy with you," she said.

"Because of me being thirty-five? And you not being?"

She shot fingers guns at him. "That's it."

"Or maybe because they think I'm a murderer?"

He watched her face when he said that. Those rumors about him…they were convenient sometimes. They let him keep people at a distance.

They weren't real, so why not use them?

"They don't think that."

"Do you?" he asked.

"No."

He could tell she wasn't sure.

"Your call, Alaina."

"I have to decide right this minute?"

"Well, Fia knows."

She bit her lip and looked back toward her sister. "Fine. Fine, Gus. I'll marry you."

Here he was, cleaning up the mess. That was typical. And he didn't know what he felt over her agreement. But then, he didn't make a business of closely examining his feelings. What the hell did feelings matter? Feelings were what drove men like his father.

Rage, the need to drink…all of it.

His father had been a horrible man. A worse dad. An awful husband.

Given to fits of anger and violence. Dark, destructive violence.

Gus had never wanted to be a husband or father, but he had also purposed early that he would be everything his dad wasn't.

His dad would have found a way to crush Alaina in this moment. He excelled at that. Hurting people when they were at their weakest.

It made Gus more determined to shield her.

"Then let's go," he said. "Hunter and Elsie won't be the only ones making an announcement tonight."

Something in her eyes sparked then, and he knew she liked that. Knew that whatever feelings she had for his brother were still strong enough that she wasn't above taking another chance to get at him.

Luckily, Gus didn't care. Because he might be willing to marry Alaina, but he didn't have any feelings for her.

Angus McCloud didn't have feelings at all.

CHAPTER TWO

THIS WAS INSANE, and so was Gus. But she didn't know what else to do.

You're actually going to marry Gus McCloud...

She hated all her other options. She was afraid of doing this on her own. Afraid of everyone's reactions. Yes, her sisters would help her, but things were challenging enough as it was. And it might be the modern era, but people were still judgmental as hell. Not even Sawyer and Wolf had let their babies be born into a situation where they'd remained unmarried. And they were men. And the thing was, Alaina had spent so many years telling herself that she didn't care what anybody thought. Telling herself that she didn't need to sit in bad feelings. That she could change things. For the better. That all it took was determination and a strong will, and everything would be okay. But nothing about this had gotten better. Not for any of the amount of time she'd let it sit. It just hadn't gotten better.

She had hoped that it would. She had hoped that something would change. That something would come to her. Some new idea of how to spin this. Maybe part of her had even hoped Travis would come back. Not because she loved him but because…it just seemed like it

would make things easier. At least then her baby would
have a father.

At least then she wouldn't have to admit that she'd
gotten pregnant having sex one miserable time with a
guy she wasn't in a relationship with.

And what were they going to do? What were they going
to tell everybody? Most of all, who would believe it?

"You're not seriously going to announce this right
now," she said.

"Yeah," he said, looking at her with deadly serious
eyes. "Everyone's here. And it seems to me like it's got
to happen sooner rather than later."

They stepped back into the crowd, and Fia went to
them immediately.

"I cannot believe this." Fia looked between Gus and
Alaina. "In fact, I don't believe it. What's going on?"

"What's going on," Gus said to her sister, "is that I'm
marrying her. That's it."

"But are you…?"

"Do you think that's any of your business?" he asked.

"Yes, Angus," Fia said. "I do in fact think it's my
business. She is my youngest sister, and I think you owe
me an explanation. We have known each other since we
were in diapers. And you can't just randomly…"

"There's nothing random about it," Gus said. "If she
needs something, I'm there for her. That's how it's always been. That's how it always will be. So chill out,
Fia, and let me handle this."

"Alaina?" Fia said.

"It's the right thing to do," Alaina said.

And Gus took her hand, and started to lead her up

toward the position at the bonfire where Sawyer had just stood. His hands were rough, different than Travis's. Travis was a ranch hand, but Gus was shaped on the ranch, like iron forged in fire. He had been working since he learned to walk. Everything about him was…rough.

"Hey," Gus said. "Alaina Sullivan and I have a little announcement of our own. We'll be having a wedding here at the ranch right quick. So buy us a toaster or some shit."

There was a ripple through the entire crowd of people. And Gus began to lead her away from the bonfire.

Until Hunter stopped them.

"I'm sorry," he held his hand up like he was calling a time-out, "you don't get to do that and then give no explanation," Hunter said.

"I do," Gus said. "Because I don't owe anyone an explanation."

"Gus…"

"If you have something to say to me, Hunter, we can do it back at the homestead. You know where I live. So why don't we deal with our stuff in private. That's the relevant information that everybody at the ranch needed to know, because I expect them all to be there. Throwing rice or whatever the hell."

There was a smattering of very uncomfortable applause, and they were predictably rushed by her sisters. Fia, Quinn and Rory. Quinn and Rory looked… Well, they looked outraged.

"What in the world?" Quinn asked.

"I… Aren't you going to congratulate me?"

"I might congratulate you if this didn't seem so desperately random."

"How was it random?" Gus asked, slinging his arm around her like it was the most natural thing in the entire world. "People at the ranch hook up these days, right? It's what they do. Look at Hunter and Elsie. How is this different?"

"You're...*older*," Rory said.

"And...*you*," Fia added.

"I'm pregnant," said Alaina.

The explosion of curse words from Quinn was epic and Rory was looking back and forth between herself and Gus, obviously trying to decide if this was a surprise, romantic triumph, or if she was going to pick up her steak knife and launch into a rage like Quinn.

"How?" Rory asked.

"Oh, for God's sake, Rory," Quinn said.

"I know *how* but...*how*?"

Alaina wished she had a good story to tell but she felt skinned and rolled in salt. Stinging, exposed and all things she hated, and it was Gus. Gus, who had always been there for her in his way but they would never...

"All you need to know," said Gus, "is that I care about your sister. And I would never hurt her. Do you believe that?"

Fia eyed him hard. "I do."

"We need to talk by ourselves," Quinn said.

"If you want to accuse me of murder, Quinn," Gus said, "why don't you do it in front of me? I'm not afraid."

"Well, maybe I am," Quinn said.

"For the record, I didn't kill my father." Alaina had

never heard Gus outright deny it before. "It suits me to let that rumor go around. Maybe because I like a little fantasy. And hell, that's a pretty compelling one, I have to admit. There was no love lost between me and the old man. But no. I didn't kill him. I just made sure he would never come back. I made sure he signed the ranch over to me and my brothers so that we never had to see him ever again. And I made sure he knew that if his trifling ass ever wandered back on Four Corners, I'd finish what I started. Because when I handle something, I handle it."

Those words sent a shiver down Alaina's spine. He was handling her, wasn't he?

And suddenly, she was brimming with questions. She had agreed to this, and now it was a public announcement. News of her pregnancy was bound to get around and quickly. So she should be thankful, but she found herself wanting details.

"We need to talk," Alaina said to Gus.

"I expect so."

"Not tonight," Rory said, grabbing hold of her arm, and Alaina felt like a rag doll, being pulled between things.

"Out of respect, sure," he said. "Alaina. We'll talk tomorrow, okay. You come out to McCloud's Landing nice and early. I'll have some coffee for you."

"I'm not sure if I'm supposed to drink coffee," she said.

"Have you been drinking it anyway?"

She squirmed. "Well. Yeah."

"Then I'll be there with coffee on."

And he tipped his hat and walked away from the circle of Sullivans.

"Back to the house," Fia ordered.

And that was how Alaina found herself bundled up into a truck, driven back to the house and marched inside like she was a prisoner of war. The little eclectic farmhouse was always going to be the place that Alaina loved most. They had built the most beautiful life here, she and her sisters, after their parents had left them on their own.

Their dad had gone off to start a new life because their life here wasn't enough.

Their mom had gone six years later because she'd never been able to accept this place without him.

Fia, Rory, Quinn and Alaina had stayed.

This was Sullivan's Point. It belonged to the Sullivan family. It had been her father's responsibility. The responsibility of those that carried the Sullivan name, and Sullivan blood.

Their mother was gone, and yes, it stung a little. But they were adults and she'd at least raised them all before she'd gone. She didn't have Sullivan blood; the land wasn't hers.

But their dad…he had a responsibility to this place. To the land. And he had simply left it. Like it didn't matter. Like it didn't mean anything.

When their dad had left, the house had gone gray. Their mother had been like a ghost. Fia had held things together, but the sadness had been inescapable.

When their mom left, the first thing Fia had done was take the antique table that had sat in the dining room forever, and put it right out in the yard. She had sanded it, and then she had painted it a bright blue.

That had begun the process of adding color to everything in the place. Now Alaina could hardly remember it not being this way.

When it had all been wood and white paint.

Now it was red, yellow, tangerine. Spots of magenta, teal. They ate every meal on an eclectic set of china, mismatched teacups, carnival glass tumblers. They had decided that if they were left to their own devices, they would do it in style. And they had done so. And they had made... They had made a life. They had managed by hiring good ranch hands that they could trust, by working toward opening a farm store on the property that would be like a continuous farmers market.

They made pie and jam, they made cakes and they gardened. And while Alaina preferred working with horses to that, she loved what they did because it was part of them.

Because it was part of what they had done to survive.

It wasn't her, though.

Fia had done everything she could to unite them, to bring them together.

But the longer it all went on, Alaina felt lost in it. Fia had been part of making Four Corners. And then she'd done something with Sullivan's Point. She'd done it for them, and Alaina loved her for that.

But she wanted to know where she fit in this world. In this life.

It hit her right then that if she was going to marry Gus...

Well, her place would be his.

Her place would be Gus McCloud's.

She was torn by that realization. Because it still wasn't hers. But it was…a chance to be somewhere different. Do something different.

You're really going to marry him?

Marrying Gus. Marrying Gus.

It was insane. But was it any more insane than the situation she found herself in?

"Now can you please explain what's going on?"

"I'm marrying Gus," she said. "He…he made that perfectly clear."

"Yes," Fia said. "He did." Fia looked for a moment like she might implode, then she turned and gripped Alaina by the shoulders. "I need you to look at me and tell me that Gus McCloud did not take advantage of you."

"No," Alaina said, horrified, tugging away from Fia. "Look, first of all, I'm an adult. I'm allowed to have sex." She sounded more defiant about that than she felt. "Second of all, no he did not. Gus is a good guy. And I don't care what kind of rumors go around about him, he's never hurt anyone who didn't deserve it. He's only ever been kind to me."

There was a slight pause and then Rory fixed her with an extremely piercing stare. "It's not his baby, is it?" she asked.

"Rory… I…"

"We don't care," Quinn said. "No one is judging you."

Quinn's lofty tone annoyed Alaina a little. Quinn was the only one of the four sisters that had gone to college and sometimes her know-it-all streak got a bit irritating.

"Yes, you are," Alaina said. "You're judging me about Gus."

"It depends on the circumstances," Quinn said. "Because I know you, Alaina, and you're tough and you're…impulsive. And I have to say, I'm a little worried Gus took advantage of the impulsivity."

The very thought of that made Alaina feel like she wasn't quite in her body. But she hadn't felt in her body for at least a month now.

But she knew one thing: she couldn't let her sisters think that about Gus. Not when he was helping, and not when all the decisions that had taken her here were… hers. She couldn't blame anyone else.

Well, Travis was an ass. But it was better this way. The idea of being stuck with him *forever* because of *fifteen minutes* that hadn't even felt like much of anything wouldn't have been fair.

So she was happy to take the consequences on herself if it meant not dealing with him.

And she wouldn't pass any blame to Gus.

"No, it's not Gus's baby. Please don't tell anyone. Please… He knew I was in trouble. He offered to help."

She could sense a ripple of disappointment in her sisters. Wow. This was why she was keeping it secret. This was why Gus was helping her.

"You're all judging me," she said.

"No!" Quinn and Fia shouted.

Rory, for her part, was silent.

Quinn punched Rory in the arm. Rory looked at Quinn. "What? I was thinking about if I was being judgmental. At least I'm honest."

"*We'll* help," Quinn said. "This ranch is full of broken families. Who's going to…"

But for her it mattered. For her it would be unbearable. For her it would mean being that object of pity all over again, that girl she'd been whose dad had left and…

No. She couldn't deal with that.

"That's just it. I don't want that. I don't want that for my baby. I never wanted this at all. I was trying to do better than our parents. I was trying to do better than all the broken-ass shit around this place. And look at what I did. I went and got myself in trouble. I did exactly what I said I was too smart to do. And Elsie warned me. She said to be careful. And I kept telling her I knew what I was doing. I kept insisting that I did."

"Who was it?" Quinn asked.

"Doesn't matter," Alaina said. "Really. He doesn't matter. He isn't worth a damn. He doesn't want anything to do with me. And he doesn't want anything to do with the baby. And he isn't here anymore. And Gus… Gus was there for me. He's been there for me."

"So you're just going to marry him," Rory said.

"Yes. I'm going to let everybody think it's his baby. Because he wants that. But I can't lie to you. You're my sisters."

"Who are you going to lie to?" Rory asked.

She had to consider that. Really carefully.

"Not Elsie," she said.

She didn't have it in her to be irritated with her friend at all now. Not when things felt so real.

That was it. Tonight she had to face the fact that this was happening. That it was real, and the baby was coming whether she was prepared for it or not. She made the decision to keep it, and now she had to face what that meant. But when push came to shove she'd realized that she didn't want to do it alone.

"The broader ranch community does not need to know. I have a feeling it's going to be unavoidable that the Garretts know. And the McClouds obviously. And us."

"So basically, we're just keeping the secret from the Kings," Fia said.

"That should suit you," Alaina said.

"Alaina," Rory asked, suddenly looking grave. "It must be asked, because we are descended of great female warriors and witches, priestesses. Do we need to find the man responsible for this and cut his nuts off?"

Alaina laughed. Not so much because she thought it was funny. It was just… She should have known this was the kind of support she would receive from her sisters. It was how they were.

"I mean, you could. But the thing is, I don't want his nuts around the house."

"He didn't hurt you, did he?" Rory asked.

Alaina grimaced. "Not the way you mean. I wanted to do it. It sucked, though."

Fia grimaced. "Well. At least you won't miss it."

And yet again, Alaina wondered if it was a Landry King reference.

"The thing is," Quinn said, "you don't have to marry Gus."

She thought about it. For a long moment. Over the ticking sound of the clock. She let a whole minute pass.

Quinn wasn't wrong. She didn't have to marry Gus. She would be okay. It might not be ideal, but it would be fine.

"You could do a lot worse than Gus McCloud for a dad," Alaina pointed out. "And at the end of the day… that's what he's offering. It's not just about me."

"But why is he offering this?" Quinn asked. "I can understand why you'd take it, I'm just not sure why he's giving it."

"Well, ouch, Quinn. Anyway, I'm not sure that I can answer that. I haven't actually talked to Gus. I'm going to. Tomorrow I guess. He told me to come to McCloud's Landing."

"Look," Fia said. "I know that you already…made the announcement in front of everybody and all that. But you don't have to do anything."

Rory nodded. "She's right, you can quit. Trust me on that. I'm an expert. If something is hard? You can just never do it again. Like rope climb in PE."

Alaina cleared her throat and pointed at her stomach. "The rope has been climbed, Rory." She sighed. "Look, this is my mess."

"However you choose to clean it up," Fia said, "you have our unending support. Celtic warrior priestesses and all that."

"I know that."

"You don't have to keep it," Fia pointed out.

"I do, though," she said. Because of all the scenarios that she'd gone over in her head, this was the only one she knew she could live with.

"Just wanted to make sure you knew that…we've got you. We've got your back. I know that all these men around here think that we need them to protect us. But we are not insignificant, and we are not weak. We took our ranch and we made it into something great. Something that we could do. Something that made the most out of our strengths."

She didn't say anything. It was just that the thing was, they made the most out of Rory's, Quinn's and Fia's strengths. And she was more than able to do all of it. It was just that she…she missed the ranching. Now that they were leasing it out, the ranch piece was worked entirely by people who weren't Sullivans.

Sure, everyone at Four Corners had additional staff help run the ranch, but the McClouds had their horses, the Garretts had their cattle and so did the Kings.

They had some rental properties—which Rory ran. They had the plans for the farm store which Quinn and Fia were so enthused about.

And they had hazelnuts at Sullivan's Point. *Hazelnuts*.

There was nothing glorious or rugged or Western about *hazelnuts*.

"Just… I'm going to talk to Gus tomorrow."

"All right."

"I'm tired," she said. "I'm going to go to bed."

She trudged up the stairs, and she knew the creak of every single one. She had lived in this house her entire life. She had been planning on moving somewhere else, but she didn't… She hadn't thought that it would be this soon. And there would be a baby. And there was Gus.

She reached the top of the stairs and froze.

He wanted to marry her. Did that mean…?

Her breath rushed out of her lungs in a gust. She couldn't imagine that. Gus, so large and hard. Touching her and… She squeezed her thighs together and walked down the hall, feeling very much like she had just done something naughty, and she couldn't quite say why.

She hadn't ever thought of Gus McCloud in that way. He was… Well, he had been a *man* as far as she was concerned ever since she'd first met him.

When she was a child.

She'd never thought about him like that before.

She walked into her room quickly and shut the door firmly behind her, lying across the handmade quilt that was still on her bed.

She groaned. Eventually, she had to call her mother, let her know she was going to be a grandmother. Maybe she'd be willing to leave her beach life for a while to sit in a rocking chair holding a baby?

That made her chest tight.

No. She wouldn't be doing that now. Not right now. She just needed to sleep.

She threw her arm over her eyes. Sleep was elusive, and she couldn't grab hold of it in spite of her best efforts.

Finally, when the light was beginning to turn pink, she went downstairs and out the front door. She went right to the barn area and took her horse out of the stall, grabbing hold of a bridle and some reins and putting them on the old gelding. She decided to skip the saddle, pulling herself up and riding bareback across the field. She had it on good authority—meaning the internet—

that as long as horse riding was something she was accustomed to, it was just fine to do while pregnant.

It was such a strange thing. She'd felt like she was in some sort of denial about this from the beginning, but she had been trying to take care of herself. To take care of the baby. Because it did matter. It just did.

She decided that as weird as everything had been... she needed to see Elsie. She had to go to McCloud's Landing anyway and she figured that's where her friend was. So she headed that way, as fast as her horse would take her.

The wind blew in her hair, and she closed her eyes for a moment and just felt.

Felt it all.

It was early, but she knew that Elsie would already be up. Her friend was always up with the dawn.

She was a horse girl, after all.

Alaina got off her horse and stomped up the front porch of Hunter's cabin. She knocked on the door, swift and hard, and it opened abruptly. And there was Hunter, shirtless and looking irritated. And really, she should've realized that they might be in a partial state of undress. And that Hunter would be the one to answer the door, but she just wasn't quite prepared.

"Hey," he said, his lips turned down into a frown.

"Hi," she said.

She felt awkward. Because she knew that *he* knew that she'd had a crush on him, and also, he knew that she was marrying Gus. And... She let herself take a slow perusal of his bare chest. It was weird.

He was aesthetically a beautiful man, and she could

see that and appreciate it. But now… Well, she wasn't a virgin anymore. She couldn't say that she passed for anything like *experienced*, considering her sexual adventures had been muted to say the least. And very brief. But she didn't feel a real sexual stirring along with the appreciation of his aesthetic.

Maybe it had to do with him and Elsie being together now. That would be good and right and fair. But she had a feeling it was something else that she couldn't quite put a finger on, and it made her feel disoriented.

But then, everything about this moment was disorienting.

"Should I get Elsie for you?" he asked.

She sniffed. "I didn't come here to see you."

"You're going to be my sister-in-law."

"Sure," she said, feeling a little dizzy at that.

"Who's that?"

Elsie appeared, and then stood still for a moment, staring at Alaina through the crack in the door.

"Hey," Elsie said, looking surprised.

"Hey," said Alaina. "I just wanted to talk."

"Okay," Elsie said.

She stepped outside and closed the door behind her. "Are you all right? I wanted to know what happened. With…with Gus. Since I'm having trouble making sense of this."

"I know. Because when last we left off, I had slept with Travis."

"Yes. When last we left off."

Elsie stared at her for a long moment and Alaina decided to just…let it out.

"I'm pregnant, Elsie," Alaina said.

Elsie's eyes went wide. "You're *pregnant*?"

"Yes. I know there's no way that Gus is going to keep all the details secret from his family…"

"Did you sleep with Gus?" Elsie somehow managed to shout that whispered sentence.

"I didn't sleep with Gus," Alaina said. And she felt jittery and warm just saying the words. Just thinking about it.

It was too jarring. She'd been through way, way too much in the last two months. Really.

"But he…" Alaina sighed. "He's doing what he does. He's rescuing me. And I wish that I had the fortitude to not need that. But I really need it. Can you imagine? All the questions that people are going to have about who the father is, and how sorry everyone's going to feel for me because he's gone. I just… I can't bear it. I really can't." She bit the inside of her cheek. "I didn't come here to have a fight, Elsie. But…what you did with Hunter, it made me feel stupid. That was the problem. It didn't make me feel brokenhearted. But when my father left, we were blindsided. It was such a shock. I thought everything was perfect, and it wasn't. And then it turned out there were people at Four Corners who knew. Other people knew that there were cracks in our family and it didn't ever once occur to me that there might be. I couldn't bear that that happened again. I couldn't bear that that happened in our friendship. And I can't take the humiliation that is going to come with all this, because even if everybody is well-meaning, and I know that they are…"

"Slow down. Please don't marry Gus just because of what I did. I'm really sorry. I shouldn't have lied to you and…"

"No, they're separate issues. Kind of. They're separate issues kind of. I just feel raw and very reminded of that place that I was in. And Gus reached out a hand, and I don't think that I can tell him no."

"You can," Elsie said, looking defiant. "I'll be your baby's surrogate dad if I need to."

"I know you would. And I'm sorry… I'm sorry that the last couple of months I haven't been honest with you. And that I've been distant. I haven't been able to be honest with anybody. That's the truth. I haven't been able to articulate any of this. And then it all came to a head last night when I puked and Gus found me. He quite literally picked me up off the ground. He's offering a life for my baby that I can't give apart from him."

"Is this about your dad? I mean, I know what you just said, about me and Hunter, and making you feel stupid. But I mean is this about…?"

"Me not having a dad? Yeah, kind of. Look, you know what it's like. To not have parents. At least, not functional ones. And yeah. I want something different than that for my kid. And oh, dear God, Elsie. I'm having a kid. I don't know what to do. I don't know what to do. Maybe this is the problem. I need an adult, and Gus is basically one of the few functional adults that we know."

"Did you want Gus to be the baby's daddy, or *your* daddy?"

"The baby's." And she felt weird and warm. And she didn't like it.

"You're marrying him. *Marrying* him." Elsie's eyes bugged. "What's that going to look like?"

Well, Alaina had thought of it in terms of living at the house. Managing the ranch.

"I figure," Alaina said, "I'll actually get to work on the ranch. Manage the house. I kind of like that idea. I've always shared the farmhouse with my sisters, and I love them, but you know how Fia is. She runs a tight ship, and I don't know. I guess lately I've been wondering what it would be like to run my own ship. And I feel like with Gus I have the chance to do that."

"Sex, Alaina," Elsie said, looking at her intensely.

"Oh," Alaina said, her stomach squeezing tight. "I… hadn't thought about… Hadn't thought about sex."

That wasn't totally true, she'd thought about it for a little last night and had made herself spiral. But…she'd had sex. The once. It wasn't that big of a deal.

If Gus wanted sex…

For some reason, she pictured Gus's hands. They were very big. Her mind got stuck there.

"If he wants sex…" She shrugged and tried to make it look casual. "I guess it's all part and parcel, right? I mean… He'd have to. He's a man." She bit the inside of her cheek.

"I guess so. But…"

"What?"

"I don't know. He's just…"

"I don't want to talk about this," Alaina said. Because somehow thinking of him like that, thinking of them like that, and then talking about it, felt like a weird betrayal. "He's helping me. And Gus has certainly never done anything to hurt me. All he's *ever* done is help me. I trust him."

"Yeah. Well, he's a good guy. A scary guy, but a good one, as far as I can tell."

Alaina put on her bravest face.

Sure, somewhere deep down in her heart, she was a romantic, who'd fantasized about maybe someday falling in love, but she'd limited her own options. She had to accept that. "I didn't have a whole lot of dreams about getting married or anything like that. Getting married for the sake of a baby seems as fine a reason as any. And he's *good*. He's never going to abandon me. This place is in his blood. He ran his father off rather than leave. I can trust him. At least in that way."

"I'm glad that you feel good about it," Elsie said. "And I'm glad that you trusted me to tell me. And to tell me how I hurt you. I'm really sorry, Alaina. I shouldn't have been a coward. I didn't know what to do with my feelings for Hunter, because they were very new, but that isn't an excuse. Because our relationship isn't new. We're friends. Best friends."

"Yeah," Alaina said. "I certainly can't afford to be in a fight with you. Not when everything in my life is completely turned upside down. I need you, Elsie."

"Well, me too. *This* is totally new territory for me." She gestured at the closed cabin door behind her. "This being-in-love business. This... All of this."

"I guess we are going to be sisters-in-law."

"Well, if anything could make this perfect, then that's it."

Alaina reached out and hugged Elsie. "I have to go. I'm going to talk to Gus. Get all this *stuff* ironed out."

"Make sure to ask him about sex."

"Believe me," Alaina said, her cheeks going hot, "I fully intend to."

She walked away from Elsie and got back on her horse, riding out toward the main house. She felt better for having talked to Elsie, but that didn't solve everything. Even if it did solve most things. There was still the whole logistical… Everything.

There was still Gus.

And when she arrived at the main house at McCloud's Landing, Gus was standing out on the porch.

Waiting.

He was wearing a tight black T-shirt that emphasized just how muscular he was, and had a dark cowboy hat pulled low over his eyes, and it made her feel…uncomfortable. Much like the feelings she'd had last night that had sent her running for her bed feeling guilty and vaguely dirty.

"I came to talk to you about wedding details," she said. "I mean, most importantly, *everything* details."

"You want some coffee?" He asked the question slow and deliberate.

"Yes. It is okay for me to have a single caffeinated beverage at this stage of the pregnancy. I looked it up."

"Okay then," he said, opening the door and ushering her inside.

She couldn't remember the last time she'd been in his

house. Maybe when she was a kid? Back before it was his. When his dad had still been here. Maybe her dad had brought her over to discuss some business? It was a foggy memory. She would have been maybe four or five.

The place was…rustic.

Not hugely messy, but she could just tell that it wasn't all that lived-in. It was a huge house, and she bet Gus didn't make use of half the rooms in it.

They walked into the kitchen, and she stopped.

There was a long wooden table with benches at it, and the tabletop was covered in paperwork, envelopes, maps, all kinds of things. Like it hadn't actually been cleared off in weeks.

"Find a spot," he said, gesturing to the debris.

She did, down at the end.

He brought her a little blue speckled camp mug full to the brim with piping hot coffee.

"I need cream and sugar," she said.

"I could stick my finger in it?"

If she hadn't felt so tense she might've found that riotously funny, as she stared up into his completely unsmiling, craggy face.

"No thanks, Gus," she said. "We wouldn't want to oversweeten it. I'll just take regular sugar."

He grunted, went to the fridge and opened it up, grabbed a carton of half-and-half and put it down in front of her. Then he did the same with a bag of sugar.

"You don't have a sugar shaker?"

"I do not," he said.

"Spoon?"

He opened up the silverware drawer, grabbed a spoon

and chucked it to her. She caught it, then took a small scoop of sugar out of the bag, put it into the cup and stirred, putting half-and-half over that and watching it bloom into a milky flower.

"So the wedding…" she started. "Actually, the whole marriage. Why do we need to get *married*?"

He leaned against the counter, the muscles in his forearms shifting. "Alaina Sullivan, I have known you since you were born. Which means you've known me since you were born. You oughtta know, I would never get a woman pregnant and not marry her."

"Really?"

He frowned. "You can ask me that?"

"I don't know, Gus. I don't really know anything about your personal life."

He was…mysterious. He wasn't a player, not like his brothers. He didn't go out much. It was common to go to Smokey's and see Brody and Lach, and before they were in relationships, Tag and Hunter too.

But Gus kept to himself.

He *could* be fun.

During the annual Game Day on the ranch, he played just the same as everyone.

"Because I don't have one. Not at Four Corners, I don't, and not in Pyrite Falls. I don't screw around in my own backyard. But I guaran-damn-tee that if a woman contacted me and said that she was pregnant with my baby, I would be on the way to get her and take her straight to town hall. I don't shirk my responsibilities."

"Well, I can see that. I'm not even your responsibility. I… Why are you doing this?"

"I'm not ever going to get married, Alaina. It's not in the cards for me. Babies, all of that stuff… But look, I've got land, I've got this house. I'm not my father."

"I know you aren't," she said softly.

"Right. Well. I might as well, right? I'm not going to leave a kid fatherless, not when I could be one."

"And what do you get out of it?"

"Snow White. You're going to clean up my ranch house, right?"

She narrowed her eyes. "Only if I'm in charge of it."

She hadn't known she was going to say that until the words came out of her mouth. But if she could be in charge of the household, of all the things in the house, that would be a great deal. That would be something she wanted. A kind of dream, even. "And I want to work at the equestrian facility."

They were starting equine therapy up on the ranch. And getting all their ducks in a row for it. She had been so fascinated by the whole process, infinitely more interested in it than what was going on with the farm store at Sullivan's.

"Fine with me."

"And there's…" She wasn't timid. She had never been timid. She was the kind of girl who faced things head-on. Hell, she'd been a virgin, and when she'd decided she was done with that, she'd gotten a guy to deal with it in five minutes in the cab of his truck.

Okay.

She wasn't quite able to recast that one yet. But she was *working* on it. Eventually, she would see it as a triumph. Difficult considering the consequences, but she would figure it out.

She would make it a boon.

She was nothing if not resourceful, and she could find a boon anywhere. She could find one here. She *would*.

She was not going to be bashful.

"There's the matter of sex," she said.

He looked at her for a full second.

Then, he laughed.

Rich and low, rolling over her like thunder. *Like it was funny.* Like sex with her was *funny.* "Hard pass, sweetie."

She sputtered. "I'm sorry, what?"

"That's not why I'm doing this."

"Okay then," she groused, crossing her arms. "You could have said that nicer."

"Sorry to disappoint you, mite. I am not nice."

"Oh no, how could I ever have thought that you were nice, Gus? You're just saving me from a future as an unwed mother. Offering the protection of your name to my child. Why would I think that you were nice?"

"I have honor," he said, pointing at her. "There's a difference."

"All right. So what if somebody else needs your honor? Why me? Why spend it on me?"

He looked at her, long and hard. "I've been saving your ass since you were five years old. And you've been writing checks that ass couldn't cash ever since then. You need someone to save you, Alaina, and your family has been shit at it."

"My sisters are *wonderful*."

"Not your sisters. Your parents. They were never there for you the way that they should have been. Somebody had to do it. And you know what…? My father wouldn't have helped you. He'd have called you everything you call yourself. So having the opportunity to be as different from him as I can… That's the best thing. That's what I need."

"So is this about you or me?"

"Hell, of course it's about me. None of us does anything wholly selflessly, do we?"

"Gus, babies are expensive. I was planning on moving out before I found out I was pregnant. When I started looking at everything I was going to need I realized there's no way. It's scary."

He shrugged. "I have money."

"Oh. And you're just offering that to me too?"

"We're getting married."

"You say that like I should know what that means, but you also laughed at me when I asked about sex. Usually, when people get married they have sex."

"Why don't we just skip to the part where we have separate rooms and call it a day?" He smiled. "We'll be like an old married couple right off."

"Right. *Well*." She felt distinctly unattractive then. Because the whole conversation didn't seem to be having any sort of effect on him, and in fact, he seemed to find it all rather amusing.

As if sex with her were a joke.

She felt very strongly that *she* should be the one having issue with it all. As she was younger, and practically still a virgin. And he was...

She looked at his face. She couldn't even bring herself to think uncharitably about his scars while she was being mean inside of her own heart.

He wasn't ugly, anyway. She felt guilty for having let herself think that the other day. It was wrong. He wasn't.

He was him.

Broad and strong and tall. Head and shoulders above other men, pretty much literally. He had a square jaw, and half his face had gone mostly untouched by flame.

"Name only," he said. "But you got the full benefit of my name. This house, this ranch, my name on the birth certificate. You're a McCloud. And so is the baby."

A McCloud.

Given how attached they all were to their names, and what they meant to be each individual family, even though Four Corners was a somewhat blended endeavor, it was a very strange thing to think of. The idea of not being a Sullivan.

Of becoming a McCloud.

Elsie was also going to be a McCloud.

It was very weird. It was very, very weird.

"This is a lot to take in."

"We can do it whenever you want. There's no rush."

"There is, though. I don't want him coming back. I want us to be married. I want your name on the baby's birth certificate. He lost his right. To anything. He wanted me to get an abortion."

"Damn," Gus said, his words hard. "Did he try to pressure you?"

"No. Worse, he laughed, and just wanted to know if I needed a ride. Like he didn't even care that much one way or the other. Not desperate to make it go away… Because if I had the baby it was obvious it wouldn't mean anything to him. I would prefer it if he had been terrible and tried to talk me into it. He didn't even care that much. I don't know that I want to be a mom. Not now. But my parents left me." And suddenly, she felt a burning conviction in her chest that hadn't really been there before. "My parents left me. They left me here and… I want more for my child. I'm not going to make them feel like an afterthought. I want them to feel like they're the most important thing. I don't know how to do that. Because I'm selfish, and I'm just now trying to figure everything out. I'm twenty-four years old and I've never been off of this ranch. I don't know anything, I… I was going to make my own way. But I think I have to do that in a different fashion now. I'm going to make my own way by being the best mother that I can be. And I just don't ever want this child to feel that kind of dismissive… If he were here, if he had decided to stay, he would've become someone like my dad. Just able to up and walk away never thinking of his kids again. I hate it. I hate him. Not because he hurt me. But because he doesn't care about…" She put her hand on her stomach.

Gus's face softened. Just a little.

"Alaina, I don't know that I'm going to be any good as a dad. I don't know anything. Except I know how not to be one. What I do know is how to protect people. I've been doing it all my life. Plus, the uncles will be pretty good."

That made her laugh. "Uncle Hunter." And then she felt immediately guilty. "They'll have to know, though."

"Yeah. But that doesn't matter. It's not going to matter."

"Thank you," she said.

"Let's get married down at the lake."

"Okay."

She'd lied to Elsie. She *had* dreamed about getting married. She loved romance novels. And she loved the passion in them. She hadn't found any of that passion in the cab of Travis's truck, nor had she found thundering climaxes, crashing waves or opening flowers. It had just been perfunctory. It had been *friction*. And it had not been something that she was all that interested in repeating.

And she wondered if...much like that, all she was going to get out of her wedding was... The lake. Not the gauzy glorious wedding of her fantasies.

Nothing that she had dreamed about when she was a girl.

Well, it was time to stop being a baby. Dreams were for girls who didn't go out and make stupid-ass choices. Dreams weren't for her. Not anymore. She had to make do.

"Yeah. That would be good," she lied.

"We can drive down to the county and get paperwork."

"That sounds...fun."

"You don't think it sounds fun."

"I mean, it's always fun to get out of Pyrite."

"Get off the ranch."

They looked at each other. She still really…didn't know what to think about any of this. "When?"

"Today. I've got work to do this morning. Around lunchtime, let's go to Mapleton."

"Okay."

CHAPTER THREE

"ALL RIGHT," Hunter said, glaring directly at Gus. "It's time for you to explain."

"Seriously," Brody said.

Lachlan said nothing; he just stared, along with Tag.

Gus shrugged. "No explaining to be done. I'm marrying Alaina Sullivan."

"Why?" Brody pressed.

"She's pregnant."

"Fucking *hell*," Lach said. "You are the biggest dick in the entire world. You lecture us about our behavior all the time and you knock up *little Alaina Sullivan*."

"*He* didn't knock her up," Hunter said, looking far too confident in his opinion. His opinion was correct, but that didn't make it less annoying. "That much is clear."

"I'm hurt, Hunter. You don't think she'd have me?" He did his best grin, and he could feel his scar tissue pull tight.

"That isn't what I mean," Hunter said. "And I think you know that. You were warning me off Elsie like it was your hobby. I think you're a whole lot of things, Gus, but I know you're not a hypocrite. So you might as well come clean."

He shrugged. "Biologically, no, it's not my baby. But

my name's going on the birth certificate. So as far as I'm concerned, the kid is mine. I'm protecting her. I will not hear a damn thing said about the parentage of this child, or about Alaina, or anything. *She's* mine."

He could tell that his ferocity shocked his brothers. He hadn't meant to claim her along with the baby. But it was true.

The thing was…there were a few things he cared about in this whole world. She was one of them. From moment one.

She was too wild to be contained, from the time she was born. She'd been like a little firecracker roaming across the land, and he'd always known that if she caught alight, she had it in her to destroy the whole place. And herself along with it.

Here she was, in a whole pickle, and he was going to help fix it.

Because that was what he did. Because it was who he was.

Maybe then people wouldn't say Gus McCloud, possible murderer. They would say Gus McCloud, all-around decent guy, and a pretty good dad.

A *dad*.

The word made him uncomfortable. Fact of the matter was, he *hated* the word. As much as he hated his old man.

He had never thought that he'd be a father.

But again, this was different. He was offering protection. And he knew how to do that.

"So you're just going to marry her and… Why? I

don't get it, Gus. You've never seemed interested in having kids," Brody said.

"I'm not. I wasn't. Look, I never would've set out to make one. This world is shit. Our blood is… No offense meant to you loved-up idiots."

"None taken," Hunter and Tag said.

"You guys procreate all you want. I wouldn't have done it. But as for leaving a vulnerable woman who needs help to flounder on her own…"

"It's not your job to fix the broken things in the world," Hunter said. "Just because Dad was a dick doesn't mean that you can fix it by…"

"Maybe not, but I can fix something. I swear, if that little weed Travis comes back here, I'm going to make him a new asshole."

"Oh," Hunter said, grimacing. "I was afraid of that."

"What?"

"That it was *him*. I hate that guy."

"Yeah, you just hate him because Elsie was hung up on him there for a while," Gus pointed out.

"All right," Hunter said. "I get it. I really do. Because there but for the grace of God went Elsie."

Lach snorted. "I think you mean *there but for the lack of self-control in your pants*, Hunter."

"Hey," said Hunter. "I may or may not have seduced her, but it kept her away from *him*. And I'm going to marry her. *And*, I didn't get her pregnant." He smiled. "Yet."

"Yeah, you're a real prince," Brody said.

"Look, Gus," Hunter said, getting serious again. "You spent our whole childhoods saving our asses.

You've always been there for us. I guess my biggest question is…don't you want a break? Don't you want to quit doing that?"

Gus sat with that for a second.

But he couldn't imagine what the hell a break would look like. He lived in this house. He used the living room sometimes. His bedroom and the kitchen. There were whole sections of the place he didn't go into. He didn't care about much of anything other than the ranch. Other than his brothers.

He just felt like he had a whole bunch of unused space and resources.

And Alaina *needed* him.

He thought back to that moment she asked him about sex. His whole body went tight.

That was something he *didn't* want her to know.

That he'd wanted her since she became a woman.

Hell, he didn't like admitting it to himself. Because what the hell kind of asshole felt that way?

He'd felt protective over the little girl she'd been. But he *wanted* the woman.

Now that woman needed protection, and while he would never, ever give in to his desires for her, he could save her. Maybe along the way it would save him too.

SHE WAS EXHAUSTED and sleepy by the time lunchtime rolled around. And she hadn't even done anything. It was just that she'd slept badly, then had gone to meet with Gus, had fallen into an uncertain and irritating nap, and now was crabby.

He'd texted her to say that he was going to meet

her at Sullivan's Point, and she was sitting out on the porch in one of the white wicker chairs with her knees pulled up to her chest and her eyebrows cinched tightly together.

He pulled up in his battered old pickup and got out. His boot hit the dirt first, then the rest of him unfolded out of the cab of the truck. He put his hat on his head, and walked up to the porch. "You ready?"

"I guess."

"You feeling okay?"

"No," she said. "I feel sick and angry."

"You want to wait to do this? Because it can wait."

"No. I don't want to wait. I just want to get it out of the way."

"Right then. Let's go, princess. I might buy you lunch if you play nice."

She huffed as she walked around to the other side of the truck, but he went around the front, which was much shorter, and met her there, with the passenger door held open. "I'm nice!"

With her irritation on high, and not even really directed at him, she got into the truck. She pulled her knees up in the same position as he started the engine and peeled out of the driveway.

It wasn't a terribly long drive down to the courthouse in Mapleton. It was always nice to go there. There was actual shopping and restaurant options. Pyrite Falls wasn't exactly a booming metropolis. It was a collection of ramshackle wooden buildings along the highway. Smokey's Tavern and the general store, a gas station, a diner and an ice cream shop. Not much else.

"Can we play music?" she asked.

"Be my guest."

She found a pop music station—she'd never been a huge fan of country, which mortified Elsie—and started to sing along with the song. Some of her irritation faded away as the beat picked up. She shook her hair out, laughing as she did.

She felt better already.

About halfway through, she peeked over at him, and saw that he had part of his attention directed at her.

"You're supposed to be watching the road," she said, suddenly feeling self-conscious.

"You're a changeable little thing."

"I don't like to feel upset. Sometimes it's unavoidable. But… I've always tried to just make the best of things. I was tired, but music gives me energy. So, I don't need to sit in my tiredness. I just need to deal with myself. Find a way to be happy."

"Is that what you're supposed to do? I just learned to like the feeling of being burned at the stake for my sins."

She blinked and stared at him.

"Intentional reference," he said. "But if I can't make a good joke about being burned at the stake, who can?"

He grinned, and the smile tugged at his scars.

She huffed a laugh. "Yeah. You're a real Joan of Arc."

Except, she had to wonder if he was. Given that he was sacrificing to marry her. Though, maybe he wasn't really sacrificing anything. Like he'd said, he didn't really do personal life here in town. Which must mean he did it elsewhere. Well, he'd kind of said that too. And that meant that he would probably keep on doing that.

They were on their way to get their marriage license. She should probably ask.

"Are you still going to...do your business out of town? Like you do."

"Are you asking me if I'm going to sleep with other people?"

"Yes."

"I don't have a need all that often, Alaina, if I'm honest with you. I'm not out every week the way my brothers are. If I have a need, I go off and take care of it. Don't like to talk about it. Don't like to advertise it. I expect I'll do much the same. You won't know about it. Nobody will."

"Okay."

Well, that answered her question. About as good as anything could. He wouldn't embarrass her. Nobody on the ranch would know. Their child wouldn't know.

Their child.

Isn't that handy? You can erase your mistake, just like that. Pretend that Gus McCloud is the father of your baby.

Except... Gus never touched you.

No. And he never would. And that was fine.

She felt breathless again, and she did her best to ignore it. When they drove into the town of Mapleton, she started to pay close attention to all the restaurants they passed, trying to figure out if she had a craving of any kind. She was kind of looking forward to cravings. In general, food had been mediocre for her for the last few weeks.

"What are you thinking about?"

"Food."

"I knew I liked you," he said, the corner of his mouth tipping up into a grin.

They pulled up to the curb, and got out. Then they went in to the office and found that there was no line. They filled out the paperwork required, and left with the instructions that the license had to be filed within three days.

"I didn't realize we were going to have to get married in three days," she said.

"Well, sooner rather than later. Like you said."

"I don't have a dress or anything, Gus." She felt small and silly then.

His eyes took on a strange light. "Did you want a dress?"

She looked at him for a moment. His eyes were different than Hunter's. His eyes were green. Deep like the forest. His hair was dark, a little long, touching the collar of his shirt. Probably just because he was too lazy to go get it cut all that often. Or maybe *lazy* was the wrong word. He just didn't care.

That was probably closer to the truth.

"Well, yeah. I'd like to look nice. So maybe your brothers know it's not real, and so do my sisters. And so do the Garretts. But the whole rest of the ranch doesn't, and neither does the town. And I want to look like it means something. I want it to mean something. This is…this is changing our lives. Whether we really want to marry each other in *that* way or not. It's changing our lives. And that has to matter for something, doesn't it?"

"It matters," he said.

"Well, okay then."

"Let's get you some food. And then we can stop at one of the shops in town."

"I'd like that."

They decided on a little café that served farm-to-table food, and Alaina got a hamburger, which wasn't adventurous, but was safe. The stoutness of the burger and the salt content in the fries provided just about everything she needed. And she felt bolstered by the time they were through.

They walked down the street, and lingered in front of some of the shop windows. But it was a thrift store that had a dress that really caught her eye. Lacy and old-fashioned, and since they were getting married in three days she didn't have to worry about whether or not it would fit because of her expanding waistline.

Gus wasn't standing with her when she found it, and he didn't go with her to try it on. Which, she supposed, was a good thing. Given that it was bad luck for the groom to see the bride. Or something. It was also probably pretty bad luck for the bride to be pregnant with another man's baby. But, she wasn't lying to him about it.

He *did* know.

She went into the dressing room and tugged the blue curtain over the opening, then she undressed quickly, slipping the simple dress up over her shoulders, and zipping it. She was extremely satisfied to see that it fit. It came just to the middle of her calves, sort of a 1950s style. Not terribly bridal. She didn't know why she cared.

Would she and Gus stay married forever? Would they stay married just long enough that they would be established as a family, with him fixed in everyone's mind as the baby's dad? She supposed there was no real way to project that. He might not want to fall in love and get married someday, but she sort of had.

She stared at the mirror, at the girl there who looked scared and hollow-eyed and a little bit tragic.

"Pull yourself together," she said to herself.

She stripped the dress off and got dressed again, coming out to see Gus holding a frying pan. "This is a damn good pan," he said, pointing to it.

"Well, let's get the dress and the frying pan. That seems…wedding appropriate."

"I ought to get you a ring," he said.

"Oh. I…"

"We need rings," he said. "For the ceremony."

"Gus," she said, feeling slightly uncomfortable. "We don't need to go to all that trouble."

"I'm marrying you, Alaina. If that's not the chief trouble in all this, I don't know what is."

"We can get rings here," she said, pointing to the glass case by the registers. Where there were rings, necklaces and…

A doll head.

There was a doll head.

"No," he said, clearly spotting the doll head when she did. "Not doing that."

They bought their items, and walked out of the shop. "Let's drive over to Gold Valley."

"It takes like three hours to get there," she said.

"I know. But there's a jewelry store there that's supposed to be really good."

"You just *know* about a jewelry store?"

It seemed unlikely Gus had a thing for jewelry.

"I happen to know that Wolf bought Violet a ring there. Yeah."

"I'm not Violet," she said, looking up at him. "And you're not Wolf."

Wolf and Violet had gotten married last year, after Violet had gotten pregnant during an affair they were carrying on while he was visiting family in Copper Ridge. She had come back to Four Corners and married him, and Alaina couldn't imagine the place without her.

But the big difference was, the two of them were... romantic.

She and Gus were very not.

"Our marriage license is as legal as theirs," he said.

"Yes but..."

The man was offering to buy her a ring. Maybe she should settle down and quit protesting. They got back to the truck, and he opened the door for her again. She climbed up inside. Waited for him to get in the cab. "What are we going to do on the drive?"

"Play slug bug?"

She looked at him and saw that the corner of his mouth had turned upward.

He thought he was hilarious. Clearly.

"Gus McCloud, if you punch me because you see a VW Bug, I will bite you."

"I'd like to see that."

"I'm not afraid of you," she said.

She'd meant it as a joke, but it settled between them, sort of strange and long.

"You never have been, have you?" he asked her, sounding vaguely mystified.

"No," she said. "But then, you've never been all that scary around me."

She thought back to when he had picked her up and carried her over the goal line on Game Day. Her and the ball. And the point had counted too.

The bastard.

His hold had been strong. He'd lifted her like she was nothing. But he was gentle with it too. She had always seen that in him. He would lead with what was right. He could crush someone. But he could hold someone gently too.

"Well, I'd better up my game then," he said.

"I mean, or not. Since we're getting married. You could just be nice to me."

"I could." He sounded like he was considering it. As if *not* being nice had been on the table.

They kept on driving, the scenery flying by. She leaned back, resting her head on the seat. The seat belt was scratchy against her neck. "People are going to wonder where we went."

"We *are* newly engaged."

She wrinkled her nose. "It's almost funny. Because it seems so weird."

"Yeah. So I'll tell you, Hunter didn't believe it. Not even for a second."

She sat up. "Didn't believe what?"

"That I got you pregnant."

She felt *wretched* again. What was it about the Mc-

Clouds that made them think she was utterly unremarkable, and completely unbeddable?

She slumped and crossed her arms. "This is all harming my self-esteem hugely."

"Why?"

"You laughed at me when I mentioned sex. And apparently Hunter also thinks it's unbelievable that you would ever touch me."

"Alaina," Gus said, like she was a silly child. "Hunter didn't think that *you* would ever come near *me*." He snorted. "Well, he also didn't think I'd touch you, but for different reasons. Mostly because I read him the riot act over Elsie."

That sparked her interest. She turned toward him. "You did?"

"Yeah. I didn't like him messing around with her. I don't care about him marrying her obviously. But I just wanted him to be careful."

"I see."

She shifted uncomfortably, because she also knew that Gus had known about her crush on Hunter. She didn't want to mention it, and she really hoped that he didn't...

"Also, I didn't want to see you get hurt."

Oof. And ouch.

"Please don't," she said.

"Why not?"

She squinted and frowned. "It's a sore spot, okay?"

"Okay." There was no sound for a while, just the tires on the road. "Okay," he said again. "I just need to know one thing."

"Okay," she said, exasperated now. "What?"

"Are you in love with my brother?"

"No," she said. "He's marrying my best friend."

"Is she still your best friend?"

"Yes. She's my best friend. Yes, the whole thing was not great. But I got over it. And I'm certainly not hanging on to it now that they're getting married. Anyway, what would it matter if I was in love with him?"

"A man can tolerate a lot of things, Alaina. But his wife being in love with his brother is not one of them."

"I'm not a wife you want to sleep with," she said crisply.

He didn't say anything. She looked over at him, saw a muscle in his jaw jump. The muscles in his forearms flexing. "It's a pride thing."

"Oh. Sorry. I guess I just don't see how pride fits in all this. But I'm not a man. So I'm not ridiculous."

He laughed. "You're not ridiculous?"

"I mean, maybe we're both ridiculous. We're driving out to a town that's three hours away to go and grab some jewelry for a wedding that we're having in three days. For a marriage that isn't even…"

"What?"

"I don't know."

"What do you want?" he asked.

She tilted her head. "What do you mean?"

"For the house. For anything. Everything. The house is yours, like I said. All I know how to do is make frozen pizza. I never much learned my way around the kitchen. But that was the kind of thing my dad said was for wimps. So… I've suffered these long years."

"You expect me to cook for you."

"Yeah. In exchange for my protection, my house and all of my money. Seems fair."

"Fine. Your dad really didn't want you to know how to cook?"

"I think defining those kinds of things was one of the ways that he kept my mother with him. Women's work and all that. Things he didn't know how to do. He could be charming sometimes. At least, there was a time when he could be. I think toward the end there he quit bothering. Once my mom was gone. There was never any effort. With her it was an endless cycle. Apologies and helplessness. Before the violence started again. Yeah, he beat that shit into us. Mostly, though, I… Cooking in the kitchen reminds me of her and I don't like it."

She'd never really talked to Gus like this. Like they were…equals, or whatever this was. Sure, his burns couldn't be hidden. Everyone knew he'd suffered terrible abuse; it was written all over his skin. "Oh. Well, is me cooking in the kitchen going to…?"

"I've got demons," he said. "I don't pretend I don't. That's the thing about my brothers. They don't look like they lived through hell. So they can smile, and they can flirt and they could do whatever the hell they want. People don't know. They don't know the shit that they went through. Me? Did you see the way people were staring in the store?"

"No," she said.

"Well, they were. They will when we go out to Gold Valley too. It's one thing to hang out in Pyrite Falls. Everybody knows me. Nobody looks at my scars anymore. I mean, you guys make fun of them sometimes, but that's preferable to looking at me like I'm..."

Her stomach twisted in a knot. She hadn't ever thought of that. Of people staring at Gus like that. Openly. Because they didn't know, or because it was shocking.

But he went out of town to...to hook up. So it made her wonder...

"So how does it work?" she asked, her curiosity suddenly piqued.

It wasn't that she didn't understand why women found Gus attractive. She did. Looking at him now, it was undeniable. Broad shoulders, tall, big hands, muscular. The issue wasn't his scars. It was that he was older than her, and she'd never thought of him as...as *that*.

He'd been larger than life to her from moment one. His status in town was more myth than man, the one who'd gotten rid of Seamus McCloud. He was too *much* to be a mortal.

But as she stared at him, at his profile in the truck, she could see he was incredibly appealing. Big and strong and masculine and he had an edge. He wasn't pretty like his brothers. He was something else. Something that was a little darker. A bit more dangerous.

"How does what work?" he asked.

"You go out of town to...to hook up. But when you leave town people stare at you."

"Yeah," he said, and looked at her sideways. "There's a kind of girl that's into it."

She frowned. "Into what?"

He shook his head and laughed. "Honey, I am not having this conversation with you."

"I am about to be your wife, Angus McCloud. Who better to talk about your extramarital sexcapades with than me?"

Not that they'd ever discussed such things before. But they were engaged. She was pregnant.

Things changed.

Oh, how things changed.

"All right," he said. "If you're so curious. I look like exactly what I am. I'm a big rough beast." His lips curved into a smile that seemed to catch on her midsection and make it go tight. "And there are plenty of women who want to go on that ride. I'm happy to take them there. *Pretty boys* don't cut it." His smile turned rueful. And felt pointed, quite frankly. "At least, not for everybody."

Her throat suddenly felt tight, and she was restless.

A big rough beast...

That didn't sound like something you could even... do in the cab of the truck.

She would not characterize the sex she'd had as *rough*. Just brief and deeply unsatisfying.

Gus was so big. Strong. It was far too easy to imagine those big hands wrapped tight around her wrists...

"Don't think too hard about it," he said.

"I'm not," she lied, her face getting very very hot.

"My ass."

She wheezed. "Well. Okay, I thought about it a little bit. I'm human, Gus."

He chuckled. "Great."

They sat in silence for a beat.

"Put your music on," he said.

So she did, pumping up the volume and singing. Eventually, she rolled the window down, and let the warm air filter through her red hair, blowing it all around them.

She laughed when some of it got in his face, and he smacked it away.

And when his rough fingertips made contact with her arm, she pulled away like she'd been burned. And hoped that he hadn't seen it.

It was a beautiful drive out to Gold Valley, and the town itself was lovely. Redbrick and Western, and with so many more shops than were in Pyrite Falls.

It didn't take long to find the little jewelry store. When they opened it and went inside, they were greeted by a bohemian-looking woman with a baby on her hip, and a toddler running around. "Welcome in," she said, smiling.

"Hi," Gus said. "We're here for…for rings."

"Of course. I'm Sammy. Sammy Daniels. I'm happy to help."

She took out a few pieces of jewelry, and the one that caught Alaina's eye was rose gold, the band a woven Celtic knot, a gleaming sunstone at the center.

"That's beautiful," she said. "But of course, it might be very expensive…"

"I don't care about the price," Gus said.

The woman looked up at Gus and beamed. "That's what I like to hear. And not just because I sell jewelry for a living. I like it when all a man cares about is seeing his fiancée happy. There's a matching band for the groom." She pulled out some black gold. It had a rosy color on the inside of the band, and there was the same Celtic knot impressed into the metal.

"It's made so that her ring locks into his."

"We'll take them," he said.

But it was so romantic. It was way, way too romantic for them. But Gus was getting them anyway. The sample fit her perfectly. She had to go in the back and quickly adjust Gus's. It needed to be made quite a bit bigger.

When she came back, she handed them the rings.

"Congratulations," she said.

"Thanks," Alaina muttered.

When they left, they stopped by the kitchen store.

"For a man who doesn't cook, you're fascinated by this kind of thing," she said as he touched a couple of brightly colored baking dishes.

"I'm just imagining how different it's going to be."

And there was something about that that hit her deep. She didn't let him know, though. She kept that to herself. And they bought the deep blue baking dishes, and took the drive back to Pyrite Falls. Back to Four Corners. When they pulled up to Sullivan's Point again, it was dark. And Alaina hadn't even thought to check her phone. She had about ten texts from her sisters. She sighed.

"Wait," he said.

He got the ring out, and held it out to her. "Wear this."

He wanted her to wear it now? Already? Well, why not? They'd announced their engagement to everyone and all.

"Okay." The word came out scratchy.

She took it from his hand and put it on, flexing her fingers.

"Guess you'd better tell your sisters that the wedding is Saturday."

She wrinkled her nose. "Should we tell the preacher? You know, so we make sure we can actually do this in time."

"He's never busy," Gus said.

"Well, good point. But we should tell him."

"I am going to tell him to not wear flip-flops. I don't like that."

She laughed. "I think he's supposed to be accessible," Alaina said.

"No. Nothing about flip-flops on a clergyman is accessible to me. Sorry."

"Okay. Your clergy issues are noted. See you tomorrow, Gus."

"You should probably start moving your things over."

"Oh. Right."

"You'll have your own room. There's…there's another room, near the master, that has its own bathroom too. You can have that one."

"Thanks."

"Yeah. No problem."

And she got out of the car, looking down at her hand, marveling at the fact that she was inheriting a large grumpy roommate that she was going to call husband.

Who was apparently an aficionado of rough, edgy sex, but thought the idea of sex with her was hilarious.

Yeah right. Like you want to do anything with him

anyway. That would be...hideous and needlessly complicated.

She walked into the house, and was immediately set upon by the Sullivan girls.

"Where the hell have you been?" Fia asked.

"All day," Quinn said.

"All damn day," Rory continued.

"I was out," she said. And she waved her hand so that her sisters noticed the ring.

"OMG!" Quinn said, grabbing her hand. "That's beautiful."

"Thank you," she said. "Gus... Gus got it for me."

"Wow." Quinn looked stunned. "Alaina... He's taking this very seriously."

Suddenly, she didn't want to tell her sisters that this was a marriage in name only. Why should anyone know the details of their lives? It wasn't their business.

"Well..." Her hackles were up now. "We're getting married. It's real. We have a real marriage license to prove it. And we're getting married Saturday. At the lake. I got a wedding dress." She held up the bag with the dress. Gus had taken all the kitchen supplies back with him.

"Saturday," Fia repeated, looking shocked.

"Yep. Be sure to invite everybody. And bring a plus-one. I bet Landry would love to come with you."

"Bite your tongue," Fia said.

"I will never."

"Awfully sassy still," Fia grumbled.

"And I always will be. Because Alaina Sullivan always lands on her feet."

Rory elbowed her. "I think this time you landed in Angus McCloud's arms."

And as she walked up the stairs to go to her room, that kept on echoing in her head. And when she finally slept, she dreamed about those arms. And how strong she knew they were.

CHAPTER FOUR

IT WAS THE night before his wedding, and all the arrangements had been made. And his jackass brothers had decided to throw him a bachelor party. So there he was, sitting in his mess of a kitchen, with Wolf and Sawyer Garrett, Brody, Hunter, Lachlan and Tag. There was a giant cake in the middle of the table, and a mountain of steaks. Baked potatoes, and rolls, courtesy of Sawyer's wife, Evelyn.

"Another one bites the dust," Wolf Garrett said cheerfully, slinging his arm around Gus as if Gus wasn't liable to punch him for that.

"Not the same," Gus muttered, moving away from him.

And he didn't know why he felt the need to say that. It wasn't anyone's damn business.

For all they knew, he had feelings for her.

So what.

What the fuck was it to them?

He cleared his throat, uncomfortable with what that thought had done to his chest.

"Yeah, Elsie filled us in," Sawyer said.

"Champion martyr, buddy," Wolf said.

"I'm not a martyr. She's going to move in and cook

and clean. Hell, all you boys said that I should do that," he said, looking at his brothers. "Around the time Sawyer mail-ordered his bride, you were thinking I needed to do the same. Get someone to clean this place up."

"It is a pigsty," Brody said.

"So there," he said, gesturing to Brody. "I'm doing what you said. I'm getting myself a wife. I'm *domesticating*."

"Why do I not believe that?" Brody asked.

"I don't know, *Brody*," Gus said. "Why don't you believe it?"

"Once an asshole, always an asshole?"

"Hey," Sawyer said. "I, for onc, am happy for you. Evelyn might not be Junebug's biological mother," he said, speaking of his wife and daughter. "But it doesn't matter in the end. She loves that little girl more than she loves anything. And Junebug couldn't be more bonded with her...no matter what. Blood doesn't mean a thing. And we all know that. Because we're all from some shit blood."

"Hear! Hear!" Wolf said, and they all lifted their glasses.

"The only thing that really matters is..."

"Not beating your kids when you're pissed off?" Lach asked.

"Well, that," Sawyer said. "But also being there. Loving them. Kids don't care about DNA. That's all adult stuff. Hang-ups about stupid things. I'm here to tell you, I've got the best kind of blended family in the whole world. And nothing about it is less."

That actually made Gus feel...not better. Not at all.

Because it sounded like something he hadn't bargained for. Sounded like something a little bit deeper than he'd been intending. But then, Evelyn had wanted children. She was very maternal. And she was already pregnant with baby number two. They loved having kids.

It was different. Different for him. Different for Alaina.

"Well…thanks," he said to Sawyer. Because there was a certain kind of mean he would be to his brothers, but he'd be a little bit nicer to Sawyer.

"To Gus and Alaina," Wolf said, lifting his glass.

"Gus and Alaina," they echoed, raising their glasses.

And he looked around the table, and marveled at the thing they'd built. The truth was, he'd always felt outside of every group he was ever in. Well, maybe there was a time he hadn't. But then, that had been before his dad had set him the fuck *on fire*.

Everything had changed after that.

He was the kind of tragic that made people uncomfortable, and he didn't have the stomach for being tragic.

He didn't want anyone's pity. Any more than he wanted their fear or their disgust. But there was…nothing he could do about it. Nothing he could do about the way people reacted to him.

It was what it was. But right now, he didn't feel quite so distant. Right now he didn't feel like a whole other species, or those men who got to hide the fact that they'd been through hell.

He often wondered what that was like. To not have to wear what you'd been through on your face.

To be able to protect your privacy just a little bit more.

To be able to protect your pain.

Maybe that was why he left town when he wanted to hook up. Maybe that was why he was so private about certain things.

In some ways, his choice about whether or not to keep things to himself had been taken from him.

So he wanted the ones that he could have.

"Where's my stripper?" he asked, leaning back in his chair.

"I just need another drink, then I'm good to go," Brody said, pretending to stretch, like he was limbering up.

"No," they all groaned.

"Wow," Brody said, feigning hurt. "I've been practicing all week."

"No one wants to see it," Lach said.

"There's a lot of girls down at the bar that do."

Leave it to Brody. He had a way of lightening everything up. Of keeping things fun, or making them fun when they shouldn't be. He'd always been like that.

He loved his brother. But he knew that Brody's particular pain cut deep.

Because their father had never touched Brody at all.

Their father had *loved* Brody.

And in the end, Gus sometimes figured he'd rather have been despised by the old man, just as he was.

Rather be the one he'd tried to kill.

Brody's demons were dark, lurking beneath the surface of his laughing green eyes.

And Gus had a feeling they were no joke.

"Tomorrow you'll be a married man," Wolf said.

Of course, it wasn't going to change half as much as they thought.

Really, he shouldn't notice her at all.

He'd gotten so good at ignoring her over the years. The way that he felt about her.

And sure, the whole thing with her wanting Hunter had kind of messed him up. Then he'd made a little bit too much of it to Hunter, which he had regretted later.

But he'd been *worried* about her. That was the thing. He might want her, but he'd never been under any illusion that she was for him.

It was a weird sort of punishment bringing her into his house. A way to torture himself. With her right there, but still out of reach.

His, but not his.

But it was just the right kind of torture.

You really are a mess.

Yeah. But he knew that.

Whether he married her or not. It didn't change anything.

Alaina Sullivan wasn't for him. And he would do well to remember that.

It was her wedding day. That she couldn't quite…come to terms with. She put on the white lace gown and looked in the mirror, then started to try and arrange her hair.

There were definite benefits to curly hair. She could get a tumbled effect with an updo without having to engage in much precision. If she wanted something sleek, she was out of luck, but tumbled… That was easy.

Slowly, she started to put makeup on. Trying to imagine how the day would unfold. They would say their vows.

They would… They were going to have to kiss.

Which they hadn't discussed at all.

She had a feeling that Gus just wasn't worried about it. That it didn't bother him. That it had never even occurred to him to worry at all. He would just grab her and kiss her and not feel a thing.

Maybe the pastor would tell them to kiss and Gus would *laugh*.

She felt miserable.

She went downstairs looking miserable.

Her sisters were down there, all dressed up in mismatching dresses—her bridesmaids, even if they weren't in formal wear.

They shrieked when they saw her.

"You look beautiful," Rory said, her eyes shining with romance that was not merited.

"My baby is all grown up," Fia added.

"I still can't believe you're marrying him," Quinn said, looking sharp.

"Hey," she said. "Can you stop with that?"

"Everything's going to be fine. But if you need to leave him, you can always come back home," Fia said.

"Well, thank you for helping me plan my divorce before I even walk down the aisle."

"It's always good to know that you have an escape route," Fia said nodding. "I don't forget that I have a 30-06. I can handle Gus McCloud."

"Settle down," she said. "Honestly."

The flowers that she would carry to walk down the aisle were from the garden. Her sisters' garden, which she hadn't been as enthusiastic about as she should have been.

She suddenly felt wistful and sad leaving their crazy mismatched house with all of its brightly colored paint. She'd been so focused on the fact that it wasn't hers, that she hadn't really realized how much she would miss it.

Maybe she'd done them all a disservice by not asking for what she'd wanted.

She suddenly felt very young. And a little bit tragic.

She'd been behaving poorly; that was the bottom line. She hadn't been open with her sisters. She'd thought hooking up with Travis was maturity when it just… wasn't. She'd needed Gus to step in when she was absolutely panicking…

And she'd never talked to her sisters about what she'd wanted, or what she wished was going on and…

Maybe it had all been a mistake.

Should she have leaned on them instead of him?

But you didn't. You said you'd marry Gus, and here you are. This is where your choices took you and you have to follow through.

"I love you guys," she said, wrapping her arms around them and standing out in the yard for a long moment. "I can't believe I'm leaving."

"Me either," Rory said, wiping at her eyes. "I wish you weren't."

"I'm literally moving to the next ranch."

They all laughed at that.

"You'll be a McCloud," Fia said.

"No." She shook her head. "I'm a Sullivan. I'm a Sullivan by blood. No matter if I'm a McCloud in name."

"You could also *not* take his name."

"I want the same name as the baby."

"Fine," Quinn said. "I guess that makes sense."

"But don't worry. I won't forget where I came from."

They all piled into one truck, and drove the little ways down to the lake. What she saw made her jaw drop. Because everything there was already set up. For her. For them. Food and a cake and it was beautiful. It wasn't like a last-minute thrown-together fake wedding.

It actually was like a romance novel. Everyone that she cared about right there, each one of them putting so much work into all this.

Even the Kings were standing there grilling. Even the Kings had contributed.

"Don't be mean to Landry," she hissed at Fia. "He brought meat."

"I'm not always mean to Landry," Fia said archly. "Mostly, I avoid him."

"Yeah, God help us if she ever drinks too much when he's around. I have a feeling the end result would be bad," Rory said.

Fia's grin went sharp. "Because I would tear him a new one?"

"No," Quinn said. "Because you'd be walk-of-shaming home the next morning. And I think you know that."

Fia huffed inelegantly, and parked the truck. The other girls piled out and then Fia suddenly regained her speech and opened the door, hanging halfway out. "Gross! And no!"

"Convincing," Alaina muttered.

Fia glared at her, then got out, following Rory and Quinn.

She hung back until her sisters got assembled down by the lake, until Gus was standing there in his position. He didn't have anyone standing up with him.

A couple of the ranch hands who played music at the town hall meetings got out their guitars and started to play a song.

Alaina scrunched her nose, trying to keep her emotions at bay as she walked away from the truck, down toward the lake. Down toward Gus.

And when she got there, the way he looked at her... It was really something.

Her heart was pounding, and Fia reached out and took her flowers from her hand. Which meant she had to...

"Join hands," said Pastor Flip-Flops.

She had to smile, because he *had* come in flip-flops, and she didn't know if Gus's threat had reached him. But if it had, he clearly hadn't cared.

"Join hands."

She stepped forward, and took Gus's hands in hers. His hands were so rough. And so much bigger than hers. The vows went by so quickly. Far too quickly. How was it so easy to pledge her entire life to another human being? How was it so fast?

It didn't seem right.

She was breathing hard by the time they finished, and she was waiting. Waiting. Because it was going to come.

"You may kiss the bride," the pastor said.

And she waited to see what he would do. But the wait wasn't very long. Because he didn't hesitate. He wrapped his arm around her waist and drew her up against him. He was so hard. Like a mountainside. Like a whole mountain range.

And then he brought his head down, and kissed her.

His lips were hot and firm, and even though it wasn't a deep kiss, wasn't an intense one, there was a certainty to it that wasn't like anything she'd ever experienced before.

Not that she had a vast array of kissing experience.

He was only the second guy she'd ever kissed.

Guy.

Angus McCloud wasn't...a *guy*.

He was a *man*.

Not a rock. Or a mountain.

A *man*.

Solid and unyielding and warm.

And then it was just over.

And she was...she was not happy. She was confused. How could she have this little tiny sliver of what he was, of what *kissing* him was? It left her with so many questions. Why hadn't he at least...why hadn't he let it go on longer?

She wanted to explore it. The texture and taste and feel of him.

"Alaina," he said. "Pay attention."

"Oh," she said.

They were being presented. And everyone was cheering. And then the music and the food was going, and the wedding was…over. Well, the wedding proper anyway.

They were married. The pastor pulled her and Gus aside, and they signed the license. "I'll file it tomorrow. Thanks for having me out for the wedding."

"Yeah," she said.

Well, okay, now they were married. Totally married. All signed and everything.

And she was…

She suddenly felt light-headed.

"Alaina?"

She swayed, and Gus picked her up, and parted the crowd of people, setting her down in the chair. "Are you okay?"

"Yeah," she said faintly.

He got down on his knee, and held her hand in his. "Mite," he said. "You don't look so good."

"I'm so overwhelmed," she whispered.

"It's all right," he said. "We're the same as we were before."

Except she didn't feel like they were. Nothing felt the same as it did before. They felt altered. Unutterably. And she wasn't sure why he didn't feel the same way.

"I'm fine."

"I'll get you a water."

"Thanks."

He came back with a glass, and she drank from it, but it didn't do anything to help with the light-headedness. But thankfully, everyone was lost in their revelry now, and they weren't paying attention to the small break-down the bride was having over in the corner.

She peered up at Gus. He didn't look... *Worried* was the wrong word. She didn't think he did anything half so uncertain as worry. But there was a little bit of concern etched into his face, and that was...sweet. She supposed. Not a word she would normally use to describe him. He knelt down in front of her.

"What are you doing?" she asked.

He looked up at her. "How are your feet?"

"Fine." She frowned. "Why?"

"Pregnant women. Their feet hurt."

"When they're big their feet hurt," she said, feeling flustered. "I don't even show yet."

Still, he stayed where he was, and then he slipped one of her shoes off, pushing hard into the arch of her foot, and she flexed her toes. *"Oh."*

It felt good.

No one had ever...rubbed her feet before. And there were people all around them. "Relax," he said.

"Gus," she said. "We're..."

"I'm making sure you're comfortable."

But she was... They had kissed. And suddenly, all she could think about was his mouth. And the way it had felt.

It was funny, to compare. She shouldn't. It was weird and wrong and kind of messed up. Travis had been confident. His kisses forceful. But they were choppy and the rhythm was off. It was a confidence that seemed to *insist* upon itself.

That wasn't the way that Gus's confidence worked.

His was slow. Deliberate. Controlled. Like there wasn't a thing in the world that he had to prove.

Not a thing.

And it was the same with this.

He hadn't asked. Not really. He was just…making her feel good. Handling her body like he knew just what to do. And it was strange, the way that he had anticipated something she hadn't even thought she would enjoy. But it turned out her feet did feel a little bit sore, and this felt good.

"We don't have to stay," he said.

"It's our wedding." She sounded sulky. And she was annoyed with herself. And she wondered where the hell all her certainty had gone. "There's cake. The Kings brought meat."

"Well," he said, his tone flat. "Far be it for us to turn down the generosity of the King family. So rarely is it shown."

She was pretty sure Gus was actually funny. You just had to pay close attention.

"They're not that *bad*," she said.

"Jury's out," Gus said.

"We've known them all of our lives."

"Yeah. Jury's still out."

He transferred his attention to her other foot, removing her shoe slowly. She bit her lip, goose bumps breaking out over her arms, and she looked around, feeling like they were doing something outrageously scandalous.

But no one was even looking at them. And she didn't know why she was reacting this way. Why it felt like something erotic.

"Don't be jumpy," he said.

"I'm not jumpy," she said.

"You are jumpy." He continued to work her sore muscles, his hands moving up her calves.

She moaned. "That feels good."

Then he pulled his hands away. Almost like she'd burned him.

Well, probably not that. He knew what real burns felt like. She couldn't be that powerful.

"Well. I hope you feel better," he said.

"I do. Thanks." She curled her toes into the grass and cleared her throat, then shoved her feet back inside of her shoes.

"I am looking forward to...getting properly settled in the house."

Over the last few days all of her stuff had been packed up and moved over to his place in boxes. Where everything but the furniture remained in that state.

"It'll be nice."

New roommate, she *almost* said. But she didn't.

"You have a doctor?" he asked.

"What?" She shook her head, jarred by the subject change.

"I was thinking. Because I was just thinking about... all the things we need to settle. The house. Stuff for the baby. It connects."

"If you say so."

"I do."

"Not yet," she said. "I was thinking I would go to one over in town."

"Yeah. Well, let me know if I can help with anything. With that."

"About the ranch too," she said. "Just while we're settling business."

While music played in the background, and they were at their wedding, and he had been rubbing her feet a moment ago. "I want to help. I know that you're getting the cabins set up and remodeled, and everything opens in a couple of months. I just… I'd like to help wherever I can."

"You don't need to."

"I want to. I like ranch work. I… I've missed it. I did it with my dad when he was there and after he left… Anyway we don't really do that at Sullivan's Point anymore. The Sullivans don't. We've been really focused on opening up the store. Rory is into the rentals. And Fia is all about her baked goods, and her garden. It's just…it's not the same."

"You can do whatever you want. If you want to be part of exercising horses…"

"I do. Horse chores. I'd like that."

"Then that's my wedding gift to you. Physical labor."

"Thanks. I mean, I guess that means that I won't be cooking three meals a day for you. But I'm sure that I would rather eat my cooking for dinner than yours. And whatever I don't do… I'll bring. From the Sullivans. My family can help feed us. Since Fia cooks something savory every night anyway."

"Right."

She could picture that life a little bit clearer now. And maybe that was a wholly appropriate thing to be doing at their wedding.

They stayed to cut the cake, but declined to make a

big ceremony out of it. She hadn't been able to eat. Not anything. She wasn't sad. That wasn't it at all. She was just… Things had changed. They were changing. And she wanted to hurry up and get to the part where it felt certain and settled. Because right now it was… She was trying to latch on to a picture of it all, and it was a little bit difficult. Right now it was all very weird.

When they were through with the wedding, it was dark outside and the whole crowd of people cheered them on as they headed to Gus's truck, which thankfully hadn't been vandalized in any fashion. Probably because they were just driving up the road on the same property. And she knew that they weren't headed for an actual wedding night, and still. Her body felt jingly with nerves.

Maybe because he took her hand. And it was as rough and hot as it had been at the wedding. And it was just a strange thing to have him touch her like that.

When they got in the truck it seemed especially quiet.

He started the engine and they went down the road, and suddenly he sang a line of the pop song that had been on when they'd driven out to Mapleton. Then stopped. Just as suddenly as he'd started. As if he realized that he'd done it out loud. Not embarrassed really. Just done.

"We did it," she said.

"Yeah," he responded.

"Married."

"Yep."

They pulled up to the house, and got out. And she was suddenly...very nervous.

"Relax," he said, anticipating her mood again.

It was...comforting in some ways when he did that, and a little bit disconcerting, also. Because she felt taken care of, but at the same time extraordinarily exposed.

They walked into the house, and she didn't know what she had been expecting, but it wasn't there.

Maybe a sense of warmth. A sense of homecoming. But it just felt like Gus's house, that bachelor pad that it had been before.

"You need anything?"

"No," she said. "I'm actually really tired. I think I'm going to go take a shower and go to bed."

"All right. See you tomorrow."

"Yeah. See you tomorrow."

He went into the kitchen, and she went upstairs. She wondered if he had gone into the kitchen just to avoid going upstairs at the same time she did. She walked into the bedroom, and stopped. There were just stacks of boxes. On her bed. And it wasn't nice or special or hers at all.

It was his.

She sat down on the edge of the bed and closed her eyes.

"You've got this. This is your new life. Make it yours. You don't need to feel bad about it."

She was done with her shower and ready to get in bed when she realized she still hadn't talked to either of her parents. Maybe one of her sisters had told them. That she was pregnant. That she had gotten married.

She didn't know why she felt an obligation to them.

It just didn't go away. No matter how angry or upset she felt, no matter whether they felt like parents.

She felt like their daughter and it made her think she needed to tell them.

And that was a feeling too complicated for her to dig into. A sensation she didn't like at all.

CHAPTER FIVE

GUS GAVE UP on sleep pretty early and went out to the stables. There wasn't a whole lot of shit to do, but he couldn't stand being in the house.

Touching her had been a mistake.

He stood there in the dark, hanging on to his hay fork, breathing hard. She was so soft.

And he'd kissed her.

Hell.

There was no way around it. It would have looked ridiculous for him to not do it. But she was so *sweet*. He'd known that she would be. But it wasn't anything like he'd imagined. Mostly because he never let himself fully have that fantasy.

Impressions of wanting her were one thing, but he didn't let it get graphic. But hell. *Hell.*

Now he'd kissed her. He'd tasted her. Sure. It had been nothing like the kind of taste he'd wanted to have. But it had been damn sweet.

She had melted against him. Pressing her breasts against him. She was a curvy little handful. And it was way too easy to imagine…

He cursed, and went back to breaking out the stalls. Hell.

Yeah, this was a special kind of hell.

One with pretty green eyes and fiery red hair.

A particular kind of hell that he sort of wanted to linger in. Because it was…

Well, maybe because he was a martyr.

But when you wanted the wrong things, and you also wanted to be a decent human being, he didn't know what the alternative was.

She didn't see him that way. That was the thing.

He could touch her and get a reaction out of her. She was passionate. But…it wasn't the same.

She'd liked that pretty boy. That pretty boy that was smooth and her age, and not…jacked up. Of course, that guy had been a terrible asshole, but that had nothing to do with how he looked. Or maybe it did. Maybe having it too easy, being far too pretty, had made him into that kind of jackass.

Gus wouldn't know.

Well, his brothers were pretty boys, and they managed to not behave that way. So who knew? And it wasn't his business. The guy wasn't his problem. And they were just doing this for the baby. That was it. And he had to remember that. He had to remember that there was a reason for this, and it wasn't his own satisfaction.

Hell, Gus didn't even know what his own satisfaction looked like. He wasn't sure he'd ever be satisfied. He didn't feel sorry for himself particularly. But he'd been born into a relatively shitty life, and he'd done the best with that that he could. His life was better now. Had been ever since his old man had been run off. But there was still shit that lingered on. That was the thing. And it made things difficult.

Well. It made things difficult where she was concerned.

He shook his head. He was sick of himself. He was being a whiny-ass bitch.

And he didn't deal in self-pity. That wasn't his thing.

So he kept on working. Until his brother showed up. And they didn't have to know that he'd been out here all night. And Alaina never had to know either.

WHEN SHE WOKE up the sun was high in the sky.

She sat up with a start and looked around the room. She wasn't in her room. Because she was at Gus's house.

Because she had married Gus yesterday.

And all of it came back to her in a flood of memory. She got out of bed, and gave thanks that at least she didn't want to throw up.

Then she looked at the stack of boxes around the room and felt...heavy. There was a lot to do.

And it was late.

How the hell had she slept in this late? She hadn't slept in this late since...ever.

It was 10:00 a.m.

She was a farm girl. She didn't do that lie-in-bed-for-half-the-day stuff.

She got dressed quickly, pulling on her blue jeans and grimacing when she realized they were a little bit tight.

And then she went downstairs, and stopped.

The house was a mess. There was a layer of dust over...most things.

It had a hollow, unused feeling. And then she went into the kitchen. And that table was still covered with papers. And everything was just...

The space of a man who wasn't really inhabiting his house.

It was the weirdest thing.

And he hadn't fixed it up for her.

Why should he? She didn't really know the answer to that. Especially because she had said she wanted to be in charge of all of this.

But she also wanted to work the ranch. And she suddenly felt overwhelmed by all the things that she wanted to do. They would have to make a room for the baby.

You're getting ten steps ahead of yourself.

She huffed. First things first. She needed some coffee. That little bit that she was allowed to have today.

The coffeepot was cold. Whatever had been in it was long gone. It didn't even look like there had been any made in it today.

She opened the top and saw that there was an old filter full of grounds in it and grimaced. She dumped out the remainder in the carafe and went hunting around for beans. It took forever to find them. The little bag of grounds was halfway rolled shut. She got the pot of coffee going, and then proceeded to hunt around for some breakfast.

She opened up the fridge.

There was…beer. And the half-and-half she'd used here the other day. The corners of the carton opening were ragged, the half-and-half nearly gone. There was no milk. There was an onion. She had no idea the hell why.

So there was nothing to eat. *Fabulous.*

What kind of farmer—rancher—didn't even have eggs in his fridge?

She opened up the freezer and laughed. There was toaster strudel in there. And pizza. And ice cream. And the man obviously ate entirely out of his freezer. She took out a toaster strudel and the little packet of icing. Stuck it in the toaster. She wasn't going to be a beggar or a chooser. And this was just fine.

But she was going to have to go get some supplies. Maybe she would just go back to Sullivan's Point and get some things there. She would be able to see her sisters.

Of course, they might be waiting for details on her wedding night.

Since she had *not* told them that Gus had outright said he didn't want her. Because her pride wouldn't allow it.

She huffed. Again. She was feeling very huffy and it was his fault. Because the house was a mess.

What she ultimately decided on as she crunched the toaster pastry and drank the coffee with the scanty cream was that she would go down to the ranch. Work for a while, and then she would co-opt Gus and make him shop with her. They could go to a grocery store, and choose some things that he liked. And maybe they could go out to dinner. That seemed like a nice thing to do.

Yeah. Happy couple time.

That's not weird at all. And completely unlike what you said you were going to do.

Yeah. That. Completely unlike that. Weren't they supposed to be like roommates? But he wanted her to cook for him, so she had to know what he wanted. She finished eating, dumped the rest of the coffee out, because the grounds were old and it was all disappointing anyway, and she was going to fix that.

And get the man a sugar shaker.

Because she was not fussing around with this old bag of sugar every morning.

She went outside and took a deep breath. The morning air was crisp and clean. And later today she was going to have to have him help her get her truck too, to bring it back. Maybe this was being an adult. This endless list of things to do.

She hadn't been in charge of the household at Sullivan's Point. And it felt different now.

Look at you. Being in charge. Making your life.

This was the right choice.

She kept herself focused and walked quickly down to the barn area. It wasn't Gus that she found first. It was Brody. Brody was so good-looking he scared her a little bit. He crossed over a tipping point into being intimidating. Because mortal men should not look like that. "Good morning," he said.

She blushed. "Hi, Brody."

"Elsie's around if you're looking for her."

"Oh. I was actually looking for Gus."

She really had been. She hadn't even thought of the fact that Elsie would be working here. But of course she did now.

"Oh," Brody said, his eyebrows lifting. "Well, he's growling around somewhere. He's in a bear of a mood. So good luck with that."

"Is he ever *not* in a bear of a mood?"

That was what Gus reminded her of. A big grouchy

bear. And his house was his den, and it was sort of set up for a summer he wouldn't be spending in it.

"Yeah. But it's a little growlier than usual."

"I'm not scared of him."

"Great. We got some stuff happening today. Elizabeth Colfax, the equestrian-therapy expert that we hired, is coming down to see the place today. We've got to spruce up her living quarters still. But…"

"Right. Well…that's cool. I… I actually wanted to do some work. I wasn't only looking for Gus."

"Charity's going to be here soon to do a vet check. Did you want to help her? I mean, she'll have Lachlan, but we've got to get all the horses out and get them ready for her to look at."

"Yeah. I can do that."

Lachlan's best friend, Charity, was the vet in town, and she was assisting with the equine project. She knew a little bit about all of it. But it was neat to come and see the inner workings.

"Did you still want to see Gus first?"

"Oh. Yeah."

"In there," he said, gesturing to the barn.

And she didn't know why he hadn't said that in the first place. She now couldn't escape the image of Gus as a bear. But yes. That was accurate. Sort of brutish and big and utterly uncaring of what anyone around him thought. Because why did he have to be? Because he was a bear.

And he made the rules.

"Good morning," she said.

She was greeted by a grunt.

"You're *cranky*," she said.

"Yep. But you were cranky the other day. So that's fair, right?"

"I guess. I would like to go grocery shopping with you later."

He straightened and looked at her. "What the hell do you think this is, mite?"

"A partnership, Angus. I want to know the kind of food that you like. And then you can take me to dinner."

He looked like she had hit him with a two-by-four. And she had to admit it was sort of satisfying to see that. Because... Bear. Therefore difficult for him to ever be thrown off his game.

"Well. *Well.*"

"Well indeed," she returned.

"Sure. We can do that after work."

"Great. I already have my assignment for the day. We will reconvene when everything's done."

She turned on her heel and felt...good. Because she had taken control of the situation. She was not going to leave the house a squalid den. And today her room wasn't going to get unpacked. So that was a little bit unfortunate. But she was amped to be helping with the vet check.

She went down to the main paddock, and Lachlan was already there. Leading a horse out of one of the stalls.

"Hi," she said to him.

"Howdy," he returned. "You here to help?"

"I see Brody's been in touch."

"Yeah. Charity's almost here."

And a few moments later, a big truck with modified

racks on it pulled onto the property. And a very small woman climbed out of it.

Charity had always reminded Alaina of a mouse. She was quick and able in her movements, fine-boned and bright-eyed. She had wispy blond hair that fell in ringlets from a bun piled at the top of her head. She was wearing a pair of serviceable jeans, a T-shirt, and as soon as she got there, put on some gloves. "All right. Vaccines, checkups and all the rest ready to go."

"All right," he said, elbowing her. "How's it going?"

She frowned. "My dad's not doing great."

"Sorry."

And for all that Alaina knew they were just friends, she felt slightly uncomfortable witnessing the intimacy between them. They were close. And it was obvious.

"We'll talk later," Lachlan said.

She nodded. They got twenty horses checked and given a clean bill of health, and when they were finished, she went and found Elsie, who was exercising a horse in the paddock. She leaned up against the fence and looked at her friend. "How's it going?"

"Great," Elsie said. "Great. How are…? You didn't… you didn't tell me how the whole…the whole you-and-Gus convo went."

"Which, um, one?"

Elsie's eyes went wide. "The…sex one."

Alaina's throat went dry. "Oh, that. Well. Because. Because he laughed at me and said he didn't want to… do that."

Elsie stopped the horse. "Oh."

"Right? I thought men were all for that. *Gung ho* for that. But apparently he is just wanting to help."

"Is that why you didn't ask anyone to be your bridesmaid?"

Alaina's heart slammed against her ribs. "Yeah. It wasn't a real wedding. Were you... Did I hurt your feelings?"

"I was a little worried. I thought maybe you were still mad at me."

"I'm not. It's just...this isn't real and we didn't spend a ton of time planning it. It was a hurry-and-make-it-legal thing. That's all."

"Good. Because I want you to be in my wedding."

Emotion made her chest feel like it was expanding. "I want to be in your wedding."

"Good." Elsie paused for a second. "I know your wedding happened quickly, but it was real. Are you really never going to...?"

"He said he isn't into it." She thought of the kiss and her cheeks warmed.

"Are you into it?"

The thought made her brain short out. "I don't... He's Gus. I trust him more than I trust anyone. I... Sorry. He's not my best friend or anything but he's a protector. He's..."

"It's okay that you have a different relationship with him than you do with me. You trust him. He's always been there for you."

He had been. A strong silent presence that she somehow had always known would back her up.

"That's what this is," she said. "It's just more of the same. Him protecting me."

"Do you want there to be more?"

"I think that would be one too many things on my to-do list. I'm already his farm wife. His house is a wreck."

Elsie laughed. "Yeah. I'm going to have to do some work to civilize Hunter. I know he's not quite as feral as Gus, but…"

"There are whole packs of wild animals that are less feral than Gus," Alaina said.

And they smiled at each other.

"Are you happy?"

She shrugged. "I think I have to wait and see how everything pans out. I'm just kind of anxious to get to the changes. Like get them over with. So he and I have moved in together. But I need to get the house in order. And then when the baby comes… I just need to be able to get a handle on where this is all going."

"I think unfortunately you'll find your feet and then more stuff will just change."

Alaina didn't like the sound of that at all. She wanted to arrive at a place of certainty. Where everything was well ordered and it was a perfect and proper place.

"Don't tell me that."

"Well. With your busy schedule let's actually hang out. Let's not be those people that get…lost. Because of men and all of that."

"All right. Let's make sure."

And she left feeling a little bit lighter than when she'd arrived. She went hunting for Gus around five o'clock, and found him standing out in the driveway with a pretty blonde woman that Alaina had never seen before. She was elegant. Something Alaina had certainly never been accused of. Wearing pearls and a very understated sheath dress with navy blue sling-back shoes. And she was just...*pretty.*

Gus looked at ease with her. In a way that he never did with her. Of course, she'd never really seen Gus when he wasn't with her, so she didn't know that he could look like this. Relaxed.

She skulked into view, and made her way over to the two of them. "Hi," she said. "I'm Alaina. Alaina McCloud. Gus's wife."

The other woman grinned warmly at her, and did not respond to the slight spikiness in Alaina's tone.

"Elizabeth Colfax," she said. "I'm going to be the licensed therapist and consultant at the facility."

"Once we get everything cleaned up." Brody's voice came from the barn, and a second later he appeared. And Alaina watched as Miss Elizabeth Perfectly-Put-Together went stiff. Her smile was still there, but she had gone rigid. Obviously, she was bothered by Brody McCloud. "Yes. Well. I look forward to that. Thank you for the productive meeting," she said. "But I have a drive back to Portland. So... I'll see you in a couple of months."

Gus took his hand out and shook hers. "See you then, Elizabeth."

"A pleasure. Thank you, Angus."

"Angus," Brody said as soon as Elizabeth left. "*A pleasure.* She's got a stick up her ass."

"She's professional," Gus said. "Something you wouldn't know anything about."

"It's something I don't need to know anything about," Brody said. "Because all this kind of stuff isn't my problem. The uptight therapist girl is your issue."

"Not unless I make it yours. Because I'm your boss."

Brody scowled. And Alaina didn't think she'd ever seen Brody scowl.

"Are you ready, Gus?"

"Yeah," he said. "Sure."

They headed to his truck, and got inside. And for the first time, Alaina wished she would've gone back to change. Into something a little bit nicer. Because that Elizabeth had made her feel like a troll.

"What was that about?"

"What?"

"Alaina McCloud. You haven't changed your name, mite, at least as far as I know."

"I will," she said, sniffing. She buckled her seat belt fiercely and stared out the window. "Anyway, I *am* your wife. I was introducing myself is all."

"Yes. You are my wife. But that was…that was a little bit of jealousy there, wasn't it?"

"I am not jealous. Of her. She…she looks like she should be on a yacht. I don't want to be on a yacht. I'm not seagoing. I am of a mountainous people. And I have no desire to be… No. Not a wayfarer."

"Okay," he responded, his tone indicating that he very much thought that she was unhinged.

"Let's just go to the store."

"You want to go to John's or…"

"I'd rather not. I'd rather just skip over to town."

"All right."

"Hmm, I need to feed you first. Because you're being a feral little demon."

She slapped her thigh. "I thought you were going to be nice to me."

"That *was* nice."

They didn't speak as they made their trip toward town. And he took her to the same restaurant for the same burger, and she almost groused about it, except that it really was very good, so her grousing would've been disingenuous. They got to the grocery store, and Gus, in his cowboy hat, grabbed the shopping cart and steered it toward the automatic doors. And seeing him do such a mundane act was about the strangest thing she had ever experienced. This domesticated act of being in a grocery store. Pushing a shopping cart. And it made it harder for her to ignore the fact that he was a man. A human man.

Not a bear.

Not a mountain.

And definitely not out of reach.

Her fingertips felt strange.

"Okay. Let's do this thing," he said.

"What do you like?"

"I eat almost exclusively frozen pizza."

"How do you look like that?" she asked, knowing that she had just betrayed that she had in fact noticed his body. All hard-packed muscle, without an ounce of fat.

"I don't know," he said.

"Do you secretly do a thousand sit-ups every day?"

"No."

"You don't…you don't work at that?"

"No. What the hell do I care? I just need to be able to get my job done. I'm not some gym bro out trying to get gains or whatever else. I don't care."

And she didn't know why that was compelling. It just was.

"Well. Fine. But we're not doing frozen pizza."

"Oh, I wasn't suggesting we should. I'm sick of it."

"Okay. So I'm not a gourmet or anything. But spaghetti? Pot roast?"

"Like I said. It's all good."

They stopped by the produce and she grabbed onions and some potatoes.

"I assume we can just get steak from the Garretts?" she asked.

"Yep. Direct. I actually have a flat freezer outside and there's plenty of meat in there."

"Oh. I didn't check there."

This was mundane. This was skipping to be an old married couple. And she felt…weirdly charged. She couldn't say that she cared for it.

She grabbed the front of the cart and guided it toward a small section that had dishes. "You need a sugar shaker," she said.

"I do?"

"Yes," she said. "I am not a savage, and I will not live as one."

"I think you mean *we* need a sugar shaker."

And he was messing with her. She was pretty sure. But he grinned, and it was irresistible. And she wondered if it mattered whether he was teasing her or not, since the end result was the same. It was their sugar shaker. Everything that they were getting today was going to be theirs.

The house was theirs.

She stared at him. "Fine. We need a sugar shaker."

They went over to look at them, and there was a white one with flowers. And a cowboy. But sugar that came out of his hat.

"You know which one we have to get," he said.

"*No,*" she said.

"Marriage is about compromise. You think we need a sugar shaker. I think we need no such thing. We have to get a cowboy."

She stared up at him, trying to see if he was smiling. She swore she could hear a hint of humor in his voice. It was so very hard to say.

"Are you messing with me?"

"Yes. But we are getting the cowboy."

"You're a child," she said.

"I thought I was an old man."

"Angus McCloud," she muttered, grabbing the cowboy and putting it in the cart.

Then she stepped back toward the produce, and chose some avocados and other things that they weren't able to grow in the garden at Sullivan's Point.

If she got caught buying pitted fruits, she would be disowned forever.

"What are we having tonight?"

"Tacos and guacamole?"

"Yeah. I can dig that."

"All right. But I hope you are not expecting homemade bread and the kinds of things that Evelyn Garrett comes up with. Or Violet. Or my sisters. I am not my sisters."

"I know," he said.

"You should learn to cook," she said. "It would be fun."

"I don't think it would be. And why would I do that?"

She lifted a shoulder. "Because. You have someone to cook for now."

CHAPTER SIX

HER WORDS RANG in his head the whole rest of the next day.

He had someone to cook for now.

He wasn't sure how he felt about that. But if anything made him want to learn how to fry an egg, it was that.

The thing about his house. He had a well-worn path he moved through. Rooms he went into every day, rooms he didn't go in at all. It was a necessity, like sleeping and eating. The thing about eating was it was something he had to do to fuel himself for work.

He just didn't think a whole lot about his own comfort.

He had always rationalized that with the fact that he had gone through a horrific injury and a hellish recovery.

His dad had been mad about that too. Had to declare medical bankruptcy after Gus's long-term stay in the hospital.

Burns were a bitch. They didn't just heal.

He'd had rehab and recovery and all kinds of shit. Surgeries. He didn't have feeling in the place where the burns were the worst. And he sort of figured...it was the kind of thing that guarded him against good and bad sensations. Pain and pleasure.

He figured it had translated into other areas of his life. So he didn't think much about what he ate, what he wore.

He liked sex, but he wasn't obsessed with it. His life didn't revolve around his own desires. That was the thing. But…she wanted to work at the ranch. And could he really ask her to do that and cook all the meals? They were having a kid. He wouldn't want his son to do anything like that to a woman he married. And he sure as hell wouldn't want his daughter to accept that.

He stood still for a moment, his heart frozen in his chest.

He'd committed to being a father and that meant modeling behavior.

He could have a little girl. And he knew…he just knew how terrible men could be, and the very idea of it terrified him.

. So yeah. He supposed he needed to learn how to cook.

This was a lot more complicated than he'd antici-pated. A lot more involved.

Down to grocery shopping with her last night. He looked across the field and saw Elsie and Hunter, on their horses, talking to each other, looking…settled.

He wondered what his life would be like when they were all settled.

He supposed he was settled now. Well, and he had the kid to look after.

All of his life he'd had to look after the boys.

All of his life he felt an intense, fierce protective-ness over them.

Because he knew his parents wouldn't protect them.

His mother couldn't. She'd been way too beaten down by his father, and the thing was, Gus knew just how lethal the man was. Gus knew. He didn't blame Hunter, even though Hunter blamed himself. That was just youngest-kid bullshit. He wasn't here for it. Youngest kids always did that. Managing to make it all about them while trying to take all the guilt on board at the same time.

Useless. It wasn't anyone's fault but Seamus McCloud's. He was a dick. And he was the only one that had to answer for the things that he'd done.

But the fact remained…he left a whole lot of broken people in his wake.

What he did wonder sometimes was whether their mother was still alive. Because Seamus was gone, and she could come back to see them…

The thought filled him with a strange sort of dread.

His mother hadn't seen him since he'd been set on fire. She wouldn't know him. Wouldn't recognize him.

Wouldn't think he was her beautiful boy or any of the things that she used to say to him.

Shit. Why was he thinking about his mom? It was this baby nonsense. He didn't have time to sit around and ruminate.

And then he heard hooves, coming up hard and fast behind him, and he turned just in time to see Alaina riding fast down toward him. And for just a second… for just a second everything stopped. Her red hair was flying in the wind, and the look on her face was one of pure joy.

And she was coming toward him.

But then, she whipped right on past, turning the horse sideways and coming to a stop next to Hunter and Elsie. They started talking and laughing, and Gus gritted his teeth.

Yeah. That was about right. She hadn't been coming toward him after all.

He urged his horse forward into a trot and came alongside the trio.

"Good morning," he said.

"Hi," Alaina said, breathing hard, her eyes sparkling.

He knew it wasn't for him. He was sure of it now. But that didn't mean it didn't make his chest do all kinds of strange and horrible things.

"You got up a little earlier today," he commented.

"Yeah. I feel a little better."

"Good."

"So, lunch today?" Alaina asked, directing it at Elsie.

"Sure," Elsie said, looking thrilled.

"I guess we are not invited to join the ladies who lunch," Hunter said.

"I don't want to go eat salads anyway," Gus said.

Alaina snorted. "When have I eaten a salad in front of you?"

"I don't know," he said. "You bought avocados last night."

He felt a little bit like she must've felt when she had stood there and proudly proclaimed that she was his wife in front of Elizabeth Colfax like she had to stake a claim. Because that's what he was doing. Making sure that Elsie and Hunter knew she was something else to him now. Because they'd gone to the grocery store last night. They'd bought avocados. He'd weighed them. They had a connection.

And he had no idea why that mattered to him. Except it… He had his brothers. And that mattered. It mattered a hell of a lot. In fact, it was everything in some ways. If he hadn't had them growing up, if he hadn't had them going through that most horrible time of his life…there would've been no point. He would've just died in that shed. He wouldn't have tried to get out. Because it hurt too much, even at the time. Because just letting the fire finish what it started would have seemed like a much easier thing than the recovery and the survival that he had to endure. And make no mistake…he'd fucking endured it. So yeah, they mattered. But he'd always felt distant from them too. He was different.

Again, he thought of Brody. Who must feel like an outsider himself.

The brother that hadn't been beaten.

And Gus… Well, he was the one his dad had tried to kill.

"Avocados," Hunter said. "Neat."

"We had tacos," Alaina said. "We might have them again tonight."

"I like tacos," Hunter said.

"Good for you, Hunter," Alaina said.

And she did not invite him over for their dinner, and that satisfied Gus.

"Alaina," he said, "have you seen the cabins that we're renovating?"

"No," she said.

"Come on over and I'll show you."

"All right." She turned back to Elsie. "See you later."

"Race you," he said.

And she didn't wait for him to say go; she took off laughing. The little wench. And he went after her, until he didn't feel the urge to pass her at all. Because he just wanted to watch her ride. Wanted to watch her hair fly behind her.

That girl that couldn't be tamed.

He didn't want to tame her. He just wanted to keep her safe.

His chest suddenly felt sore.

He pulled in front of her as they got back to the main part of McCloud's Landing. "You don't know where you're going," he said, slowing the horse down as she slowed hers too. Then they came to the little row of cabins. "It'll be guests. Patients, I guess. And then we got a place that we're doing just for Elizabeth."

"Ah, yes. Elizabeth."

"Yes," he said. "You have a real issue with her."

"I don't."

"Back to that jealousy I mentioned earlier."

He was poking at her, and she might laugh. Instead, she sputtered. "I am not… I'm not jealous. I mean, you know, she's one of those women that seems to be effortlessly put together, and I challenge you to find a woman who wouldn't feel a little bit intimidated by someone like her. But… I'm not jealous."

"Happy to hear it."

"So…where's her place going to be?"

"Out of the way a little bit. To give her some privacy. She's got a son."

"Oh."

"Yeah. Went through a divorce a few years back. Looking to start over."

"Well, now I feel bad. Because I guess you can't really tell who has it all together. And a lot of people make mistakes…hedge their bets on the wrong guy."

"People lie about who they are," he said. "And accidents happen. And even when people are a hundred percent truthful about who they are, it doesn't mean it's that easy to get away. Look at my family. It took a lot to get rid of the poison that was here. It happens. We make bad mistakes with people sometimes and…"

"I mean, at least Elizabeth was married to him, I guess."

"And you're married to me," he said. "So I don't see the issue."

"Gus," she said, then she reached out and patted him on the hand. "You're sweet."

And he felt…somewhat emasculated by that comment.

Lucky for her his masculinity wasn't fragile, or it might've done some serious damage.

"I'm *sweet*?"

"You married me to protect me, and now you're reassuring me. Of the nine thousand things that have come up in this conversation. My insecurity around someone like Elizabeth, and obviously my deep insecurity of the fact that I did something…rash and idiotic. You're

protecting me. And you're protecting the baby. And…
yeah. You're sweet."

"I'm not fucking sweet, Alaina."

She grinned from her position on the horse. "Why
is that such a challenge to you?"

"Because no one else treats me like that."

"Maybe no one else has ever seen the real you. Not
that you show it to me constantly," she said. "I feel like
I get glimpses of him daily. Even though I do have an
ugly sugar shaker now."

"Wench."

She smiled and got off her horse, and he did the
same. Then they walked toward the first cabin and
opened it up. It had been entirely gutted. The wiring
pulled out of the walls, and rewired. They'd hired a professional for that, but he and his brothers were going to
be working on Sheetrock and texture this week.

"Wow," she said, looking around the hollowed-out
shell. "I can see where they have a lot of potential."

"Yeah. That way it'll be a nice place for people who
come here and do short- or long-term stays."

She looked at him, those green eyes too bright and
too sharp. They'd always been like that. She'd always
been like that.

"Would you have wanted to come to a place like
this?" she asked.

She'd always been a bold thing, but she'd never
talked to him about anything this personal.

She had gotten closer to the heart of all of it than anyone else had. People thought that it was a smart business
venture. They knew that part of him wanted to reach out

and do something, since this land had been the site of so much violence and sadness. That he wanted to give it a different legacy.

But he never talked about the way it made him think about that thirteen-year-old boy who'd been so badly wounded. That thirteen-year-old boy that had felt lost and scared and alone and struggled with nightmares, struggled with fear. With increasingly feeling isolated from the people around him.

"I couldn't find a lot of happiness after what happened," he said.

"I don't really know the story," she said.

And it all kind of caught in his throat. Because he and his brothers just didn't talk about it as a matter of course. And the whole rest of Four Corners seemed happy to let it be a myth. Maybe a murderer. Maybe a monster. And he knew that his appearance added to that.

He also knew that in the telling of the whole story, it revealed that there was only one monster in the Mc-Cloud family.

Just the one.

Just the one that let it all go free.

"It's not really a secret," he said.

That much was true. But she was looking at him, and he was caught between two things. The desire to tell her, and treat her like it wasn't a big deal, because the more he refused to talk about it when asked directly, the more it made it…made it seem like his father had succeeded in at least part of what he'd tried to do.

He did. He killed part of you and you know it.

Didn't mean he had to show it.

There were things he had to show. The scars. And he wore them boldly because he had no other choice. He wore his hatred for his father that way, and if people wanted to believe he killed his dad? Fine with him. If they wanted to believe that when he was eighteen he'd lost it completely and driven the old man into an early grave, it was fine by him.

It kept his truths hidden. And he prized those. The personal things. The things he could keep to himself.

But even though there were things he couldn't hide, he wanted to protect Alaina. Because there wasn't a single part of that story that was pretty. Not remotely. And he knew that Alaina had been through her share of pain. That her parents had a lot to answer for. But he also just wanted to protect her. From anything ugly.

"Stop," she said. "Stop…whatever it is you're doing. You can tell me what happened. I'm not… I'm not five. I know that you pulled me out of the pond then, but I've grown up since then. Remember. You married me. I'm pregnant. I'm not a child."

"I don't think you're a child," he said, his voice sounding rough even to his own ears. "There's just… There's things in this world that no one should have to hear about. That no one should have to know about. Least of all thirteen-year-old boys. And I didn't have a choice. I went through what I did. It's inflicting it on other people that bothers me."

"All of it's your dad. All of it's his fault. You don't need to take a single thing on board. And you certainly don't need to hold it in on my account."

"I don't feel like I'm holding it in. Not anymore."

He wondered what would be right here. To hold back, or to give it to her? She was his wife, and it might not be a traditional sort of thing, but didn't she deserve to know the man she was living with? The man who'd be raising her baby?

Maybe you just want to say it. Finally.

Maybe.

"I just never told the whole story," he said. "My brothers were kids. And it's one of those things I think when you…were kind of around when something happens, you kind of think you know. Nobody really questions it. They all talked about it among themselves, but they never talked about it to me."

"What happened?"

"He…he was beating Lachlan. I thought it was going to kill him. Lachlan asked where Mom was. He got furious. Just…absolutely furious. I was thirteen and tall and skinny, and didn't have an ounce of muscle. And I flung myself at him. Punched him right in the face. I told him he was the reason that Mom left. And he sure as hell didn't have any kind of a right to take it out on Lachlan. He started to run after me…and I… I gave him something to chase. I like to think that I was leading him away from Lach, but you know. Most likely I was just running to save my own ass."

"I hid in the woodshed," he said. "I heard the door rattle, and I was scared. But he wasn't opening it. He was shoving a broom handle through the door catch. To hold the door shut. And before I knew it… I could smell smoke. I could hear them outside. He was drunk. And he said…he said he'd let me out if I said I was sorry.

If I said I was wrong. If I'd go tan Lachlan's hide the way he deserves. He said I didn't understand discipline here, being the head of a household or being a man. He said I didn't understand being a father. I wouldn't say anything. I wouldn't give him the satisfaction. Then I started to realize it wasn't just smoke, and there were flames. That's when I started to yell for help. I didn't have pride, Alaina. I didn't stay brave. I screamed and cried like a baby. Especially when the fire burned to me. I don't know why I didn't pass out from the smoke. I had a hell of a lot of damage on the inside of my throat, my lungs. The fire burned me all the way down. I remember the way it felt against my face. And I remember fighting against it, because if I died…who was going to protect them? So I threw myself against the fire. Where it had already burned the shed and weakened it. And I was able to get out. I ran down to the river, threw myself in. Lachlan called for help. I think he's… I think he's the only one that really knows. Because he saw it. The ambulance came, and the story was that there was an accident. Accidental fire and I got trapped. And I just think it never really got investigated."

"How? How did everyone fail you like that? In a town this size, how did they not know?"

"It's because it's a town this size. Some people knew and didn't do anything because they didn't want to get involved. Other people knew and were afraid of him too. Some refused to know because they worked with him and needed him to help pay their bills. There are connections everywhere you look, everywhere you step. And at the end of the day so many people prize the rights of a man to do what he wants to the people around him over the safety of the people in his path. Now, they don't let themselves see how bad it is. I don't think anyone thought he'd try to kill one of us. No. There's a lot more denial involved than that."

Alaina had tears on her cheeks, and that was what he hated. She took a step forward, her hand outstretched. "Gus…"

And he pulled away, because he couldn't stand for Alaina Sullivan to put her hands on him because she felt sorry for him. That was just a bridge too far. He'd rescue her from anything. But he didn't want her pity.

"I can't believe he did that to you," she said.

"I can. It's right in his character. It's who he is. Believe me on that. He was just waiting for that moment. He was just waiting. For an excuse. To let it boil over like that. Better me than them. I'm the oldest. That's the point."

"Who protected you, Gus?"

He smiled, and he felt that tightening in his skin. "No one. They didn't need to. I'm all right."

She looked down. "And now you're protecting me."

"It's not a hardship. Don't worry about it."

She looked back up at him, her face too pretty for him to bear. "What do you want, Gus? Because you asked me what I wanted. From life. From this. Do you want to be a father?"

The question was uncomfortable, and tore at him, and forced him to look at things that hurt. Because the thing was, he was obviously trying to find a way to make up for some of the stuff that he'd been through.

"I don't know. What I want is to be better than my old man. And it's not just for me. I want to… I want to make up for him existing. For the fact that I didn't kill him. I want to do good stuff. I want to…"

"You are good," she said. "And you already made more changes in my life than I can even believe."

"I won't be like him, Alaina. I won't. I don't even know why he had kids. I don't know what he thought. I don't know what he wanted. Not from his wife. Not from us. Why? Why do you do that? Tie these people to you just so you can abuse them? Why have kids if you can't…protect them?"

Those last words cost him.

They weren't about his father.

They weren't about the scars anyone could see.

They were private scars. The ones he kept buried.

"I don't know," she said. "And I know you aren't like him." She made a move to touch him again, but he rebuffed her.

Not now.

Not when she wanted to comfort him like he was a wounded, sad animal, and he wanted to touch her like she was a woman.

"Don't pity me," he said. "It was a long time ago. I wouldn't call me sweet, Alaina, but I have a lot of empathy for people who are going through something tough. If I can help…then great."

"Did horses help you?"

He smiled, but this was an effortless one. "Horses are about the only thing on this earth that haven't let me down. It's the reason I feel strongly about McCloud's

Landing. About keeping it. Cultivating it. Finding a way to move forward with it. So that it's something other than what it was. The only reason I care about our legacy at all…is because I believe we have resources that we can make matter. Mean something. And the horses are the biggest part of that."

"It was when my dad left that I really realized how much being outside, tending the land, finding connection meant to me. Because when he left, I lost that. He was my companion out there and I… I didn't have it anymore. That was when Elsie and I really became great friends. I found a way to hang on to what I loved even without him there. Sometimes losing things shows you what matters. What you really want to hold on to. The horses were certainly therapy for me."

"I'm glad you're here. To help with this."

"Thanks. I still don't know what you want, Gus."

For a minute, he sincerely thought about telling her. *I want you. Naked and begging for me.*

But he didn't.

"I don't want a whole lot, mite. But when I think of something I'll let you know."

"Okay. I'm going to go meet Elsie for lunch."

"All right."

And as he watched her exit the cabin and get back on her horse, he wished that he'd let her touch him. Even if it had been out of pity. Pride and martyrdom weren't all that satisfying when the ache of wanting another person was so damn intense.

Yeah. That pretty well sucked.

And it was a hell of his own making.

Just like most of the ones he found himself in.

"Champion martyr," he mumbled to himself. "Champion fucking martyr."

"I GUESS I need to make a doctor appointment," she said, sitting cross-legged on the sandy beach across from Elsie. Their lunches were just the ones they'd packed themselves that morning. Alaina had a sandwich and chips. Elsie had rolls and cold chicken.

Alaina was appalled by the cold chicken, and every time her friend took a bite of it she wanted to gag. But she didn't say anything about it. Because she was trying to build bridges. Not be a chicken bitch.

"So how are things going?" Elsie asked.

All she could think of was her conversation with Gus, but she knew that wasn't what Elsie was asking. Since Alaina had just been talking about making a doctor appointment, she was pretty sure she was asking about the pregnancy.

"I don't feel as sick. At least not today."

"That's good."

Her heart hurt. The story that Gus had told had horrified her, and part of her wanted to tell Elsie about it. But she also wanted to keep Gus's confidence. Wanted him to be able to trust her with whatever he needed to.

Her loyalty to Gus was becoming something real. Big. She wanted…she wanted something from him, with him; she just wasn't sure what.

"How are other things going?" Elsie asked.

"Do you mean living with Gus?"

"Yes. I do."

"I… It's going well." She wanted to share about her feelings. About the way things were shifting. But she didn't have words for it. "We got a sugar shaker, so that's really revolutionized things."

"Okay," Elsie said. "I didn't realize sugar shakers were quite so revelatory."

"Yeah. And he said that I could order stuff for the house. But I just keep looking at things and not really pulling the trigger. Because it freaks me out. The idea of spending his money. But he says that I can. I mean, I'm working at the ranch now. But we haven't really talked about me getting paid. I don't know if it's just… sharing all of our stuff. And I want to teach him how to cook. Because he doesn't know how."

"Really? Hunter does."

"Oh." She wondered why Hunter could cook, but Gus wouldn't.

"Though, only breakfast," Elsie said. "Which I have a feeling has something to do with the one-night stands he used to have."

"Ah right. Yeah. Gus doesn't cook anything. Everything's just in his freezer. He's uncivilized."

Elsie said nothing for a moment, then finally asked, "So how long is this thing going to last?" Elsie's eyes were keen and Alaina squirmed beneath her friend's gaze.

"Well, it's marriage, Elsie, so you tend to plan on it lasting forever."

"Yeah, the people banking on forever are usually romantically involved."

"We have an agreement. He's…just going to go about

his—" she wrinkled her nose "—sensual business. Like he always has."

"And you're okay with that?" Elsie asked, her lip curling.

"I… No." As soon as she said that, she realized she wasn't okay with it. Gus felt like hers. And if she really thought about it, Gus had felt like hers for a long time. Her protector. Her special…scary guardian mountain man who was always there when she needed him. Up to the point of marrying her. But what category did that fit in? And yeah, there was the kiss. And there was the way that he had touched her when he was rubbing her feet after the wedding.

And then there was him talking about rough sex.

But there was also him laughing at her when she'd asked about the two of them sleeping together.

"It's complicated. If we add personal stuff between us… I'm worried. I'm worried about changing too many things. I mean, I guess we don't really have to worry about it, right? Maybe someday we'll…fall into that kind of thing. Naturally, you know? Maybe it will feel right someday. I don't know."

"So you, Alaina Sullivan, who are all about taking control of your life and your feelings, just want to wait and see what happens? Even though you don't like the idea of the guy sleeping with other women?"

That made her furious. But she refused to show it. "Yeah. Sums it up."

"Do you want him?"

A deep, profound pang went through her body. And it was like her whole brain turned away from even thinking about it. Like it was dangerous ground, and she was too afraid to walk on it.

She didn't know how to answer it.

No was the wrong answer.

Yes felt sharp and thorny and terrifying. Like it needed a wall built up around it. It was too big, too scary to face head-on.

Still, she couldn't say no.

"He's…him. He's been a part of my life for so long and…"

"You're not answering my question."

She looked away. "Well… I don't know…"

"You were happy to inform me that you were going to sleep with Hunter. And that it would be fun. And that it wouldn't be a big deal. And then you were all about Travis. And you're not acting the same about this at all."

"Because it's not the same," she said, looking back at Elsie, spreading her arms wide. "Because it's Gus."

And the way Elsie looked at her, it made her feel like she had to keep talking. "It isn't because he's scarred, Elsie. He's…too much. He's just too much."

"Oh," Elsie said. "I know you feel judged right now, but I promise you, I'm not judging you. Not about him, not about what happened with Travis. Remember, I wanted to do the exact same thing. I feel like you got caught up in something that just had…deeper consequences. And if you hadn't gotten pregnant, then no one would think it was a big deal. Including you. But I'm not judging you. Not if you do or don't want Gus. Not about Travis or Hunter, or anything."

"Well, you're right about one thing. I judge myself.

And I don't want to think about being with Gus for some reason. It…it scares me."

"Maybe the issue is that you like him a lot."

"He married me," Alaina said. "He's taking care of me. That's what he does. He laughed at me when I asked if we were going to sleep together. He said no."

"Since when do you accept a no when you want something else?"

"And why exactly are you invested in this?"

"Because I'm invested in your happiness. And if you told me absolutely definitively you were happy with this *in-name-only* thing, and he could hook up with other people, and so could you, and it was all just about protecting the baby and giving it a dad, then that would be great. And I'd support you in that. I'm worried you won't be happy, though. I'm worried you want something more."

That was a terrifying thought. She refused to entertain it.

"Don't be worried. I'm taken care of. I think that's the biggest thing. I'm completely and totally taken care of. And you don't need to worry about me."

"If you say so."

"Don't condescend to me, Elsie. As you just reminded me, you were about to make the same dumb mistake that I did. It's just that Hunter got in your way."

Elsie cringed. "Does that… Does it still bother you?"

She thought about it. Really. Because she thought she owed it to both of them to give that deep consideration. She didn't want to be with Hunter, though. She just didn't. Sleeping with Travis hadn't made her want to sleep with him again. But it had also clarified some things for her. Just thinking someone was cute wasn't actually chemistry. And some flutters in your stomach could be manufactured by your own determination. But even though she was in the kind of predicament she was then, she didn't wish it had gone differently. Not in the way that Elsie was saying.

But what she really didn't want to think about was the direct question about whether or not she found Gus *attractive*.

For some reason, it sent up a wall inside of her, which she really didn't want to deal with or address. It…it scared her. Of course, if she didn't want Gus to sleep with other women…

She finished up her sandwich and threw a rock into the lake. And remembered all the times they had done that when they were children. And things had felt simple. And nothing felt simple now.

"How come everything is such a mess here?" Alaina asked.

"What do you mean?"

"My parents, your parents. Hunter and Gus's parents. Honestly, the weird thing is that the Kings seem the most even-keeled. And I think we all know that's not true."

"Yeah, I'm pretty sure they have their own demons. I don't know, though. I don't know why things fell apart here. But what I know is that all of us—our generation— we're trying to make something better out of this place. We're trying to make a real family. I think we've done a pretty good job. We stick together when it's tough. We don't abandon each other. We never have."

Of course they didn't. Because she and Elsie were still here together, even after everything. And she wasn't by herself. Travis had left, but Gus was with her. Gus had married her. That was loyalty. That family loyalty they had here at Four Corners, that they had knit together between the four families, because of the way their parents had been. They had decided to be better. And they were doing a damn good job.

She and Elsie hung out at the lake for a little while longer, and then they loaded back up into their trucks and headed back out to McCloud's Landing. Elsie back to work, and Alaina to the house. She had promised Gus tacos, and she had boxes to unpack in her room.

She started with her room, sorting through as much as possible before she began to get hungry again. Then she went downstairs and started hunting around in that flat freezer for some ground beef, which she found directly, and began to cook up a skillet of taco meat. She threw in some spices, and then mashed up the avocado, throwing in some of the homemade salsa that Fia had put together, garlic and a bit of citrus. She took out the stack of corn tortillas and started to fry taco shells, slightly irritated she hadn't had time to cook her own dry beans. But she had brought cans as a backup. She just preferred homemade.

She got everything finished, then covered it with a cloth, and went outside, hoping that she might catch sight of Gus.

Again, she felt slightly disquieted by the domesticity of it all. Or maybe just how much she liked it. But really, wasn't this the point? They were partners. Friends.

Working together to build a family. To make something new and better than what they were given. And they would do it.

They were doing it.

She walked around the back side of the house, and stopped. Because there was Gus, pitching his cowboy hat onto the ground and grabbing the bottom of his shirt, wrenching it over his head. And then he picked up a bucket of water on the ground in front of him, straightened and dumped it over his head.

And all Alaina could do was stand there and stare.

Water rolled down his perfectly defined chest. His—dare she be so cliché—rippling abs. She had known that he was rock-solid. She had known that he was muscular. But she hadn't realized that he was so beautifully formed. Tanned skin with scars here and there. Dark hair scattered across a broad chest. He was lean, but big.

And it could not be denied, as she sat there feeling parched as hell, that Angus McCloud was a whole thirst trap.

Did she *want* him?

Well, the thing was, she had never even thought she could aspire to a man like that.

He was a *man*. Not a green boy like Travis had been. She couldn't even muster up any enthusiasm for the flutters that she'd once felt for Hunter, who was definitely a more mature kind of handsome than Travis had been.

But this was something else.

Gus McCloud was something else.

And maybe that was why. Maybe that was why she had always pushed the Gus situation to the side. Because this was big. And terrifying. And she kept on staring. At that lean waist, at the dramatic cuts that seemed to point straight down below the belt line of his jeans. And then he turned, just partway, his biceps and shoulder muscles shifting with the motion, little tiny muscles all along his ribs popping out.

She needed to retake anatomy. Because she was seeing a whole lot of muscles with names she wasn't even certain of. And she would like to be able to catalog them as she stood there staring at him like he was a hamburger.

"Hey," he said, tilting his chin up. And of course he had no idea. No idea that she was literally slack-jawed in awe over his masculine beauty. Because why would he? Why the hell would he?

He thought it was silly. Absolutely ridiculous that she might engage in that sort of relationship with him. So of course he wouldn't think it was any less silly that she would be staring at him feeling like she had no idea what sexual attraction was before this moment.

"Dinner's ready," she said.

"Great," he said, grabbing his T-shirt and dragging it over his face. "I'm starving."

"What were you doing?"

"We had a horse spook, and I flat out killed myself going after that thing. I have concerns. I thought he had a placid enough demeanor to use him in the therapy program. But now I don't know. We cannot have that happen with a kid."

He looked so concerned, and that did something to her too.

But mostly, it was his chest.

"Well," she said, coughing. "I don't want dinner to get cold… But if you need a shower or…"

"No, I'm good," he said. "All I needed was to cool off."

"Right. Cooling off. Well. Guess you did that."

"Guess I did." She stared dumbly at him. He stared back. "You get any closer to making a doctor appointment?"

"I'll call. I'll call right now while you get changed for dinner."

"All right," he said.

And she scampered off like her ankles had caught a light, and the rest of her was liable to catch it too.

Because that was how she felt.

It was damn well how she felt.

CHAPTER SEVEN

WELL, DAMMIT ALL.

He could've gone his entire life without experiencing *that* moment. Without turning and seeing Alaina Sullivan looking at him like she wanted to eat him. Lick him. Do all the things to him he'd wanted to do to her for years.

Gus didn't have any illusions about his looks. His face either freaked women out or it didn't. They were either into the rough thing or they weren't. But his face aside, he knew they liked his body. He hadn't lied to Alaina when he'd said he didn't work at it. Other than doing labor.

He figured it was his compensation.

Well.

There were other things. Other areas where he was blessed generously, and women liked that too.

But he didn't *know* those women. And it wasn't often they looked across the bar and stared at him like he was a treat.

And that was how she'd looked at him. Alaina Sullivan.

Alaina McCloud.

She might not have changed her name yet, but it was how she'd introduced herself to Elizabeth the other day in that little fit of jealousy.

The look on her face...

It had not been an innocent expression. And hell, he doubted she had any idea she was putting that out there.

He waited a minute, then went into the house, stopped at his room and pulled a fresh T-shirt on.

Then he went back downstairs to find her standing next to the table. Which was clean.

And there was food on it. And even though they'd made a plan, he just... He wasn't used to this. And he didn't know how long it would take him to be.

"Have a seat," she said.

She went to the fridge and opened it and got out a bottle of beer. And *brought it to him*.

"Thank you," he said.

"I have a Sprite. No beer for me. Obviously."

"Yeah," he said.

She seemed flustered.

"Anyway, the doctor said that I should come in soon. I've got an appointment scheduled in a couple of days."

"Great. Tell me when. I'll go too."

"Oh, you don't..." She tucked a strand of coppery red hair behind her ear. "You don't have to do that. I mean, it's probably boring."

"Why would it be boring? I'm committing to this. To this kid. To this life. Tacos are not boring. This isn't boring."

She bit her lip. "Thanks, Gus. That's... Thank you."

"No problem."

She sat down at the table, and started to build herself a taco, and he did the same. She was skittish now. Because she'd noticed him. Noticed his body.

Well, she was absolutely welcome to join his hell. He'd been in it for a number of years now. Didn't mean there was anything to be done about it. Because if it got like that… Well, if it got like that, it would go to a place he couldn't. That was the problem. That was the thing.

If he actually knew at all how to love. If maybe there was a fundamental break there, caused by the extreme conditions that came about living with his dad.

From losing his mom.

He really did wonder that. Often.

He could sleep with Alaina. Could let her warm his bed. Could enjoy her body. But it would never…it would never go beyond what they were now. It would just be them, but with sex. He didn't want to do that to her.

And anyway, it would cause stress, and then it would make the whole situation feel difficult, and then, it would become next to impossible for them to be together, because she would be miserable, wanting more.

Or hell, maybe she wouldn't. Maybe he was thinking too highly of himself. Just because she was looking at his chest. Didn't mean she would ever fall in love.

But either way, it would introduce a complication that neither of them could afford.

They could do tacos. They could do this. And frankly, it was more than he'd ever had.

No matter that she seemed attracted now, it had only strengthened his resolve. He had to make sure they stayed on neutral ground. He had to make sure that this stayed… Well, for her and the baby. And not for him.

She was young. And she was inexperienced. She had just come off of a bad time with a guy who deserved to be drowned like the wretched alley cat that he was. He would never be part of hurting Alaina. That was the most important thing. That was what mattered to him.

And he would sacrifice everything, including his own desires, to make sure that happened.

SHE COULDN'T SLEEP. So she'd been unpacking boxes ever since she'd come up to bed. She felt hot and fractious and more than a little bit irritated by absolutely everything. But most of all, by the fact that she now knew Angus McCloud was sexy as sin, and she couldn't forget it. And he had just sat down at the table with his tacos like he didn't know he was hot.

How could he *not know*?

It seemed like he had to know. It seemed like he must be fully aware that he was built like the kind of mountain any woman would want to climb.

He was hot. He was just so hot. His body was… He was like a fantasy that she didn't even know she'd had. And he had been emphatic about nothing happening between them.

And nothing will.

Well. That was the thing. Gus McCloud was *hers*. Her rescuer. He was making this terrible situation right. And if she had ever needed another person, it was now. Desperately. And the mystery of sex had been solved for her. She wasn't a virgin. She wasn't an innocent. She knew how it went. She'd seen a penis. She'd done it. And it just hadn't been all that great. What had he gotten her? Pregnant. That's what it had gotten her. And she had no desire to repeat the experience again. The mystery was gone. And so, Gus might be hot, but she already knew that sex wasn't worth destroying the kind of thing that they had.

He had said that he would just keep doing his thing. And she could keep doing hers. Maybe someday she would want to flirt again. Try again. In the meantime, she would be protected by him. Live here.

It had been good.

And that was what she had to remember. That this was what was real. And it was what mattered. The fact that he had plucked her out of the pond. The fact that he was here now.

And in the meantime she could look at his body. Because it was fun. So there. She didn't need to be sleepless about it.

She was resolute. Determined. Decisive. Elsie didn't know her. Or what she needed or wanted.

Well, okay, she did. Because they were friends. And Elsie did know her really well. But they just weren't the same. Elsie and Hunter were in love. She and Gus had each other's backs.

And maybe she needed to work on having his a little more. But that was how she would think of it.

She had Gus McCloud's very, very broad back.

She abandoned the boxes and climbed into bed.

It was fine. Everything was fine.

She turned over onto her stomach and huffed. And then finally fell asleep.

WHEN HE TOLD Hunter that they ought to come by for dinner that night, he realized a little bit late that he probably should have asked Alaina first. Because Hunter and

Elsie became Hunter and Elsie and Tag and Nelly and Brody and Lachlan. And that was a full house.

And he felt a little bit chagrined when he found Alaina at lunchtime.

"How much spaghetti did you buy?" he asked.

"Enough for a few different meals."

"Think you could cook it tonight?"

"Why?"

"I figured it would be a family thing."

The words stuck in his throat. A family thing. Like she was family. Like they were family.

Well, they were in a way. She was…she was his. He was protecting her. Distance notwithstanding.

"Yeah," she said. "Sure." She grimaced. "I'm going to need to leave here pretty early."

"That's okay. You know you don't have to do any of this."

"I want to," she said. "I like working on the ranch, Gus."

"Do you like cooking?"

"Yeah. I mean, in that I don't mind it. I like doing it for you." She smiled at him. So winningly that he thought maybe she was teasing.

"You seem a lot less feral than normal."

She scowled, and it was cute. And he really needed to get a grip. "I'm never feral."

"Liar."

"Well, I'm not feral now."

"Why?"

"Well," she said. "The thing is that I am renewed in my appreciation for what we are."

Oh great. He was always happy to hear Alaina make proclamations.

Except, no.

"We're *friends*, Gus," she said, gesturing broadly. "We are. I mean… Look, I like Elsie, but she never offered to marry me."

"Well, she is previously engaged."

"Yeah, true. But the way that you stepped up. The way that you always have. I was right. You're just sweet, Gus."

Right in the testicles. Really. Just right in 'em.

Didn't that silly girl know that the only sweetness he had in his entire body was reserved for her?

Only her.

No. She doesn't. And what difference would it make?

None. Absolutely none.

He needed to get out of town. He needed to go screw someone else. Because he was…he didn't even know.

Maybe after her doctor appointment. Maybe then he would go out of town, spend a few days away, find himself a couple of women.

Women who wouldn't call him sweet.

And if they called him daddy it would be in an entirely different context than the one he'd been thinking of the word in lately.

And he would be fine with it.

"Great. Well. See you at dinner."

"See you."

And the rest of the day passed pretty quickly. At least he wasn't chasing down horses.

And when he and his brothers went back to the main

ranch house, he was...blown away by how clean the place was. And it felt...different. Warm. There was a candle lit. On the coffee table in the living room. There were pieces of fabric draped over things. Making it all soft and...*different*. Some extra lamps. Light.

"Wow," Tag said, looking around. "This is...different."

For some reason, Tag using the same word he'd just thought irritated him.

"Oh, Gus." His sister-in-law Nelly looked at him with big liquid eyes. "This is so wonderful."

They were treating him like he was a small child who had done something amazing, and he hated it. Because yeah, as far as they were all concerned, getting a woman to come live with him probably was amazing. Even if they knew the circumstances behind it.

"Damn," Hunter said, coming in with Elsie.

"Wow," said Lach and Brody at the same time.

"Yes," he said. "It's clean. Be bigger dicks about it, all of you."

"Sorry," Tag said.

Hunter, Brody and Lachlan said nothing of the sort.

"It smells great too," Brody said, walking into the kitchen. And then he grinned. "Now, that is a sight for sore eyes. Gus, did you know such a pretty woman was in your kitchen?"

Gus came in behind Brody and stood just close enough for his brother to feel his presence. "Don't flirt with my wife, dumbass."

Alaina scrunched her face and laughed.

"Oh, Gus," she said. "Be nice."

And everybody piled in around him, and he felt decidedly disgruntled.

There was a huge pot of spaghetti on the table, a steaming red pot with sauce and meatballs, Parmesan cheese and garlic bread. There was also a green salad. And it really was just...

"Perfect."

His eyes had drifted to Alaina, and he hadn't realized he'd said it out loud. But there she was, standing in front of the window in the dining area, the light illuminating that red hair of hers. Making her look like she was on fire. And she was just the damn prettiest thing he'd ever seen.

And his brothers, who had their women, were sitting next to them at the table, touching them. Casually. Like it was just another day. Another moment. Like any other. And he had to stand back from his wife. Because he wasn't the same. Because they weren't the same.

Why is that?

He gritted his teeth. It was because he didn't need to enter into some kind of transaction with her. Because the distance was necessary. Because he had offered this, and he couldn't go making it seem like he needed sex in return.

Martyr.

He called himself a lot of things. He told himself a lot of stories.

He was honest. That was the thing. He didn't bullshit. He knew what he was. That was...that was part of being a man, accepting all that.

He knew who he was. And he knew why he and Alaina had to keep things this way.

"Sit down," she said.

He did, at the head of the table.

There was a seat available next to him, and he figured she could sit there if she wanted to. But it gave them just a tiny bit of distance putting her around the corner of the table.

Or she could take the foot.

That would make them like lord and lady of the dilapidated castle.

He started to serve himself some food, and quietly, she took a seat next to him, sticking a beer right next to his hand.

He looked over at her. "Thanks."

She shrugged, the expression on her face shy.

"Of course."

Why was she being so nice?

He liked her scrappy.

Liked her with her passion emanating from her like a scorching flame. Because it was who she was. Because it was all the things he could never let himself be.

He shoved that thought to the side.

"Hey, since we're all together," Tag said, lacing his fingers through his wife's, "Nelly and I have an announcement. We're having a baby."

Cheers erupted around the table, and Gus sat there, feeling…like he was in another world. Tag and Nelly were having a baby. And that was great. Good for them. But they were married for real. And they were having a baby. And there was a kind of joy to the announcement that he and Alaina hadn't gotten. They'd gotten suspicion. Which was fair enough, all things considered. And they'd gotten tolerance, but no one had been all that excited.

And then…he hadn't gotten to sit there holding her hand like that.

He looked at her face, tried to see what she thought about it. She looked sad, and he hated that. So he took action.

"A cousin," he said, looking at her. "For the baby. Cousins close to the same age. That's great. That's… that's great."

And her eyes went round, and then a little bit liquid. "Yeah," she said. "Cousins. Thank you…thank you, Gus."

And she realized everyone was looking at them.

"When are you due?" Elsie asked.

"May."

He and Alaina still didn't know their exact due date. And he realized he hadn't even ever asked her for a projection.

He didn't know how to do *baby math*. Otherwise he might've been able to figure it out. Since he knew the exact day the kid had been conceived. He'd been there to pick her up.

"They'll be really close to the same age," Alaina said.

"That'll just be the best," Nelly said. "And I just… I don't know, I feel like this is… When you had such a difficult childhood, like I did, like you all did… It feels especially miraculous. To get to experience it again. Through the eyes of your child."

He felt a stillness grow in Alaina. A quietness.

"Well, you guys have fun with your babies," Elsie said. "I am in no hurry."

"Me either," said Hunter.

"You think we planned this?" Tag asked. "Practice safe sex, kids."

"Always," Elsie said, looking lofty.

And he looked at Alaina, wondering if she would feel offended by that, but instead, she laughed. "Doesn't always work."

Well, that answered *that* question.

"That's chilling," Elsie said.

"Sorry," Alaina said. "Reality's reality. I made dessert," Alaina said, getting up from the table and bustling back into the kitchen. Where she pulled the most beautiful cake he'd ever seen out from underneath her cake platter. Pineapple upside down cake with caramelized pineapple and gleaming bright cherries. "And I've got homemade whipped cream."

"Gus, you really did hit the big time," Brody said.

Except he couldn't get those little interactions between Elsie and Hunter and Tag and Nelly out of his mind. He couldn't... They couldn't be that. They just couldn't be. And they never would be. They were something else. She'd said it earlier. They were friends. By necessity. They were friends, because he couldn't afford to let his emotions off leash.

Here we go.

No. He knew. He knew that only his father was responsible for his behavior. He did know that.

It was just…he was also well aware of his own behavior. Well aware of the kinds of things he did when he was pushed too far.

He could be a lot of things. Older brother. Protector.

The word *father* got caught in his mind and spun there.

Would it be fair to ask the baby *not* to call him Dad? No. He'd offered to be the baby's dad. But it wasn't the same. Because he wasn't the same. As any of the men sitting around him.

He looked up at sweet Alaina, who just had no idea what the hell kind of messed-up place his brain was. What the hell kind of wasteland his heart was.

But all of this made it clearer. What they *weren't*. What they couldn't be.

And he worried. He worried if she could be happy. But she seemed happy. She had seemed happy earlier. So why he was borrowing trouble, he didn't know. Why he was comparing, he didn't know.

He knew that he was different than them. They didn't have to be this way. They didn't have his weaknesses. He'd gone at his dad swinging when he got himself locked in that shed. Because a thirteen-year-old boy had been no match for a grown man. But hell…

When he'd been grown, and his dad had gone after Lachlan one last time, one final time, Gus had snapped.

And yeah, there were rumors all over the place that he was a murderer.

They might be serious, but mostly he suspected people thought it was funny to claim extreme violence on his part without ever thinking it through too deeply.

Nobody knew how close he'd actually come.

Beg.

Beg for your life like you made me do.

Another hit. And another. The feeling of him giving way beneath his knuckles.

Damn, that had been satisfying.

Cry for it. Like you made me do.

I won't set you on fire, though. I'll just let you burn in hell. But first, let me bring you up to the gates.

The memory made something metallic flood his mouth. Made him feel almost ill. And he took a bite of the cake to try to banish it.

But it was still there. Even though he could tell the cake tasted great. It was still there, and he was still Gus.

And it didn't change a damn thing that the cake was wonderful, and so was she.

Because he was Angus McCloud. Angus Evander McCloud, chip off the old fucking block.

The boy who'd been left to heal from all those burns, and God help him if he'd healed twisted. Who'd been left with no one, and nothing.

So no. He didn't worry about the taint of his father's blood swimming through his veins. He just worried about the fact that the temper was there. That his own conviction in his rightness was enough to blot out everything else.

He wasn't his dad; that would be a cop-out. He was himself. Filled with all the rage that his life had instilled in him, and he knew just how big the anger was. How bad it could be.

And those were things his brothers didn't know about themselves.

Brody might worry. He might worry what their father had seen in him. But Brody had never tested it.

Gus had.

They might see him as a hero. But he couldn't see himself that way.

The only good thing was that in the end of all things, he had protected them. Was that he had done the best he could for them.

That he never hurt any of his brothers.

But he had to watch himself. He had to.

That day he'd sent his father to the hospital. And that day he'd made a decision. To disengage any of the emotion that was left in him.

Because he had to. Because he had no other choice.

"Do you like it?"

"Yeah," he said.

They didn't touch, but they sat next to each other, eating the cake.

Nelly was sitting on Tag's lap. Public gestures like that weren't really in Elsie and Hunter's wheelhouse. Something Gus was grateful for. Because any more of those displays and what was on edge inside of him was going to get pushed over completely.

And when they were finished, everyone said their goodbyes, and he got up and started putting plates in the sink.

Then he filled up the sink with water, and started to wash them.

Alaina came in a moment later. "Oh. I didn't think you…did kitchen things."

"You were going to teach me, right?"

"Yeah."

"Well, I don't need to be taught how to do this. It's pretty self-explanatory. I used to do the dishes for my mom."

And then he realized what he'd said and looked back down in the sink.

"Oh."

"I mean, once the place was mine I just started using paper all the time. And I don't cook so…"

"Sorry," she said. "I…"

"Don't apologize for doing something nice."

It was a weird thing, this distant space. Because he wanted to be grateful for what she'd done. But he also felt intoxicated by her nearness. By the fact that he found her so beautiful. By…everything.

"We always did the dishes. Us girls," she said, picking up a dishcloth and starting to dry. "And we used to sing. My dad was in the living room with the paper, and my mom would sit there with her romance novel. And then he left. He started a new life. Without us. Like our life didn't matter. And we kept doing the dishes, but Mom stopped reading romance novels. Of course, at that point, I had started reading them. So, I stole them. And sneaked them off to my room. I can't really blame her. For stopping. But I wanted to believe in something that had a happy ending." She looked like she was off somewhere distant, and she blinked rapidly. "Do you ever feel that way? Like you just need to believe that things will be okay?"

"No. I've never really thought that way. In terms of okay and not okay. There were times when I just thought in terms of…surviving. Surviving the life that we had. It was a hell of a thing. With my dad."

"Yeah. I'm sorry. It's not the same."

"It's bad enough. To believe that someone's on your side and have them leave… It's a terrible feeling."

"That's what your mom did. To you. To all of you."

"It's complicated. And I do have sympathy for her."

"She shouldn't have left you behind. You were just a kid, Gus. She shouldn't have left you all behind."

"Maybe not," he said, his throat tightening up against the words. Words he needed to say. Words he needed to feel, even though something in him wanted to push them back. Erase them. Deny them. "What she did… And I think she felt like she had to. At least some of the time. I think she felt like… I think she felt like there would be no escaping him if she took his sons. And hell, I know that Hunter feels responsible for her leaving. But he was a monster, Alaina. He would've killed her. Eventually. She had to make the break that she could. And I don't judge that. I don't. I can't."

"But?"

"There's no but," he said, feeling his chest hitch with it.

"I think there might be."

"Sometimes I wish she'd come back. That's all. Sometimes…" That tightness got almost impossible to speak around and he tried to cough and push it away.

His mother had been a victim of domestic violence. That was it.

"It's great that Tag and Nelly are having a baby," she said. Rescuing him from the moment, and he was grateful for it.

"Yeah. I'm sorry... I'm sorry this hasn't been *that* for you."

She blinked. "What do you mean?"

"They just seem so excited."

"I'm getting there," she said. "Really. I am."

"Good."

And then he really needed to get the hell away from her, and thankfully that came to a head when he finished washing the last dish. "I'll see you in the morning."

"Yeah," she said. "I'll see you."

And then he walked back upstairs, and straight into the shower. Cold.

And stood under the water until his body was numb, and so was his chest.

Because that distance was essential.

And he needed to find it.

CHAPTER EIGHT

THE NEXT DAY Alaina spent the afternoon helping with minor barn renovation. They were choosing new floors and all kinds of fun things.

And one of the things they decided on was to do punched tin on some of the cabinets. And they had them all set out on a worktable, with designs prestenciled on. And Alaina had spent much of the afternoon happily punching.

It was a fun project, with just a little bit of creativity, but easy enough to let her mind wander. Also, it was mildly violent, which soothed something in her.

Of course, her mind kept wandering to Gus. And she was entirely a tangle of confusion where he was concerned. Because she'd had that moment where she'd seen him without his shirt, all dripping wet and…well, sexy. And then he'd come in and helped her with dishes. And there had been this profound sadness in his eyes when he'd talked about his mother.

And again when he'd apologized to her that her pregnancy wasn't the same as Tag and Nelly's.

And she wasn't even sad about that. She'd made her bed as far as she was concerned. The fact that she wasn't in a committed relationship, and had had to solve her issue accordingly…that was her problem.

But he felt bad about it. He wanted something easier and better for her than she had.

And the only people in her life that really felt that way about her were her sisters. And that just made it all seem…special. Very special.

She moved down the line, to the next sheet of tin, punching and punching until she had the whole row done.

"Well, look at that," Gus said. "You did a damn fine job."

She looked up, feeling like she had been caught thinking about him, because she had been. But he didn't know that.

"Thank you," she said.

"I didn't know you did this kind of thing."

"I don't. We watched a video online, and I volunteered to do it. They're going on the cabinets inside."

"Great. Want me to show you how to mount them?"

"Me?" she asked.

"I'll let you use power tools." He grinned and she felt a strange buzzing feeling down in her toes. She curled them tightly in her shoes and tried to ignore it.

"Excellent," she said.

And he picked up the sheets of punched tin, one by one, and they headed into the tack area, where they were mounting them on the cabinet doors.

"This is going to look great," he said.

"Brody's rigging it up and putting lights in it so that it'll glow like punched-tin lanterns. Isn't that neat?"

"I knew I was right putting him in charge of renovation. He's good at that stuff."

"Brody is a whole thing," Alaina said.

There was no other way to describe Brody. He was charming. And he was devastatingly handsome. If she'd known him better, he might have been the one she'd had a crush on back when she'd gotten fixated on Hunter.

"Yeah, you like that type," Gus said.

Not an accusation, just a statement of fact. And he got a drill out, and started buzzing it, and it vibrated through her, along with her irritation.

She didn't want Gus to act like he knew anything about her. It made her huffy.

"What do you mean by that?" she asked, feeling sniffy.

"Pretty boys," he grunted.

"Pretty boys?"

"Like Hunter. Like Brody. Like Travis."

She sputtered. "Oh. Does anybody…not like people who are pretty?"

"Some people have a *preference*," he said, waving the drill in her direction before going back to work. "That's all I'm saying."

She pressed her lips into a thin line. "Right. Well, anyway, show me what to do."

"Come over here," he said. "You hold it up." And when she did, he marked the edges on the inner part of the cabinet. "How about you hold this one? I'll drill. Eventually, we'll switch."

"All right." She was still feeling annoyed at his accurate representation of her.

"I'll start with the high ones."

She wouldn't be able to reach them without a ladder, so it was fair. She held the tin, and he held the drill. And she watched his profile as he predrilled a hole, then put the screw into it.

"There we go," he said, talking to himself. He ran his hand over it, as if he was making sure it was a sound job. Then he turned his attention to the next one. "It's actually super easy."

"Now that you said that, I'm going to be afraid that I won't be able to do it, and then I'll feel really dumb."

He chuckled. And she stood up on her tiptoes to get a better look, and it brought her right up next to his face.

She had kissed him. Just the once. At the wedding. And right now, her lips tingled at the memory. She looked at him. Really looked at him. At his dark brown hair, shot through with one or two strands of silver, some lighter caramel colors in there. A rich mahogany. How had she ever looked at his hair and just seen brown?

And she looked at his face. Really looked. His skin was rough in parts, from where it had been touched by the fire. But he was there. Those strong features evident.

And where he had been changed…

She looked at him and saw strength.

She wanted to touch him.

And maybe she did like pretty boys. Or she *had*.

But right now the memory of them was soft, smooth and far too easy.

His lips twitched, and the groove next to the corner of his mouth deepened. And as the sunlight filtered in from the window up above, it bathed him in glory. And she wondered how she'd ever seen anything but…him.

He wasn't a good-looking man with scars obscuring his face. He was a good-looking man, scars and all.

Strong and capable, and every part of him added to that beauty.

Gus McCloud was handsome. And maybe you had to stop a minute and look at him to see it. Maybe you had to be strong enough to take in that kind of handsome. The kind that spoke of pain and struggle and everything else.

He was still him. He hadn't changed. But maybe over the last few weeks she had. And now she felt…like her eyes were open. Like she could see him for real.

"Alaina," he said, handing her the drill. "Your turn."

"Oh."

And she lifted it as he positioned the tin on the lower cabinet, standing behind her, his chest at her back, the heat radiating off of his body, his left hand pressed to one side of the cabinet, his right to the other. She was closed in, and she could smell him. His skin, the day's work. The soap that he used.

It was…heady and intimate and lovely in a way she hadn't quite known this sort of closeness could be.

"Okay," she said. "Like this?"

She hadn't really needed to ask. It wasn't that hard, after all. But she felt slightly fuzzy-headed, and when he answered with a yes, she turned to look at him, and their faces were close again.

It wouldn't take much. To close that distance. To press her mouth to his.

So she turned back and pushed the drill into the cabinet, then screwed the screw. Tight.

"Got it," she said.

And he took a step back, no longer needing to hold the punched tin.

They finished the rest quickly, and by the time they were done, her heart was finally done beating erratically. She didn't know what had just happened to her. Why everything felt like it had been turned upside down, and right all at once.

"Good girl," he said. "Good job."

And it made her melt.

"Gus," she said when he turned like he was going to leave. And she couldn't stand it.

"What do you need, mite?"

"Just… You didn't forget. The doctor appointment. Tomorrow?"

"No. I'll be there."

"Tomorrow morning. So… And we can just go together."

"Yeah," he said. "We'll go together. I've got some stuff to do." He gestured back toward the door, letting her know he was about to leave.

"Okay."

And then he left. But her heart didn't settle down for a long time after.

IT COULDN'T BE that hard to make pancakes. It couldn't be *that* hard. He built things with his bare hands. Repaired fences. Wrangled cattle. How hard could it be to make pancakes?

Well, he found out that making pancakes wasn't as simple as he thought. Rubber disks, however, were pretty easy. And by the time Alaina came down for the appointment, he had a stack of them on a plate.

"I made breakfast," he said, trying to smile and not quite managing it.

"You don't cook," she said, blinking at him.

"No. I am… I'm terrible at it. But it seemed…seemed kind of like the thing to do. Since it's your doctor appointment day and all that."

"Oh. That is… That is really…very nice."

"Don't say that until you take a bite."

He started her a plate, putting a couple of the disks onto it and handing her a bottle of syrup. She poured some on, and took a bite. And she chewed. Very, very thoughtfully. And very, very thoroughly. "Thank you."

"Let's go to breakfast," he said.

She pushed the plate away. "If you insist."

Which was how they found themselves headed into Becky's about ten minutes later.

The only diner in town, they had an all right breakfast, a halfway-decent burger, great chili and really terrible stir-fry.

They had added that to try to be a little bit more worldly. It was a very bad idea. But the breakfast was fine.

"Eggs and bacon," she said. "Toast."

"Same," he said. And he looked at her. "Not pancakes?"

"For some reason I wasn't really hungry for pancakes."

"Great. I ruined pancakes for you."

"You didn't." She laughed. "I mean, maybe for today."

He chuckled.

"We can…we can work on cooking something to-gether."

"It just didn't seem like it should be that hard," he said.

"Well, it's not. Not really. But if you don't know any-thing…"

"I like not knowing anything," he said. "Reminds me of being a kid. And being a kid is terrible."

"Oh, not to me. Being a kid was when things were simple. Everything in my family went to hell later."

"Yeah," he said.

He didn't really know what all had happened with her parents. It hadn't been all that long ago when her dad had run off. Ten years maybe. Alaina had been an adolescent. Gus had been an adult, working at making changes on the ranch. And even though he and Fia had worked together on rejuvenating Four Corners…

Fia Sullivan was a locked box. She didn't share a damn thing with anyone.

Their breakfast arrived and Alaina picked up her toast and started to nibble at the crust. He was fasci-nated by that mouth. He could remember the moment it had started.

This dark, shameful pleasure he felt when he looked at her.

At the lake, her in a bikini. Her hair all wet and curly, and backlit by the sun. And she'd smiled at him, imp-ish and mischievous. And splashed him.

No one ever did things like that to him. No one…
tried to get him to *play* with them. No one but her. She'd
never been scared of him. Never shied away.

He'd advanced on her and grabbed her around the
waist to dunk her into the water and suddenly he'd…

Become aware of her. As the woman she'd become.
That she wasn't a kid he was picking up to haul down
into the water.

She was a woman.

A woman.

The thought had haunted him all the rest of the night
and the next day when he'd seen her again, down at
the garden at Sullivan's Point, wearing a sundress with
skinny straps that showed her body right off, he hadn't
been able to see whatever he once had.

It had changed.

Forever.

He shoved a strip of bacon into his mouth. "So. Why
did your dad leave?"

He asked that to say something. To get to talking
about anything.

"He followed his dick to greener pastures," she answered. "At least…at least that is my understanding."

He frowned. "You don't know the whole story?"

"I think they were trying to protect me. Look, I don't
know what all happened. I just know…something. And
Fia was never quite the same after. She idolized my
mother and father's relationship. Our lives. And I know
she…she saw something or… I don't know. She won't
talk about it. But then, she doesn't talk about anything.
Witness her situation with Landry…"

"Yeah. Never really understood that one."

"No. Me neither. But I guess that's just my family. You ignore everything until it blows up. It all blew up. My dad left. My mom could never make sense of all the rubble, and a few years later she left too. And we just figured out how to keep going. But sometimes I worry. I mean, did I basically blow stuff up? I wonder how close Fia is to doing the same. And Rory and Quinn… Maybe the farm store is what they want. All of them. I was starting to want more. I… You know, I was always worried about getting left, but I guess I am my dad. I'm the one who wasn't responsible. I'm the one who did the leaving."

"You went to the next ranch over."

"I just meant I'm the one that started having itchy feet. It's different. They stayed. They were… I don't know. I just feel weird about it. Kind of bad."

"Well, stop feeling bad."

"You make it sound easy. But I have…trouble facing things head-on."

"You do not."

"I do! It's…it's one thing when it doesn't matter that much. But actual things I care about… I don't know if it's because I'm like my dad or if it's because of him leaving—does that make sense? I just…feel afraid. That if I get happy, if I want something too much…that I'll lose it."

"Now, that I understand."

She smiled, but it was a nervous smile.

They finished up their breakfast before making their way back to the truck and driving to Mapleton, to the doctor's office. It was a small office, with barely a waiting room, and they were ushered back almost immediately.

There were forms to fill out. New-patient ones, and they asked a whole bunch of questions. And she got to one, and her pen stopped moving. "Why did they have to ask that?"

He looked where she'd stopped.

Date of last intercourse.

"Put it down," Gus said. "You don't need to be embarrassed."

He knew the date. Because he remembered that day. Her in the parking lot looking lost…

She wrinkled her nose, but she did. He could feel her nerves amping up, especially as they moved from the waiting room to the exam room.

"Disrobe," said the nurse. "And the doctor will be in soon. Here's a gown for you."

He stepped outside, keeping his back firmly to the door and doing his best not to imagine what she was doing in there. And a few moments later, the door cracked open, and she was standing there. "Come in," she said.

She was wearing that gown, and she did a little hop up onto the exam table, where she sat, hands in her lap, swinging her feet.

"You regretting asking me to come?"

"No. I'm scared. I'm glad that I'm not by myself." She frowned. "Anyway. You need to be part of it. You need to. Because… I really can't do it by myself, Gus. I can't. I really want my baby to have a dad. And…"

"Hey," he said. "What started all that?"

"It's just very real now. And we're here. And it all feels…like a weird daydream when it's just you and me, and we're at the house. And I'm cooking. And I go to sleep in the new bedroom. And I think about all the furniture that I'm going to order and spend your money on. And it's easy to forget the *why* of it. But not here. Here I remember why. Here I know why. I know why I'm here. I know why you're here. And…and we were just talking about my parents, and you know they always seemed perfect to me. And like *adults*. That was the thing. They seemed like adults. I don't feel like an adult, Gus. And I'm supposed to have a baby. And I'm not sure if I can do it. I don't know what I'm doing. At all. I have no idea. And…"

"Hey," he said. "I don't know what the hell I'm doing either. But we are going to figure it out. And we're going to figure it out together. I'm here. I'm here."

But he didn't touch her. Because he wouldn't let himself do it. Because he knew that way lay madness, and he had to keep some level of sanity.

He didn't really know what to say. And he knew that it was his job to come up with something. Since he was supposed to be…hell, he was supposed to be taking care of her. Taking care of things.

"You don't need to worry," he said.

And he had no idea if that was true. But he figured if he said it with enough authority it would suit her. And it seemed to.

The doctor knocked a moment later, and came in. A bland-looking woman with gray hair, and he was hopeful that meant she had experience. That none of this would surprise her. That the blandness came from the fact that she didn't get excited if there was no need to be excited. Yeah. He was counting on that.

"All right," she said. "Today we're just going to do a quick ultrasound to get a look. We'll do an official one with all manner of measurements and to determine gender in a few weeks. This is just to establish the viability of the pregnancy and try to confirm your dates."

She looked at him, afraid. He wondered if it was the word *viability*. And he touched her face, even though he shouldn't have. And she seemed to lean into that touch.

"All right, go ahead and lie back," the doctor said. "Have you had a transvaginal ultrasound before?"

"No," she said, grabbing hold of Gus's hand. And his brain had shorted out already. Because he had never... They had never... And here he was.

"I'll stay right here," he said, up by her shoulder resolutely. And he fixed his eyes straight on her face. "Hey. You're going to be fine."

He was saying that partly for himself.

The doctor pulled out a wand, and quickly, he diverted his gaze again. And he just held her hand, while everything got situated.

There was a watery sound in the room, and he couldn't help but look at the screen then. He couldn't make heads or tails of anything. It was black and grainy, and didn't mean a damn thing to him. "There are your ovaries," the doctor said.

Well. Neat. So, he'd seen that now.

"Your uterus."

Also that.

"And there is…" The doctor expanded something over the top of a little blurry movement, and zoomed in. "There's a heartbeat. Yep, there's a little one in there. Looks like nine weeks. And I'm just going to get some measurements on fluid."

And all he could do was stare. At the little flutter of movement. A baby. Their baby.

Their baby.

They had decided that this was what they were doing. And the baby was theirs.

And he felt it.

When it was all finished, the doctor left and Alaina smiled ruefully. "I guess you might as well just stay in here and turn around while I get dressed. After that."

She had a point. Though, she had no idea what it would do to him.

But he did it. Because…because.

He didn't want to leave her.

And it was fine. Because he was resolute. He knew why he was doing this. He knew why they were doing this.

"Feels really real now," she said, and he could hear the rustle of fabrics this time. The clothing.

And his gut went tight.

What the hell is wrong with you? She just had a whole medical thing done and you're getting hard.

Yeah. He was. But he had never claimed to be a good person.

He was just one who was trying to do the right thing. Endlessly. And it was exhausting.

He was just so…he was so tired.

"Yeah," he said. "Everything looks good, though. So that's good."

There was a long pause. "It is. Gus, it is. I honestly didn't know how I would feel today. I was worried that I was going to be upset. One way or the other. That if everything was gone then… Well, then I wouldn't know what I was supposed to do with my life now. But I was also worried that I might see the baby and not want it. But I do. I do want this. I'm getting to a place where I can feel maybe a little bit excited and a little bit happy. I don't really know how to explain it. Except that I feel…like maybe I love it. I don't even know how that's possible."

"How nature protects the species, I think," he said.

"That is terribly realistic and unromantic, *Angus*," she said.

"Well, Alaina, I am both of those things."

"I'm done now. You can turn around."

He did, and he wasn't prepared. For the impact of just how beautiful she was, somehow different in the aftermath of what they'd just seen.

"Does it really matter why?" he asked.

"I'd like to think that it's a mystical connection to my impending motherhood."

"Then it can be. Why shouldn't you be exactly what you wanted to be? Nobody has the answer. So I say it's nature. You say it's mystical. Why the hell not?"

She smiled, if very smally. "That's almost open-minded."

"I'm almost open-minded. Sometimes."

"Is this…is this really weird for you?"

He stood there and looked at her. The most beautiful woman he'd ever seen in his life. Who might as well have been a hundred miles away and encased in glass for all that he couldn't touch her.

"Yeah. It is. But I've got time."

She looked away and was quiet for a long space of time. "You don't have to do this."

"I married you," he said. "I married you, and I made a commitment. And I aim to keep it. I'm not my father, I won't be. And I'm not your father. I stayed. I protect people. I will protect you. And I will protect this baby."

"And be his dad. Really."

"Yeah," he said, the words scraping his throat raw. Because they'd talked about that, and they'd thrown the idea around, but it meant something more now that he'd seen the little life moving around inside of her.

And it would come out all helpless and small. Defenseless. And he made up his mind that he would always be there. Always.

"I don't know if I'll be a great dad, Alaina. I've got to be real honest with you. I didn't have an example. Neither did you. We don't really know what we're doing. Kind of flying blind. But I'm willing to give it everything I have. And if there's one thing I know I can do, it's protect people who need it. The defenseless. The weak. I'm willing to go as far as I have to. So maybe I won't be…the kind of world's greatest dad that's out there with great speeches and corny jokes, and whatever the hell else you're supposed to do. But I'd go to the ends of the earth to keep that kid from harm. I swear that to you. I know how to muscle my way through anything. And you already know I'd walk through fire."

He meant that. Every word.

She nodded, and her eyes were bright. And she said nothing.

"Come on. Let's go."

They scheduled her next appointment on the way out and he felt like there was something else he should do. Something else he should offer. He felt drawn to her, and he knew that he shouldn't. Knew that he couldn't be. And so he pulled away. Because that seemed like the lesser of the evils right then.

"We better head back to the ranch. There's work to do."

"Right. Hey, is it okay if I go to town and do some shopping? Just Pyrite Falls. Basic groceries. But we are a little depleted."

"Yeah. You don't have to ask me for time off. My brothers don't. We all just collaborate. We divvy stuff up as it happens. Everyone's pretty self-directed."

"Okay. I just want to make sure that I'm not mooching."

"We're married," he said. "This isn't a transaction."

He stared at her, hard, willing her to believe it. Willing her to understand it.

"Okay."

"Good."

CHAPTER NINE

SHE STILL FELT pretty shaken up, even after she and Gus had gone back to the house, and she had drifted up to her room to change and shower.

She had seen the baby.

The baby.

And Gus had made those fierce vows to her about being a good father. And she knew that he would be.

He'd held her hand. He'd stood right near her while… Well, that had been the furthest thing from intimate, really. It had been clinical.

And uncomfortable. But he'd been there through it.

He made her feel a jumble of confused feelings.

Because he was…

Because when he got close to her now, her heart jumped. Because she was so conscious of the heat of his body as he stood there with his hand in hers.

And she was so aware of the fact that the stakes were high, no matter what he said.

That it wasn't a transaction. And maybe that was true; maybe *transaction* was entirely the wrong word. But she wasn't worried about that. What she was worried about was messing it up. Because she hadn't really earned this. She so often struggled to find a way to make things right. But she hadn't been the one in control of this solution. It was Gus.

He had given her this new lease on life. He had given her the solution. And there were so many possibilities in it. So many things that she was excited about. So many things about it that did make her happy.

From the glory of working the ranch, to enjoying having a house of her own. Even cooking him dinner.

She *liked* being Gus McCloud's wife. And she didn't want to mess that up by making a move on him. Which may have been one of the weirder things she'd ever thought, but it was a very real issue, all things considered.

She walked into the little tiny grocery store, which had a selection of prepackaged items. And after that she would go to Sullivan's Point and get some produce from her sisters.

But she would start by getting her milk, her chips and things like that. She might be a farm girl who had access to the freshest meat and vegetables, but she liked junk food. Quite often, actually.

And right now she was really craving Cheetos.

As she went in, there was a knot of young cowboys standing over by the beer. They weren't from Four Corners; rather, they were from one of the other spreads in the area.

"Howdy," one of them said, his mouth curving up into a smile.

"Howdy," she said.

And she felt a little bit pleased to get some attention. Because she was kind of obsessing about Gus, and he was immune to her in that way. Which was good, or it should be. But she was having a lot of trouble actually synthesizing that.

But hey, Gus wanted to do his own thing. And so it seemed…fine for her to get flirted with. She wasn't going to do anything with anyone *now*. That was a bridge too far. But Gus wanted their thing to be separate from romance and sex and all of that. In fact, he found the very idea of them together laughable, and he wanted to go off and be with other women, so what he was suggesting was that the two of them have an open marriage. And if they had an open marriage…

She cleared her throat and tossed her hair, then started to walk toward the chips with her basket. And she ended up getting a little bit overexcited and grabbing more dips than she possibly should have, but she was pregnant. And she was having weird cravings. She also threw in a bag of Oreos. And suddenly, one of the men was standing beside her. "Can I carry that for you, ma'am?"

She didn't know how she felt about being called ma'am, but she was happy to accept some help.

"Well, thank you," she said.

How *gallant*.

What was wrong with enjoying the moment? It had been a weird day.

And so she put a few extra things in there, and he helped carry the basket up to pay.

John at the register gave her a skeptical look. Well, whatever. He was allowed to be skeptical if he wanted. He knew that she was Gus's wife, because of course he was a busybody. And there just weren't that many people to know in Pyrite Falls.

But these guys didn't know her, because they were seasonal workers. And she was happy with that. It was… it was Gus's resolute immunity to her that…

It's good. You are supposed to be feeling good about that.

Yes. She was. She was supposed to be accepting. So she would just not think about Gus. Her whole thing with Gus was about building a life. It was totally different.

They were friends. And that was more than enough. More than enough.

With her groceries back, two of the men went over to the counter, each taking a bag. "Where's your car at?"

"I just parked out front," she said.

And she was directing them on where to put the groceries when her husband pulled in in his beat-up truck.

He rolled the window down.

"Howdy," he said, his expression as mean as she'd ever seen it.

And she could see her posse blanch. She looked at them, and then looked at Gus. If they didn't know him, she could see how he was startling. But she could no longer see what other people saw when they looked at his face.

Because she saw him. And he was…he was beautiful. This strong man that had been through so much. And she was irked that they were looking at him like that.

"What are you doing here?"

"Came to get beer," he said.

He got out of his truck and walked over to her into the

men. Then he wrapped his arm around her. Possessive, and pulled her up against him. "Thanks for helping my wife out," he said.

"No problem, sir," one of them said, practically saluting before turning around, and Alaina could swear she heard one of them mutter something about *daddy issues* as they wandered off.

"What the hell was that?" Gus asked, practically snarling.

"Look," Alaina said. "Who doesn't have daddy issues?"

"That's not what I'm talking about, and I think you know that."

"They offered to help with my things. And I said yes. Because while I'm not a shrinking violet, I also don't believe in expending energy that I don't have to expend. It was nice."

"You were flirting."

She blinked. "So what, Gus?"

"Look, I'm willing to take on this baby, but you go get yourself pregnant with someone else's kid, and we may be having a different conversation altogether."

And that hurt. Stabbed her through the heart. Because… He *did* think that about her. He did. And he could say whatever he wanted about not judging her. But he did.

She felt everything in her shrink. Wilt.

"This can't work," she whispered.

"What?"

"It's not going to work if that's what you think about me, Gus."

"I rolled up and you're standing there flirting shamelessly. What am I supposed to think?"

"You could maybe stop short of accusing me of wanting to sleep with any random guy that talks to me. How about that?"

"It's a ground rule. It's fair enough."

"*You* are going to go off and have sex," she said. "You already said it yourself. That you weren't going to stay chaste or anything like that, and you said you didn't want me, Gus. I asked. And if you don't want me, then why shouldn't I find someone who does?"

"I didn't say I didn't *want* you, Alaina. I said that I wasn't going to have sex with you."

And she couldn't quite process that, because everything hurt. Everything.

"I can't deal with being around you if this is what you think of me. If you think that I… If you're judging me because I had sex with someone else. With *one person*, Gus. How many women have you been with?"

He winced.

"I'm not. I'm sorry. That isn't what I meant." He looked so contrite she almost felt bad for him. But he was being an idiot. So that really mitigated her pity.

"Right. It's just I had sex once and I happened to get pregnant, even though we did use a condom. I don't know why that happened to me. But I am not any worse than anyone else and even if I were, what does it mean? How many people has Hunter been with?"

"I told you, that's not what I meant. But you know, it is kind of a practical issue."

"How? How is this a bigger issue for me? You could

get any number of the women that you sleep with pregnant by accident. Assuming they can track you down. Because you only sleep with strangers. You might have kids out there. You might not be any better than Travis. You just *think* you are. Because you don't know. You think you do—you think you know everything, control everything, but it's a lie. Maybe none of them called you, because they had the sense that you wouldn't be there for them."

His face was dark as a thunderstorm. "I'm here for you."

"I don't know what to say to you. I don't know what to say." Her chest felt like it was splintering. And everything just felt gross. Wrong.

He reached out and grabbed her arm and pulled her toward him. "I don't judge you. I don't. I'm sorry that I said it like that."

"Why did you say it if you don't think it?"

He only stared at her, his eyes bleak. There was a desperation radiating off of him now and it made her feel light-headed. Weightless. Then he reached out, and dragged his thumb across her lower lip, and it felt like the striking of a match. Rough, leaving a trail of fire behind.

She couldn't breathe. She wanted to lean in. She wanted that touch to linger forever.

Then he drew back like he'd suffered an electric shock. "I'll see you later."

She felt sideswiped. "You can't just leave!"

He took a step back and walked away, and she let out

a breath she didn't realize she'd been holding. When he was so close. When he was touching her.

"Gus," she said.

"If you don't want to cook for me, that's fine. There's still pizza in the freezer."

And then he got in his truck, and he drove away. She just stood there, feeling like her chest had been ripped to shreds, and he was gone. She couldn't yell at him. She couldn't fix this.

And then she just… She got in her truck, and sat in the passenger seat, and she let hot tears spill down her face.

How had the day turned into this? Because he had been so sweet and soft this morning. He had been so…

And this man was like a stranger. And she didn't know what the hell to do with it. So she just cried. And she couldn't even sort out why.

Why it mattered so much what he thought.

And then she had the nagging feeling that maybe she should just call her mom. Since she didn't want to talk to her. And she didn't want to be living in this moment anyway. That was funny. Take one bad feeling and throw another one on top of it. Maybe she should call her dad too.

She scrubbed her eyes, and dialed her mom's number. Right there in the parking lot.

"Well, I was wondering when you were going to call."

"You could've called me," Alaina said, realizing too late that she had maybe made a mistake in pursuing this interaction. Considering that she usually put in an effort to not call her mom out on her lack of contact, which had gotten more and more sporadic over the last couple of years. That she didn't get on her mom's case for not telling her about her personal life, or for her general lack of interest in Alaina's.

"I assume you talked to Fia," Alaina said.

"I have," she said. "She mentioned that you married Angus McCloud."

"Yeah. Did she tell you why?"

"No."

Oh, screw Fia. Honestly. What good was she only telling half of her secrets? Alaina didn't want to drop the bombshell, and now she had to.

"I'm pregnant. So, congratulations. You're going to be a grandmother."

"Alaina!" And to give her mom her due, the exclamation sounded genuinely excited. "Really?"

"Yeah."

"That's…that's unexpected, but it's… That's wonderful."

Well. Maybe her mom would be more interested in her now. Now that she was having a baby. Maybe that was the problem. She just couldn't bring herself to be interested in her adult daughters' lives.

"Yeah. I'm due in May. So."

"We'll all be sure to come out, honey. If you want."

"Really?"

"Yes."

"I… I'm honestly surprised. I didn't know that you… You didn't call me when you found out I was getting married."

"You didn't call me when you got engaged."

And there was a lot that Alaina could say about how maybe a kid shouldn't be in charge of all the communication with her parents. But she realized that maybe with her mom she might need to be a little bit more in charge. Whether she thought it was right or not.

And here she was, having the conversation. Not running.

At least something good had come from today. The realization over breakfast hadn't come to nothing.

"I didn't think you'd be interested."

"I'm interested," her mom said. There was a long pause. "Alaina, I don't like to talk about your dad. But when he left me… When I found out that he wasn't who he always said he was. First of all I found out he was dishonest in his dealings with Levi Granger. He took advantage of a kid who'd just lost his parents and I was furious about that. Then I found out he wasn't faithful to me. He didn't want to stay with me forever… I could never look at that ranch the same way again. I could never just be there, not again. I felt like everything that we built our life on was a lie. I didn't just question the last six months of our marriage, I questioned everything. And I tried. I tried to keep it together for you. For you girls. But I couldn't live in the house. Not anymore. Fia was so bound and determined to make Four Corners more profitable and to make Sullivan's work better for you girls. And I didn't feel like I could sell it. Not when the McCloud boys were doing so much work after everything they'd been through, and the Kings…"

"What about the Kings?"

"Nothing. It's just… I didn't feel like I could risk

anything by selling. And I knew that Fia didn't want me to. I left. I chose Hawaii because it was so different. And exotic and faraway and I thought I just wouldn't have to sit in all those bad feelings anymore. If I could just be in paradise, then it would feel like paradise all the time."

And Alaina felt that echo uncomfortably inside of her. Particularly as she sat there in her own hurt.

And hurt her own rationale for so many things repeated back to her.

"Has it worked?"

"A lot of the time. The problem is, I miss you, but I don't know how to be there, and be with all of you without…without there being pain. But I want to be there for the birth of my grandchild."

Alaina wondered how her sisters would feel about that. Another difficult conversation to be had, no doubt.

"I hope you will be. I'll try to do better at calling between now and then."

"Have you…have you told your father?"

"No. Maybe he'll find out when we send the Christmas card."

Her mother paused for a moment. "You don't have to be bitter at him just because I am."

Of course it never occurred to her mom that Alaina might be bitter at her too.

"Oh, he earned direct bitterness from me. It was the abandonment. At a critical point in my childhood."

"Well. That is fair."

Alaina swallowed hard. "Mom, I love you. I don't know what I'm doing. I'm scared."

"Of course you're scared," her mom said. "Mothers

are always scared. The whole time. I'm still scared. I'm scared that you're pregnant. I'm sorry that I've…that I've done such a bad job keeping in touch with you. That I'd let my own issues get in the way. And none of it goes away. It doesn't go away when your baby is twenty-four."

Alaina grimaced at her own reflection in the rearview mirror. "That isn't comforting."

"It actually should be. Because it's love, sweetheart. It's high stakes because it's love. Even if it isn't perfect."

And one thing Alaina knew right then was that perfection wasn't a requirement. Because she might've had some anger at her mom, and it hadn't gone away just because they'd had this conversation, but she did love her.

If she didn't love her parents, the way things had ended up wouldn't hurt. If she didn't love them, it wouldn't be complicated.

And so hopefully her kid would feel the same. Just love her. No matter what.

And maybe she would never be able to figure out all this with Gus. But he could be a good dad, and she could be a good mom…

Except for some reason that made her ache.

"I didn't figure that Gus would be for you," her mom said slowly. "Mostly just because he's so much older. But looking back… You did always love him."

The word sent an uncomfortable pang through Alaina's midsection.

"Well, he…he was fun." She fiddled with some change in her cup holder and tried not to fall right into the pit of irony of thinking of Gus as *fun* right now. "I mean in the sense that he would let me sit on his shoulders and things like that."

"He always had a particular liking for you."

And that made her feel even sadder, because she hoped that she and Gus wouldn't lose their particular liking for each other over the course of all of this.

"He'll be a good dad," Alaina said.

"I'm relieved to hear you say that. Because you know his father…"

"I know. I do know. But believe me. He's nothing like him."

And when she ended the call with her mom, she comforted herself with that fact. Whatever happened between her and Gus, he would be good to the baby. Because he promised it. And he was a man who kept his promises. That she knew.

She could hang on to her anger. He deserved it. But she wasn't in the mood to hang on to anger. Not tonight. She was going to make him dinner, regardless of all that. Because she wanted to. Because she wanted things to be better.

Is that just you not wanting to feel bad?

She shoved it aside. Because what did it matter? If the end result was that things were better, then what did any of that matter?

CHAPTER TEN

Gus stood in the dark in the new tack room, and stared at nothing.

It had taken the last several hours for the rage in his blood to cool down.

When he'd seen those men with Alaina he'd lost it.

What was the matter with him?

That was the kind of shit Seamus McCloud would've pulled. A jealous rage in a parking lot. And no, he hadn't touched her. He hadn't touched them. But he'd been on edge.

Hell, he'd been on edge.

And what he'd said to her...

But in that moment, he'd imagined it. Her being with other men. Now that she was his wife. His wife. *His*.

The rage inside him had been primal.

He'd lashed out with words.

How could he tell her that? How could he say that it was blind jealousy, ugliness in himself, not a lack of respect for her. It wasn't because he thought that she was dirty or used goods or anything like that. It was just that...he hadn't been able to stand the thought of another man putting his hands on her, and how the hell could he explain that without confessing…without confessing how much he wanted her? Without…

No. Hell no. And this was why.

He was shaking with his rage.

With his desire for her.

And this morning felt like a thousand years ago, and still, he felt that way.

"Fuck," he said into the silence of the barn.

"So, things are going well then."

He turned around and saw Hunter standing there.

"What the hell do you want?"

"I might be about to get up in your business," he said.

Gus scowled. "Don't do that."

"Well, Gus, since a couple of months ago you were professionally up in mine when I was dealing with Elsie, it seems only fair."

"Alaina and I are fine—leave it alone."

"That's why you're standing in the barn swearing at nothing? Because I don't think you're doing slam poetry."

He narrowed his eyes. "No. But I can be mad about other things."

"Sure. But are you?"

"No."

He didn't owe Hunter honesty. He didn't know why he was giving it to him, except that it was true. He had been up at Hunter's grill the whole time the stuff with Elsie was going down. Because he had seen it as a potential thing to hurt Alaina, and it had upset him. Because Alaina had feelings for Hunter at the time and…

That pissed him off all over again.

"What's up?" Hunter asked.

"It's just complicated. Okay? That's it."

"If you can't handle it you have to let her go."

He practically snarled. "I don't have to fucking let her go."

"Why did you marry her, Gus?"

"To protect her," he said, the lie so close to the edge of his lips that it was easy to spit out.

Lies.

Are you admitting it now? Why did you really marry her?

Why did you really need to marry her?

Make her yours the minute that it became clear you weren't going to be able to hold on to her if you didn't.

He gritted his teeth.

"That's not it," Hunter said.

"Just go away."

"You want her. Come on, Gus, I've been trying to dance around this, I've been trying to let you have your secrets. I've been trying to let you have…whatever this is. Because before you married her, I would've said exactly what you would have. There's no way. She's a lot younger than you."

"Yeah. She's a lot younger than you too, but she liked you." But he knew why. He wasn't charming. He wasn't handsome. "Why would Alaina want a guy who's eleven years older than her and scarred all to hell?"

"That's not what I mean. But you don't exactly scream teenage dream."

"I get it."

His brother paused for a long moment. And Gus

pondered the virtues of punching him in the face before he could speak again. But he didn't. "You want her, though."

Now he regretted not hitting him.

"Yeah, and if I could figure out a way to fix that, I would've done it years ago, Hunter. Trust me on that. Because it was never my plan to pant after that *girl*. Not ever."

"Well, good for you. You did something about it. You have her."

He growled. "I was never going to marry anybody. And here we are. *Here we are.* I can't touch her."

"Why not?" Hunter asked. "That's obviously why you married her. To touch her."

He shot Hunter a hard glare.

"Oh, I'm sorry," Hunter said. "Are we making up stories here together, or are we being honest? You want her—why aren't you having her?"

"Because I fucking can't. Because I can't trust myself. I just about killed a couple of jackasses in a parking lot that were flirting with her. That's who I am."

"Look, I didn't think we were going to play this game. The *Dad's-blood-runs-through-my-veins* thing. We've talked about it a ton of times."

The *dad* word stuck in his throat. Because it wasn't about his dad. It was about him. About what he'd already done.

"Just mind your own damn business."

Hunter huffed. "You made it my business. You were shouting f-bombs in the building."

"And you were *eavesdropping.*"

"Just… If I could say one thing to you, Gus…"

"You've said about ten things to me, Hunter, and I'm already annoyed."

"Fine. You have every right to be. But I'm going to say it anyway. There are a lot of opportunities in the world to get a shit hand. Lord knows we've had it this whole time. There aren't a lot of opportunities to be happy. Why don't you experiment with that and see where it gets you."

"I'm glad things have worked out for you," he said. "But we're not the same."

"Why do you think that?"

"Hunter, I know you went through stuff. But did Dad try to kill you?" He just stood there, and stared at his brother. Who could only stare back.

And he didn't see why he shouldn't just say it now. He was beginning to feel like he didn't have anything to lose.

"No," Gus said. "He didn't. Don't pretend that you know what I've been through. Don't pretend that we're the same. Or that we have the same place to come back from. Because you didn't spend some of your teenage years getting surgeries. And then not being able to get them because…because the person who burned you was not going to take you to the hospital to finish up the re-constructive work that you needed. I don't know how to do this thing that you know how to do. I don't know how to be that person. To give you a really bad meta-phor, it got burned out of me a long time ago."

"It doesn't have to be that way."

He shook his head. "How do you know?"

"Because I want to believe in better things?"

"Fairy tales are great, Hunter. But it's all they are. Bullshit fairy tales. I don't believe in them. I can't. We finished?"

Hunter stared at him for a long time. "Sure."

And then his brother turned and left him standing there, and Gus wasn't sure if he was glad he won that battle or not. But hell, he wasn't sure about much of anything right now.

And he hoped that Alaina hadn't made him dinner. He hoped that when he walked back into his house she might be with her sisters. That his house would be empty, exactly the way he was used to. And he'd have to heat up her frozen pizza.

As if there's penance to be paid?

He ignored himself, and climbed into his truck, driving back to the main house with his mouth set into a grim line.

He parked the truck out front, got out and stomped his way into the house. And when he opened the door… he smelled something wonderful.

He stepped into the kitchen, and there she was, wearing a frilly apron and a sundress. A flirty little dress, like he hadn't just shouted at her in a grocery store parking lot. Or maybe like what she was wearing had nothing to do with him, which frankly pissed him off. Because the fact that she had the audacity to wear something that showed her legs like that, and made him feel the way he did, and likely hadn't considered him at all, just about sent him over the edge.

"What are you doing?"

"I made dinner," she said. "Like I've done every night since I moved in here."

"I told you not to."

"You said I didn't have to. You didn't say not to. Anyway, even if you did, I don't have to do what you say, Gus. And I wanted to cook dinner."

"You shouldn't have done that," he said.

"Why not?"

"Because I was an ass," he shouted.

"Yeah. So what? That doesn't mean I'm going to punish you by not feeding you. Maybe that's what it would mean to you, but it doesn't mean that to me."

She turned around and went to the stove, and started stirring the pot. And he couldn't help but notice the way her dress flared when she did it. How perilously close it came to showing the very tops of her thighs.

He shifted, feeling like everything was at the edge. His control, his…everything.

Then she bent over, opening up the oven, and all he could do was stare at the length of leg that it revealed.

Dammit. It wasn't usually this hard. It wasn't usually *this* hard. But she wasn't usually his.

Mine.

And that was the problem. He had married her. And why had he *really* done that? Why?

She took a giant roasting pan out of the oven and took the lid off, revealing a roast, surrounded by vegetables.

"There. Not that you deserve it, after you *growled* at me like that."

"Thanks," he said, sitting down at the table.

"Now, you can get up and get your own beer," she said.

And he realized that he was anticipating her handing it to him. She had trained him. Like a damn dog. He'd lived by himself for years, and even when he lived with other people they never did a damn thing for him. And now he was sitting there, expecting to be waited on by Alaina.

He got up and stormed to the fridge in a fury.

"Now, if you're going to be in a bad mood…"

"I'm in a great mood," he said, grabbing the top of the beer bottle—which definitely required a bottle opener—and twisting it, not even grimacing as the metal cut into his hand. He got it open. He'd just injured himself doing it. Felt right. "Just a great mood." And he took a swig of the beer.

"You are a salty pain in the butt," she said.

"Maybe."

"Anyway, here's the roast."

"You know what," he said, flinging the beer bottle down onto the table. It clattered and splashed. "I don't want any pot roast."

"What the hell?" she asked.

"I don't want pot roast," he said, advancing on her. She maneuvered away from the oven, her back against the wall.

And he reached around behind her, and undid the tie on her apron.

"Gus," she said, her voice a whisper.

"I want you."

Then he grabbed hold of the apron, and tugged her forward with it, before he claimed her mouth with his own.

GUS WAS KISSING HER. Gus was kissing her. And not the way that he had kissed her at the wedding. Which had been controlled, amazing, but marked by rigid discipline. As if he had specific steps mapped out in his mind. How he was going to do it. The way that it was going to go.

This wasn't like that at all. This was…

He was kissing her like he was starving. Consuming her. His tongue plunged deeper, sliding against hers, and she moaned, coming up on her tiptoes, all the better to meet him.

And she had no idea what was happening. No idea how all that fury that had been vibrating off of him when he had come in had erupted into this. And she had no idea where it was going.

His fury was like a balm for her wounds and she didn't know why. Maybe because now that his mouth was on hers, she could taste it for what it was.

Desire.

She wasn't afraid of him. He was Gus. *Her* Gus. He'd never scared her once.

She didn't know why she felt like this either. Because she had never…

She had never felt like her heart was beating so hard it was going to come straight out of her chest.

She had never felt like the hollow sensation between her thighs was akin to pain. She had never felt like she might die if she didn't get a man's hands all over her body.

When she had set out to lose her virginity, she wanted to do it for the sake of it. She wanted to gain sexual experience because she thought it might propel her into a place of maturity.

It hadn't done that.

And one thing it had never been about was desire.

Not really.

She had thought that a few butterflies meant that she wanted somebody, and she'd been wrong.

This…this was desire. This intense, riotous pain that made her want to throw off her clothes and throw caution to the wind, and throw out every rule they had made. That made her want to dismantle all that they'd built between them.

This was that moment that she'd seen him dump the bucket of water on himself shirtless, but more.

Because he was touching her. With all that strength. And she knew what his body looked like. And she wanted it. Wanted her hands on it, wanted her mouth on it.

She didn't want to just sit back and see what Gus would do. She wanted to tear his clothes off of his body and indulge herself. Explore the ridges of muscle, the scar tissue. Everything that he was.

Gus made her forget. Everything.

Forget what few other kisses she'd had. Made her forget their rules. Made her forget everything. Who she was and why she was and what they were.

Then he wrenched the apron up over her head, and pinned her against the wall.

And he grabbed the neckline of her dress—a cute little pink one with buttons that went all the way up the middle—grabbed each side of those buttons and tugged, popping them off, and exposing her bra. Then he took hold of her bra and pulled it up, revealing her breasts, and the hunger that it created in his gaze took her breath away.

He lowered his head, fastened his mouth around one nipple and sucked hard, while he growled.

She let her head fall back, her chest arching forward. And…he proved himself to be a teller of truths. He was rough, and he was skilled. The way his hands moved over her body stoked an ever-increasing need in her that went beyond anything she had ever imagined possible.

The symphony that his mouth played against her sensitive skin was virtuoso level.

And he made her…he made her wild.

He moved his mouth to her other breast, while he continued to tease her abandoned nipple with his thumb. She was panting, breathing hard. And that was when he pushed his hand up beneath the skirt of her dress, then moved his fingers beneath the waistband of her panties, finding her embarrassingly wet with her need for him. And he started to stroke her, drawing the moisture out from inside of her body and rubbing it over that sensitized bundle of nerves there, creating a sweet, slick friction that was threatening to drive her out of her mind.

"Gus," she breathed.

"That's right," he said, his eyes burning into hers. "Who's touching you?"

"Gus," she said.

"Are you going to come for me?"

She was flexing her hips, back and forth with the

movement of his hand. "Come for me," he said, this time not a question, a command.

And she did. Fireworks going off behind her eyes as her climax overtook her.

She had never come with another person.

Ever.

Hadn't even come close that one and only time she had sex.

And Gus had called that peak of pleasure out of her body with a few strokes of his hand and a rough command.

And she was undone. Utterly. Completely.

He cursed, vile and broken, and stepped away from her.

"Gus?"

"No. That shouldn't have happened. That never should have happened," he said.

"Gus," she said, feeling tears gathering in her eyes.

"This isn't going to work," he said. "I can't… We can't."

She moved forward, her hand outstretched.

"Don't fucking touch me," he said.

Angry tears spilled from her eyes. "Don't be mean to me, Gus. Please. You can't just…you can't just do that and then tell me not to touch you. You can't just… Gus I've never… I've never…"

"I have to go."

And he turned and walked out of the room, out of the house. And he left her standing there with her dress still open, and everything in her feeling raw and bloody and exposed.

And how dare he? *How dare he?* He had stripped her naked, and he had stripped her of all her inhibition. And then he had left her there. He had taken her apart, bit by bit. And he'd left.

And then he acted angry. He acted angry at her. How dare he.

And she wasn't going to let him run away.

She was going to find him.

She turned the oven off and stormed right out of the house. Buttoning the remains of her dress up as she watched the taillights of his truck and got into her own.

Angus McCloud was a coward, and she wasn't letting him get away with it.

CHAPTER ELEVEN

GUS PULLED HIS truck up to one of the cabins and let the vehicle sit there and idle.

He had messed up. Big-time.

He found the edge of his control, right when he'd been so aware of how badly he needed it.

He... He'd messed everything up.

He'd come right at her, unleashed all that pent-up hunger on her.

He shifted, his body still hard as a crowbar. Okay. He hadn't unleashed all of it.

But he'd touched her. And she'd been like silk between her legs. So hot and glorious, and wet for him.

Not to mention those gorgeous curves of hers. He'd been in heaven. Her body was better than he'd ever imagined. Sweeter than anything he could've ever dreamed of.

She was a wonder. A revelation.

And he...

He wasn't supposed to know that.

It was supposed to stay very deep, a burning bright ball of desire, regret and anger in the center of his being, and someday, he would die. And he would never, ever have to deal with it. Not ever.

That was what he wanted.

That was what he needed. He got out of the truck, and went into the cabin. He flicked on one of the lights, and looked around. There was a bed and there was beer, but it would be a decent enough place to stay the night while he figured out what to do. While he got his head on straight.

He'd made Alaina a whole lot of promises, and he'd broken a few of them.

Mostly, just promises to yourself.

Yeah. There was that. But he'd been mean to her. And he'd made her cry.

And he'd have to deal with all that tomorrow. It was the best he could do.

Granted, right now, the best he could do *wasn't much*.

He sat down on the edge of the bed, then lay back, stretching out on it, staring at the ceiling.

And that was when the cabin door was flung open.

"All right, you yellow-bellied, lily-livered pile of horse manure, how dare you do that and leave me? *How dare you?* Were you trying to prove what you accused me of earlier? That I'm just a grasping, horny slut who can't control herself? Did that make you *happy*, Gus? To embarrass me like that? And then walk away, because you don't even want me, and you don't even care?"

He sat up, and looked at her. Her eyes were bright, her hair askew. She'd buttoned up the dress again, but it was crooked.

And she was the most beautiful thing he'd ever seen.

"You think I don't want you?" he rasped.

"Yeah. Because you laughed at me when I asked you

about sex. And because you just…you just did that to me, and you left."

"You…you foolish little termite," he said, getting up out of the bed and making his way toward her. "Why the fuck do you think I give a damn about you and your baby? Why the fuck do you think I just lost it in a grocery store parking lot over a couple of pretty boys talking to you. *Why the fuck* do you think I've done any of this, Alaina?" His voice was too rough and his words were too honest, and there was nothing he could do to stop it. To change it. "Because you think I'm sweet? You…" He was unraveling. He was at the end of himself. "You are a silly little horse girl who thinks that everyone can be tamed with a sugar cube. Well, *I can't*. And I'm not doing any of this because I'm just *so damned sweet*. I have wanted you since you turned eighteen. Fresh and shiny on your birthday and the prettiest damn thing I've ever seen. I have wanted you for so damn long that I don't remember what it's like to be free of it."

He shouldn't be saying this. Not at all. He shouldn't be letting himself get this close to losing his mind. But he was. Here he was.

And she just looked stunned. And he couldn't blame her. Because this was a lot. And he was being awful.

He knew it too. But he couldn't stop himself. Where was all that control? Where was it?

It was gone. He'd literally been set on fire, and it hadn't burned his control away. Not all the way.

But Alaina Sullivan had done it. Alaina Sullivan

had done it with her beautiful green eyes and perfect breasts and that glorious wet place between her thighs.

Yeah. She'd done it.

"*I want you.* And do you know where it's going to lead? Straight to hell. Because that's where I take people. Do you know what I *wanted*? I wanted this to be what I promised you it would be. I wanted to pretend hard enough that I just wanted to take care of you, and I hoped that if I pretended well enough, eventually it would be true. But you know what, I just couldn't stand the thought of anyone else having you. So I wanted to make you mine. And if I have to take care of a kid? Small price to pay. So yeah. That's how sweet I am. I want you naked, and on your back, and begging for me. On your back, on your knees, whether that's kneeling or bending over for me. That's what I want. Because I might not be sweet, Alaina. But *you* are. The kind of sweet that I want to get my mouth on. All over. You know what my favorite thing to do is when I leave town?"

She was staring at him like a deer in the headlights. Frozen.

"I like to find a redhead. And I never ask her name. I don't care." The next words were pulled from deep, deep inside of him. "Because I've already given her one."

"Don't," she said.

"What? Is that too much for you? Is it too much for you to know what a bastard I am? Sorry to ruin your fantasy."

"No, don't… Gus, that is… That's cheap. Why would you fantasize about me while you were with another woman? Why would you do that to *her* or *me*?"

"Because I knew I couldn't have you."

"You could've had me. You idiot."

"No. Don't lie to yourself, honey. You like a pretty boy. You were fixated on Hunter, and then you were fixated on *him*. And you were talking to those guys in the parking lot…"

"If I would've known, Gus… If I would've known…"

"Nothing. Because you're a pretty young thing, and I am certainly not. We both know it. And you can rewrite it now that I've touched you, but we both know it's a lie."

"Well… I hate it. I hate the idea that you were with someone else and thought of me. It cheapens us both."

It did. She was right. But a long time ago he'd accepted that for him sex and feelings would have to stay cheap. But it shamed him, looking at her now. With the truth of it between them.

"Where do we go from here?" he asked.

"What do you mean?"

"Obviously, this isn't going to work."

And she just stood there, her green eyes trained on him. Then she grabbed the hem of her dress and pulled it up over her head. So that she was standing there in just that white lace bra and matching panties. His breath left his body in a gust.

She started to walk toward him, kicking her shoes off as she went. "I don't know where we go after tonight. But I know what's going to happen now."

"Alaina…"

"Don't. You just said you're not all that noble. Stop acting like it."

"I don't let myself off the leash. Not here."

And that was a gross oversimplification of the real reason he couldn't have her, but better than getting into the truth.

"Shut up," she said.

She moved over to him, and put her hand flat against his chest, dragged her fingertips slowly down his stomach, down to the waistband of his jeans, and he let his head fall back, almost unable to take the sweetness of her touch even through the fabric of his shirt.

When she pushed at the hem of his shirt, he grabbed the back of it and tugged it over his head, throwing it down on the ground.

His control was shot, and it wasn't any better for having acknowledged that. Not even a little.

She put her hands on his skin then, and he groaned, reveling in the softness of her touch.

His eyes wanted to close, because it felt so good, but he had to watch. Had to watch Alaina touching him.

"I better lock the door," she said.

She turned and moved to the cabin door, locking it.

And he knew there was no turning back. Hell, he had no intention of it.

"Take everything off," he said, grabbing hold of his denim-clad arousal and trying to adjust it so the seam would stop biting into him.

"Oh," she said.

"Did you think you were going to come in and take control? No. You're going to get what I give you. You understand, sweetheart?"

She nodded, soundlessly.

"Here's the thing, Alaina. I'm only good for one thing. When it comes to this. You ready?"

"I…"

"Did you think you were going to come in here, place your hand on my chest and pin me down to that bed and ride me, baby girl?"

She licked her lips, and he couldn't deny the image of that was pretty damn hot to him too. "Well… I might've thought about that."

"Someday I might let you. But that's not what's happening tonight. You need to learn what you're signing yourself up for. So that you can make a decision. About whether or not you actually want to play this game. I'm not going to pretend to be something I'm not. I'm sure as hell not going to spare you. Mostly because I can't. I did everything in my power not to fantasize about this. Not to let my thoughts get too graphic. But here we are. And now I've got about a thousand fantasies fighting to see which one gets to win. So you take your clothes off for me. Let me see what I've been dreaming about."

He could see that her fingers were trembling, and he knew that he should feel bad. Because she was Alaina. And that wasn't lost on him, not even in this moment. And when she was a kid, he just thought she was wonderful. But then she grew into a woman, and he'd wanted that woman. But she was still special because of that spirit that he'd seen in her from the beginning. And it mattered that it was her.

And that they were changing things… That mattered too. He'd always protected her. Always.

But tonight he wasn't doing that. And he supposed he should feel some kind of way about it.

But he couldn't feel anything other than the heat pouring through his blood now.

He was reduced. To that beast state he'd always been so afraid of. Because he knew what it was like when he lost control of himself. When all he could see was red and fury, and he gave in to the worst parts of what he was.

This was different, though. The beast was hungry. But it wasn't for blood.

Her bra came off, and he got to see her perfect body again. Round and pale with light pink nipples that seemed to be pouting for his attention.

And he wanted to give them all the attention in the world.

"The rest," he said, not sure how he kept himself from crossing the room and staking his claim right then and there.

She grabbed hold of the waistband of her panties and shoved them down her legs, and he groaned.

Those copper curls were prettier than he could've ever imagined.

Glorious in every way.

He wanted to taste her. Devour her.

And he realized then there was nothing stopping him. He wasn't on a leash. It was the most dangerous damn realization he could've had. Because he wasn't going to stop himself.

On a growl, he went down to his knees, pushing her back against the wall and burying his face between her legs, licking into her like she was an ice cream cone and it was a hot summer day, and he had to get every last drop.

"Gus," she said, grabbing the back of his head. And with his broad shoulders, and her thighs draped over him, he lifted her up off the ground as he continued to eat, devouring her.

"Oh, Gus," she said, rocking her hips against his mouth. And then he pushed two fingers inside of her, and a third, while she sobbed and rolled her hips against him, while she came, and then came again.

"I can't," she panted. "I can't." And he knew it was time to make her come again.

And he did. Mercilessly.

Then he picked her up, and carried her to the bed, kicking off his boots, jeans and underwear as he did, pinning her down to the mattress and pressing his arousal between that slick cleft there.

"Gus," she whimpered. And he kissed her. Drugging and deep. So that she could taste her own desire on his mouth. So that she could taste just how much he wanted her.

She wrapped her arms around his neck, wrapped her legs around his hips. And it was just about too much. To have every inch of Alaina Sullivan pressed to him. To feel her dampness covering him as she rocked her hips against him. "Gus," she moaned.

And he wanted to wait. Wanted to tease her. Wanted to tease them both.

But he didn't have the strength. Instead, he gripped the base of his shaft and guided it to the center of her body, so that he could tease her. Rub the head of it against that sensitive bundle of nerves before drawing it back down to her entrance and filling her, but just a bit.

"Please," she said.

And then he slammed home.

And it was like a freight train had run him the hell over.

She was so tight.

Tight and perfect and everything he'd been looking for in any other partner he'd ever had.

He fit her.

And he looked down into her eyes, and couldn't deny who it was. And he didn't want to.

Because she was his. His Alaina.

And he growled out her name as he ground himself against her.

She sobbed, and he withdrew, before going back home.

And he lost himself, unable to be gentle. Unable to establish any kind of rhythm.

And he was praying. Praying that she would find her release.

That this would end, because he didn't have the strength to keep on holding back.

And then those fingernails dug deep into his shoulders and she screamed out his name, her internal muscles pulsing around him. And he lost it. "Alaina," he growled, as he spilled himself deep inside of her. As his orgasm tore something from him, something he didn't think he'd ever get back.

A piece of his damn soul.

And he hadn't had all that many pieces left.

"Gus," she sobbed, burying her face in the crook of his shoulder.

And he rolled over onto his back, holding her limp, petite body against him, waiting for remorse to hit him.

It took him a moment to realize it was there. Because it always was. But not as powerful as the pleasure that was still coursing through his body.

Then he realized she was shaking. Crying.

Panic lanced through him.

"Alaina, I didn't…"

"I should've waited for that," she said, tears on her face. "I should've waited for *this*."

No. He rejected that. Immediately. Even in his sensual haze. Because his Alaina was perfect. His Alaina shouldn't have any shame. She was his, and she was everything, and they were here because of what had gone on before.

"We would never have been here," he rasped. "Without that. We would never have been here."

She looked up at him, touched his face. "You believe that?"

"Shit has to happen sometimes, I guess. To get you where you…never really thought you'd be."

"Gus I… I didn't…"

"You're perfect," he said. "That was perfect."

"It's just that with him…"

He blanched. "Let's resist the urge to talk about other men while you're in my bed."

She pushed herself up, her hair spilling over her shoulders. "But I want to say it. I didn't have an orgasm with him."

He let his head fall back against the pillow, and absurdly, his lips curved into a smile. "You had a lot with me."

"You are an asshole," she said, smacking his shoulder.

"Well documented, Alaina. You're the one that said I was sweet. I never was. I never have been. That's your bad." But he smiled. Because he felt like smiling.

She curled up beside him, her body soft against his, her hand on his chest a dream he didn't want to wake up from.

"Gus, why did you pretend you didn't want me?" she asked, her voice small.

"I *couldn't* want you," he said. "Because I needed to keep distance between you and me. I'm kind of a mess."

"I don't think that's true," she said.

"Because you don't know me."

"What don't I know?"

"You don't know everything I've done. What I said about those other women… It was true. I wasn't just being mean. That's the kind of person I am."

"You're also the kind of person who married me to protect me. And you can say whatever you want about how that wasn't part of it, but it was."

"I've always wanted to protect you."

"From myself."

"Yeah. But I was also supposed to protect you from me, and I did a pretty piss-poor job at that."

She traced a circle on his chest and he grunted. "It was a really good pot roast, you know."

"Yeah, well, I bet it was. May it rest in peace. Because I don't want to go back for it."

"Neither do I."

Her legs tangled with his, and she let her hand drift down to his stomach.

"This should feel weirder," she said.

"Should it?"

"It's taken me some time to wrap my head around the fact that I want you. But I think I have for a while. I just didn't know what it was. It's not that I only like pretty boys, Angus. It's that I didn't know what desire was. And I thought butterflies were the same thing. It isn't. Chemistry's different."

Hearing her say that satisfied him a hell of a lot more than it should.

"Well, that is the truth," he said.

"Can we stay here tonight?"

"Alaina…whatever happens between us after this…"

"Are you going to tell me this can never happen again?"

He grunted. "I was going to."

"It's not realistic. Any more than us planning on *never* doing it was."

"Alaina…"

"How about this? Tonight there's no discussions. No plans. No baby. No marriage. No rules. Tonight, can we just pretend that I want you, and you want me, and nothing else matters?"

"Hell yeah."

And when she leaned in to kiss him, he didn't stop her. Because he was all out of strength to do anything but give in.

And so he did. All night long.

CHAPTER TWELVE

THE AIR WAS COLD, but she was warm. That was the first thing that Alaina was aware of when she woke up. Her nose was chilly. But it felt like her body was cocooned in a furnace.

Because she was sleeping with someone's arms around her.

With Gus's arms around her.

And that jolted her right awake.

She opened her eyes and looked around. They were still in the cabin. Lying on the spare bed, underneath a plaid blanket. Completely naked. She could feel the insistent press of his arousal against her rear, and turned to look at him. He wasn't awake.

She wished that he looked more carefree when he slept. But he didn't.

Instead, he looked as stern and haunted as he ever did.

Did he ever rest?

Well, last night had been…something else.

She shifted, her chest and stomach fluttering, the place between her thighs pulsing.

Gus had shown her what sex was all about. That was for sure. And he had shown her all the things that she didn't know.

Except that seemed…too clinical. *Sex.*

What had happened between the two of them had been something else. It hadn't been a decision she'd set out to make. It had been undeniable. He'd been at the end of his rope, and so had she. He'd been mean, but he'd been wonderful in turn. Which basically summed up dealing with him in general.

She'd been ferocious, and angry, and filled with need for him. And now…she just felt soft. Pliant and ready to melt into him.

He was so strong.

And so…hard.

In a sexy way, sure. But also in a way that made him and this feel impossible.

She wiggled, turning to face him, so that she could better look at his face. He groaned, and shifted, rolling over onto his back, his arm still wrapped around her, and she went partly with him, finding herself sprawled out over his chest. He still didn't wake up. She stared up at his face. The way his lashes fanned down. That was about the softest thing. Everything else was still granite.

She moved experimentally, and then stretched up and kissed his cheek. Just to see.

She felt a little spark where they made contact.

And feeling a little bit naughty, and hot, she lifted up the covers and looked beneath them. Because she hadn't really gotten to see him last night. It hadn't been all that bright in the room, and they'd come together quickly, in a fury. They joined a couple other times over the course of the night, but by then the lights had been off, and they'd been beneath the covers.

Oh Lord.

He was beautiful. His body, every inch of him. Really, every inch of him. All muscular glory and...

She suddenly sensed that she was being watched as she looked up. He closed his eyes quickly.

"I know you're awake," she said.

"Didn't want to interrupt," he said, his eyes still closed.

"I was curious."

"Hey. I support that."

They didn't say anything for a moment.

She felt a marginal sense of relief. Because he was still Gus. And she was still Alaina. And it hadn't really changed them exponentially, or he wouldn't have said that.

And she would have felt horrified, rather than just mildly, amusingly embarrassed.

"How long until everybody starts working?"

"Oh," he said, his voice rough. He sat up slightly, the better to look out the window, she assumed. "Oh, they're already out there. The sun is over the mountain. Which means it's likely they saw our cars. And will have questions. But then...no one knew the specifics of this relationship anyway."

She nodded slowly. "I guess not. Though, obviously..."

"Look, we could've got here early and started work. But anyway, what does it matter?"

"I guess it doesn't. Because we are married."

He nodded. "Yeah."

"Please don't sleep with other women." He took a

deep breath and lay back on the bed, staring up at the ceiling. *"Please,"* she said. "I couldn't stand it."

He rolled over onto his side and looked at her. "No one but me."

"I promise," she said.

"Good."

And she wondered if that was all the discussing they were going to do. She wondered what all this would change. If she would move into his bedroom.

If…

"Hey, look, we can talk later. For now, let's just drive back to the house and get dressed for the day."

She nodded. "Okay. I mean, we could just wear the clothes we had on."

"We could. But I need coffee. And that's the real reason I need to head back."

"Okay."

They got into his truck and went back to the house, and she felt…overcome by his presence.

She looked at him as he drove, at the strong column of his throat, the broad set of his shoulders, the way his large, muscular hands gripped the wheel. "Remember one time you went to Copper Ridge? With some of the other guys? And when you came back, you had a bag of saltwater taffy. And you gave it to me?"

He looked at her and frowned. "No."

"Do you really not remember, or are you being mean?"

"I don't have it in me to be mean right now, Alaina. I don't remember."

"What you did. And it was right after my dad left, and it was the nicest thing… It meant a lot to me. And it made me feel like someone was still looking out for me. And… I just… Thank you. I…"

"We don't have to talk."

"But I feel things. And I want to say them."

"Alternatively, you could sit with those feelings."

"No," she said. "That's *boring*. And I hate it."

"Is it boring, or does it make you uncomfortable?"

"What difference does it make?"

He stretched his hand across the distance and rested it on the back of her neck. And instantly, she felt quieted. More settled. But there was fear in her heart. Because something had changed between the two of them, and she was afraid that it would change back. That this moment would vanish like it had never happened. And at the same time, she was also afraid of the change. And where it might lead.

She wanted to go back to the bubble. Where they had been in bed together. And it had felt simple. Nothing but them and their desire and that mattress.

That blanket.

"Steady on, mite. You don't need to solve all the problems now."

"When will we solve them then?"

"Maybe not in this lifetime."

"And you're just…okay with that?"

He took a deep, heavy breath. "Here's the thing. I'm okay. After getting nearly burned alive, I'm not in pain anymore. But you can still tell it happened, can't you?"

"Well. Yes."

"You can't fix it. It doesn't rub off. It doesn't go away. There's a measure of it that not even time sorts out. My face is kind of an object lesson. I stopped expecting things to just feel right a long time ago. Some things are messed up forever."

"You don't mean us."

"I'm not talking about last night, no. But maybe there's always going to be a certain level of discomfort. With things. I don't know. I'm not… There's a reason that I didn't want to do this with you."

He just kept saying that, over and over. It made no sense, not when he clearly wanted her. "Well, I guess it's time to get down to that reason."

"I just can't… There's a certain amount of distance that I keep between me and people in my life. It just is what it is. I never wanted to trap you with me."

"But you did propose to me."

"Yeah, I did. Because I'm weak, it turns out. And I wanted to have it both ways. I wanted to have you without having you. And I lied to myself enough to think that I could. And… I'm a little blown away by that. Because I've always felt like I was pretty damn honest. With myself and other people. But I managed to get one over on myself pretty good with you. But I wasn't going to touch you. Except…"

"You did."

"Yeah, I did."

"You really did want me?" And she felt a little bit raw and foolish asking that.

"You have no idea." He let out a hard breath. "I know what I am. There's a reason that I go out of town to hook up. I'm sorry about what I said last night. It was an asshole thing to say."

"So it wasn't true?"

He laughed, a bitter sound. "Oh no, it was true. I just shouldn't have said it to you like that. It was unkind. And I don't actively try to be mean to you. I promise. It's just sometimes I come off that way. Because sometimes I'm... Well, sometimes I'm mean. There you go."

"But you wanted me," she persisted. "And I want to know when. How."

"I can't quite explain why it happened. I was so pissed off at myself. There you were, so pretty. Eighteen and... you made me feel like I was sick in my soul. A scarred up guy my age wanting you. But there's something about you. I don't know if you know it, or if you can see it. But you sparkle, mite. You really do. You always have. And it used to scare me, all that fire in you. Because I know how fire can burn you up. But also, I... I liked it. Because I know that I can't let myself burn hot like that."

"You were just always there to put me out."

"Yeah. But then it became something else."

"Angus McCloud," she said, her heart going tight. "Did you have a crush on me?"

"No," he said, laughing. "I wanted to strip your clothes off you and lay you down in my bed and corrupt you. And I don't think that's the same as a crush."

A heat wave washed over her. "No. It isn't. It really isn't."

She had sort of *hoped* he had a crush. Because it would've felt soft and special and sweet. Like she kept trying to say that he was.

But all of this reframed his offer of marriage. It came from a place of possessiveness, rather than affection.

And she just always thought that maybe she and Gus had something kind of special that way.

"So…does it mean you don't…*like me* particularly?"

"I do," he said. "The same way I always have. It's just that when you got grown up, then I also wanted to sleep with you."

"So, you've been into me for like six years."

"Yep."

He said it so easily. Like it was a fact. "I didn't know."

"I know. You said that already. But you didn't know because I didn't want anyone to know. Because I never intended to act on it."

"But now we have."

"Yeah."

"Should I… I mean… My room…"

"Keep your room, Alaina," he said as he pulled the truck up to the front of the house. "There's no…there's no need to rush things, or make declarations or anything like that."

"Except the no sleeping with other people."

"Yeah, except for that," he said.

"And if I came to your room tonight?"

"I wouldn't kick you out."

"Well, good." And something still felt distant, and it still didn't feel quite like enough, but maybe she just had to listen to Gus. Listen to what he'd said about the fact that sometimes things were just going to be uncomfortable. She didn't believe they had to be forever. But maybe she couldn't solve it all right now. And that thought made it feel like a huge weight had been shifted from her shoulders. Because there was just so much going on. She was having a baby, they were having a baby, they'd gotten married. They'd had sex for the first time, and they were trying to navigate what all that meant. Maybe there really was no way to fix it. Maybe there really was no way to satisfy all of their wants. And maybe it was just going to be difficult.

But she could rest in that. She could take it one day at a time. One moment at a time.

Sitting in his unsolvable problems and finding a way to be grounded without picking at all the mysteries there.

And he made her feel settled, even while he changed her.

Because he was there, to put that hand on the back of her neck and make her feel like it was all okay.

Because she worried about a lot of things. And she'd been left by people she loved. But he didn't make her worry about that. She worried about certain things, but not that. Not with him.

"Come on. Let's get that coffee."

CHAPTER THIRTEEN

Gus was completely distracted. He knew what he was supposed to be doing—finishing up the woodwork inside the cabin. But it was identical to the cabin that he'd just slept in with Alaina, and that was all he could think of.

Her hands. Her body. Her mouth.

He hadn't showered, because he still wanted to smell her on his skin.

And all he could think was having her in his arms again.

And this was…this was the problem. Right here. He was supposed to be less involved than this.

And he was not doing a very good job of that. No, he wasn't.

The other thing he should be doing was itemizing his update for the town hall. And getting his financial report together, so that he could report the expenditures to the other families—who functioned as a board. This kind of thing had been natural for Gus for years. Back when he and Denver and Daughtry King, Sawyer Garrett and Fia Sullivan had first sat down with a plan to get this place back to its former glory and beyond, they'd laid out the parameters for how it would run. From the town hall meetings, to the ways that they would pool their resources.

And it had been running great in the near fifteen years since.

So great that Gus didn't even have to think about getting all this together usually.

But town hall wasn't just a couple of days, and he was...

He barely knew which way was up as far as the whole world went, much less a sheet of financials.

He walked out of the cabin, down the path that led to the main paddock.

The place was looking amazing. He'd done this. And he knew he should feel some sense of pride, but instead it just felt like...not enough. Like he was trying to atone for something, and there just wasn't a way to atone for what you were. That was the problem. He just felt exhausted all of a sudden, because no matter how many people he took care of, no matter how much of this he tried to... No matter how hard he tried to make all this right... To make himself right... He just didn't know if it was possible.

"We have our first sign-ups."

He turned, and saw Brody standing there. He was holding a printout in his hand. "We've got an autistic child who just got adopted from foster care. He's missed out on a lot of therapy he should've had. It's been a real difficult run. And his new family wants to try this."

And something in Gus's chest went still.

"That's... great."

"You know I didn't really appreciate this," Brody

said. "That what we were doing could make a difference. I was just thinking in terms of it being a good business venture. But you thought of it, didn't you?"

"Brody…"

"You thought of it, because you're the one that's been through all that shit. I just still don't think of those things."

He stared at his brother, and he kind of wanted him to say it. To say that Gus had had it harder. They all avoided that. They all avoided throwing that at Brody. Because he lived in the middle of all the violence, so surely it wasn't actually easier. Except… Brody hadn't been hurt. Not physically.

"It's okay, Gus," Brody said. "I get it. And I know you don't want to say it. I get that. But you can."

"You know, yeah. But…do you need therapy?"

Brody looked down for a second, then laughed. "I consider a night at the bar and a beautiful woman in my bed to be therapy, but thanks for asking."

"So the answer's yes," Gus said.

"I don't know. We're not…really part of that therapy generation."

"But here we are, facilitating people getting it. Here we are, working the land, spending a hell of a lot of time with horses on the site where all this stuff happened. Sometimes I think maybe we're trying to therapize ourselves. Anyway. You still didn't answer my question. Do you probably need therapy?"

"I'm sure I do."

Gus shrugged. "Then what's the point? What's the point in me saying it? Yeah. I got set on fire. Honestly,

I think I have more entitlement to issues than any of you do. Not just you. Like sure, Lach got punched in the face. But me too. And then I needed a bunch of skin grafts. I kind of win. But we're all a different, fun kind of messed up from him. So did anybody win?"

"But you think people can come back from it," Brody said.

"I think some people have a shorter distance to walk."

And he didn't know what he said was even something he believed. He believed it for his brothers. But that was the thing. Yeah, he might think they'd all suffered. But he did know that he'd suffered the worst. And he also knew that when pushed, he made decisions that looked a lot more like his dad's than like the ones he wished he made. And he also knew that none of them had ever done anything like that.

It wasn't just anger. It was the enjoyment of it. It was the thing he got out of it. Out of the violence.

It haunted him. Lived in him. And he just had to wonder if it had been forged in flame that day, and there was nothing he could do about it.

"I was always thankful I had you," Gus said. "And Tag and Hunter, and Lachlan. We were always in it together, and you were never separate from that."

"But I was," Brody said.

"That was part of the abuse, Brody." And as soon as he said it he understood it. "It was part of what he did to you."

"Whatever. Look. I just… Thanks for this. I would never be involved in something this good if it wasn't for you. I'd just be off drinking myself to death and screwing anything that moved."

"If I had your face I'd be doing the same thing. But I don't."

Brody laughed. "I don't know that you would. Anyway, you've got a wife now."

Yeah. A wife that things had gone a lot further with than he'd intended. But Brody was right. He had her. So now the question was…what all was he going to do with her?

"Lachlan and I are going out to Smokey's tonight. You want to come?"

"No. No, thanks. I'll… Pass on that."

"That's a shame," Brody said. "You really are the best wingman."

"And you're usually a better liar than that."

"Well, just don't say you weren't invited."

"I wouldn't dream of it."

"I'll let you know if we get any more sign-ups."

"Thanks. We should be ready to open right on target. So the more the better."

"See you."

He nodded. And stared down at the paper his brother had handed to him. It was coming together. This thing.

And he wanted to hang on to this moment. Where Alaina was his, and he was going to be a father, and he was maybe doing a good thing, and nothing terrible had happened yet.

He hadn't messed it up.

And he suddenly related to her. To that restlessness she'd shown earlier. Of course, she wanted to jump ahead and make sure that everything would be okay. And he wanted to freeze the moment. But he knew that time just kept going. And there was always the possibility that something worse was lurking right around the corner. Always.

ALAINA HADN'T BEEN back to the farmhouse at Sullivan's Point since she got married, and that was just silly. She'd visited with her sisters, but always out at the barn. Or in the area they were renovating to make into the farm store. Out in the garden, where she'd gone to pick up fruits and veggies, and at the coops where they had eggs.

But she hadn't been back home.

But now she was helping get ready for town hall, which meant baking extra bread and cakes and other delightful things, and while that would never be her primary joy, she did like their big baking and canning days.

When she got there, it was a full house. Evelyn Garrett was there, along with Violet Garrett, and of course Elsie, and Nelly. Even Penny Case, the young woman who'd grown up with the Kings, was there. Then there were her sisters. Arizona wasn't there, but Alaina wondered if that was out of loyalty to Landry. Fia's Landry animosity was such that Alaina would hardly blame her.

"There you are," Fia said, wrapping her arm around her. "Miss you, sister."

And Fia threw an apron on over the top of her head, and it gave Alaina extremely filthy flashbacks to last night.

That had just been last night? When Gus had…

Her face went all hot.

"Oh," Fia said, blinking. "What's up with you?"

"Nothing."

Rory stared at her. "How is married life?"

"Good," Alaina said, trying to keep her face placid. "Just…good. Everything is good."

"You said *good* a lot," Quinn said.

"I did," she returned blandly.

She pushed her way into the knot of girls standing around in the large kitchen.

"We need to plan a baby shower for you," Elsie said. "And a bridal shower. Because you need things for your kitchen, don't you?"

"Oh… It's very early for a baby shower."

"Nonsense," Quinn said, suddenly looking bright. "I'm going to be an aunt. I would really like to buy a whole bunch of baby clothes."

"Well, you should wait until we know what it is," Alaina said, feeling twitchy.

"Yeah. I guess," her sister said. "But do you and Gus need anything in the house?"

She stopped herself from saying she would like a collection of sexy lingerie, except…she was sort of thinking she might. Just thinking about seducing Gus in a variety of different outfits made her feel warm.

He'd always wanted her.

That made her chest feel tender.

"Okay," Fia said. "You seem especially spacey today."

"I'm distracted," she said. "Or maybe I have pregnancy brain."

She had Gus McCloud brain was what she had.

She had not anticipated this.

It was so strange to think back on the Alaina that she'd been a couple of months ago. Because that girl had been a trial. Impatient, and nervous, and so desperate to push her way into the next thing. And nothing had actually been about…being in the moment. It had all been about pushing past difficult moments. The last night with Gus, she'd been entirely in the moment.

Her first time having sex had been about getting *past* the moment. Getting the thing over with.

She had never wanted her time with Gus to end.

And she felt calm here too, while she assisted with the baking, especially after everybody quit talking about her. Especially after they all started focusing on jam and bread, and pies.

"We're putting in for a big community injection of cash," Rory said. "Because we need to get this farm store up and running. And we need signage, and to get a new road."

"A new road?"

"Yeah. It'll be easier and faster to get to the farm store from the highway if we pave and excavate a new road," Quinn said. "But it has to go through the back part of Granger land."

Alaina recoiled. "You have to deal with the Grangers?"

There were other ranchers in the area, of course. Four Corners was the biggest spread. It was the biggest spread in the state. But there were others. And often, they didn't play nice with the Four Corners folk. The Grangers being one of them.

"Yeah, I could live my whole life without having to sort out easements with Levi Granger, but if it comes down to it…"

"Well, best of luck to you with that," Alaina said.

"Thanks."

"Hey," Fia said. "Would you and Elsie run down to the root cellar and get the canned rhubarb?"

"Sure," Alaina said, and she and Elsie left the kitchen, heading out the front door of the farmhouse, and making their way down toward where the root cellar started.

"They still send us on errands like we're kids," Elsie said.

But Alaina realized it didn't bother her anymore. Because she didn't feel like a kid. She just didn't feel that desperate clawing need to prove herself. And maybe it was because she had her own space now. Her own thing.

"So are you gonna tell me why you're so spacey and blushing every five seconds?" Elsie asked.

Suddenly, Alaina understood something she hadn't understood before. Elsie hadn't wanted to share about Hunter because it felt too private. Too personal. She could understand that now. In a way that she never had before.

She'd taken it personally, but it wasn't personal. Elsie hadn't been able to share because she hadn't known what to say. Because it felt like taking all of the things that had happened in the dark and dissecting them in the light would be wrong.

Because what had happened with Gus wasn't funny.

It wasn't something to giggle about. It had stripped layers of protection away from her, but left her with something else in its place. It had changed a fundamental understanding of certain things inside of her, and she didn't have the words for it.

She wanted to try, though. Because if she was going to understand what was happening, she needed to reach out. She pondered that. If it was reverting to her old ways. To trying to ease that restlessness rather than learning to sit in some discomfort.

No, this was different.

It was reaching out, saying what was happening, maybe even what she needed, rather than running.

"I… Something happened with Gus," she said, feeling shy, when she never was. They went down the stairs into the root cellar, and she felt that actually damp air cooled her off. There were shelves of all the things that her sisters spent so much time canning and organizing.

"Something?" Elsie pushed.

"We…" She spread her hands. "Last night."

She trusted that Elsie could figure out the missing words.

"Really?" Elsie looked shocked.

"Yeah. I… He's…"

Did the words even exist for Gus? For what she felt for him? What she'd felt in his arms…

"It's okay that you care for him," Elsie said, gently.

Alaina swallowed. "I do. I always have. That doesn't surprise me. It's *this*… And it doesn't feel weird, it just feels right. It's Gus, and he's so *difficult*. But he's also so wonderful. And…"

"And you don't have to know how things are going to go."

"That seems to be the theme of the last twenty-four hours. I keep trying to remind myself of that. I keep trying."

Elsie was looking at her, her expression so keen Alaina felt like she was looking into her.

"Was it good?" Elsie asked, finally.

Alaina shifted, feeling warm. It felt personal, but she was also...proud. Of him. Of them. It was the strangest feeling.

"He's amazing," she said. "I had no idea it could be... Travis was awful. Awful."

Elsie blinked, and her mouth fell open.

"Well, it's true," Alaina said, and now that she'd started talking, continuing on felt easy. "I didn't want to go bringing it up, because honestly, I'd rather forget about it. I'd rather forget about him. It was just... It was *nothing*. Just... Sex when you don't know someone or like them, or when they don't care about you at all? It's nothing. It was over in minutes, and he didn't care that I didn't have an orgasm, and I didn't feel *different*." She'd wanted to. She'd thought it was that simple. Virgin, not virgin, and you were transformed. But it wasn't. And she'd been silly. "Today I feel *different*," she whispered. "Because with Gus there was something else. I mean, chemistry first of all. But there's something else there."

It made her feel small, and a little bit scared, that something else.

And she didn't want to push to defend that, and it seemed like Elsie understood that.

"Well, it's a good thing you're married to him," Elsie said.

"Yeah." Except somehow she knew it wouldn't be that simple, and she also knew she didn't have the words to explain it. It would take too much of Gus's story to explain it. And she didn't want to do anything to reveal Gus. She felt like the keeper of secrets. Because he had told her things, said things to her, and they were hers. Just like he was.

He was her husband. That was the thing. Even if it wasn't a traditional marriage, that felt like something. It felt special. It felt important and singular. And the things that she knew about him weren't for anyone else to know.

"I'm just so glad that you have that," Elsie said. And then she laughed. "Maybe I'm being ridiculous and shallow. But I was very sad thinking that you weren't going to have great sex."

"Really?"

"Yes. Because what I have with Hunter is so great. Then… It scared me a little bit at first. Because of the feelings, that *something else* you mentioned, it terrified me."

"Except your something else was love," Alaina said.

Elsie grabbed a couple of jars off of the shelves, and then stood there, looking at her. "Can you tell me you don't love Gus?"

Alaina just stood there, feeling ironically rootless in the root cellar. Feeling a little bit unsteady.

"I care about him a whole lot."

"You always have," Elsie said.

"You know, I didn't really ever want to get married,

Elsie. Or have kids. And here we are. And I don't really know what to call the feelings I have for him."

"You don't have to," Elsie said.

Alaina nodded. "No. I don't have to."

When they left the root cellar, she felt oddly better.

Because she had affirmed what she'd been working toward this whole time. She didn't have to know.

And when they finished with all their baking, and they packed up some goodies to each take home, and she went outside, expecting to carpool with Elsie like she had coming over, Gus was out there standing up against his truck instead.

"I don't think I need a ride home now," she said.

And the look of blazing intent on his face made everything in her burn.

CHAPTER FOURTEEN

HE MOVED AWAY from the truck and walked over to her, and her stomach swooped.

This was complicated. He was complicated. This rough, gorgeous man.

He had occupied this elevated space in her mind. In her life. Almost immortal, and now she felt...close to him. Next to him.

Much more aware of all the ways they were the same. And even more intimately aware of all the ways that they were different.

She squeezed her thighs together just subtly. Something to ease the ache that spread in her so instantaneously the moment she laid eyes on him.

"Come on, mite."

And his nickname for her sent a little rush of pleasure all over her.

"Bye," she said to everyone else, scampering quickly to the truck and getting inside. He rounded the front and got in slowly, closing the door behind them and looking at her. "I brought a picnic," he said.

"You did?"

"Yeah. I thought...you've been cooking so much."

"I literally have a bushel of freshly baked bread with me."

"There's never so much food that you can't have fresh-baked bread."

She laughed. "Okay. That's true."

They started driving, but they took the dirt road that went past McClouds', way up toward the hills.

There were no fields on that part of the ranch. Not much really but wild timber and craggy mountain peaks.

"Where are we going?"

"It's just a spot I like," he said, dismissive.

But that was how he was, she realized then.

There was so much about Gus McCloud that wasn't quite what he seemed. And she had always thought that the big lie that he told was that he was mean, when in reality he was really quite a nice guy.

But now she was thinking that Gus wasn't the lie he appeared to be. He was nice; it was true. He was also mean. Intense and rabid like a wounded animal when things got too real.

He fancied himself blunt and honest, and she didn't think that was true either. And even now, he minimized whatever it was *this* was.

But Gus didn't do anything accidentally. Every single thing he did was with intent. From marrying her to setting down the ground rules.

Because he *did* want her. And he *had*. And the way that he played that off from the moment they'd gotten married had been a lie. Laughing at her when she'd asked about sex. Pretending he'd never thought of it.

So now she had to suspect everything.

She did wonder, though, how much of it was that he didn't know he was lying. Just how much he had detached himself from the truths way down in his soul.

"Gus," she said softly. "Where are you taking us?"

"I think even more importantly, I'll tell you, it was Violet who made the food."

"Violet was at the Sullivans' all day."

"I know. She made this for me yesterday."

She blinked up at him in confusion. "But you were mad at me yesterday."

"Not the whole day. I had planned ahead on providing a meal for you. Because you've been doing so much."

"Thank you."

"I do want to make sure…" He shook his head. "What are you getting out of this?"

"As of last night about six orgasms. But, I don't think that's what you mean."

"No. And I need to know. I'm older than you, and I've had fantasies about you I've suppressed for a long time, and hell… I have to make sure it's not my own enthusiasm driving this."

"It's not, Gus. Believe me."

"One thing I want to settle on is…exactly why you want to take care of the house. Of me."

"For a long time, I thought that maybe I wanted adventure somewhere else. But I think what I really always wanted was something that was mine. Something no one could take away from me. Everything changed when my dad left. My mom became a different person. And then when she left, the house became totally different. My sisters changed the ranch, and they sort of did it all by consensus, and not on purpose, but they didn't ask me. And everything that I knew slipped through my fingers so damn quickly... This, having a partnership. Having something that belongs to us both... That means something to me. The idea of having a baby...a child that I love, that no one can take from me...it actually makes me happy. I'm coming to that conclusion, anyway. The thing is... I hadn't put a lot of thought into what I wanted from my life. I just had a lot of feelings. And I avoided the difficult ones. But the problem with avoiding difficult things is you can't set real goals. You just flail around a lot and feel like things aren't fair, or they aren't right, or they aren't working. But now I feel calmer. Like I can sit back and see what truly works for me. And what truly doesn't. But this little place that I'm carving for myself at McClouds'...it feels good."

He looked pleased, and she liked to see that. "Well, I'm glad to hear it."

She looked out the window, at the dense groves of trees, the ferns down at the base of them. It was beautiful here. Rich and green. And all that beauty made her heart ache. And when she looked at Gus, her heart stilled.

"Marrying me really was a grander-than-necessary gesture, Gus. All you had to do was kiss me. Does it bother you to realize you could have had me for cheaper?"

He turned to face her, his brow lifted. "You keep saying things like that, and then you get mad if I say anything..."

She bit her lip.

"That's why I get mad," she said. "Because I'm afraid that's what you think."

He blew out a breath. "No, I'm not mad. Because I didn't want you cheap. I wanted you for keeps."

The sound of the tires on the gravel filled the cab and rumbled through her chest.

And the truck wound around the side of a mountain, rising in elevation, and he didn't stop driving until they reached the very top of it. Parked on the edge of the cliff face that looked out over the ranch below. And it was like looking down at a scale model. Bright green patchwork that made up the Kings', and the Garretts'. The big pond and endless orchards at the Sullivans'. And the lush green of the McClouds'. The river winding through it. It was beautiful to see it like this.

"It's everything," she said. "All of us."

"It sure is. I love this place. And I know what you mean. About building something that feels real. That feels like it'll last. Because so much of it… It doesn't. So much of life just keeps on changing. And I had a whole childhood of things just getting worse and worse… I wanted to make things better. There was a point where I decided I wanted to make them better."

"Was the collective…? The way that things are run now, was that your idea?"

"Not me by myself. The Kings had a lot to do with it."

"Why don't they really socialize with anyone?"

"Shit, I don't know. I assume they have their own demons. But I respect the heads they collectively have on their shoulders when it comes to managing things.

They're fine ranchers. What they do with their cattle operation is genius. It's a lot of work, and they're willing to do it. We don't need to be friends."

"Yeah. I guess not. So you and the Kings."

"And Sawyer. We went to Fia, talked to her, and that was when she laid down the law regarding how she wanted things to go at Sullivans'. Your sister... She was so young then, and having to take over with your dad being gone... Your mom didn't really want to help with it."

"I know."

"But that's how it all came together. Us just deciding to make something new. To make something that was ours. Would last."

"That's how I feel now."

"I never thought I'd have kids. So there's something...something meaningful to the fact that this thing I've been working on... There's someone who can have it. I had to throw my dad out in order to take over this place. But I'm gonna give it gladly to our child."

"That's...that's... Thank you."

"Yeah. Well. You really got to quit thanking me for doing the bare minimum."

"Nothing you've done is the bare minimum."

He shrugged. Then he reached into the back of the truck and pulled out a picnic basket and a blanket. "You game?"

"Yes."

She grabbed some of the bread and jam that she brought, and they spread the blanket out outside right on the edge of that cliff, the view stretched out before them.

She was filled with a sense of purpose then. A sense of direction. That this was theirs. And that they would grow it and share it and pass it on.

But then mostly, she was just filled with interest in the picnic basket, and the sandwiches that were inside, which were beautifully made.

They ate in silence, and she moved a little bit closer to him when she was halfway through the sandwich, then a little closer still, so that her leg touched his. And she noticed when he closed his eyes and let his head fall back at the glancing contact.

And when she did it again, he made a low sound in his throat.

"Yes?"

"Stop being a tease," he said.

"Who said I'm teasing?"

"You are a problem."

"So are you."

She popped the last piece of her sandwich in her mouth, chewed and swallowed, and that was when Gus kissed her. Slow, deliberate. Nothing like the way he had devoured her last night. He was exploring her, like he had nothing better to do, his tongue sliding slowly against hers, his rough hands moving up to cup her face, stroking her cheeks. She wrapped her arms around his neck and pressed her body against him as best she could while she parted her lips, allowing him to take the kiss deeper.

He acted like he had nothing better to do, and nothing else on his mind. Then he moved his hand slowly down her back, his thumbs coming around to skim the undersides of her breasts. And she ached. The slow, maddening seduction, the sensuality of it. Her nipples went tight, ached for his touch, but he didn't give that to her. He kept on going slow, moving those hands all the way down to her hips, his thumb still stroking her as he moved across her curves. They parted for a moment, and she looked up at him, deep into those green eyes. Familiar, unfamiliar, all at once. Seeing that hunger there. And that spark that was all him.

She wanted to capture that moment. That moment when he was her protector, her lover, her friend from all these years and a stranger all at once. When he exhilarated her, made her feel like she was flying off the edge of this cliff, and made her feel comforted at the same time. Because he was everything. And this was everything. And she wished there was a way to capture it like fireflies in a jar, so that it could glow in her hands for the rest of forever. Because part of her was afraid. Afraid that she would lose it. Afraid that she would lose him. Because nothing in her life had ever stayed. Everything gold turned brown eventually and faded away. And she wanted this to last forever. Their own little world made of happiness. And every pass of his mouth over hers added another layer to that conviction, that determination. To everything they were. It didn't erase what they'd been before, it added to it.

Because this was the same man she'd always known. He wasn't a stranger. She was just learning something new about him.

Finally learning everything.

He pushed her back onto the blanket, his big body

covering hers, and she arched, her breasts pressed against his muscular chest. She moved her hands over his shoulders, down his back, at the same time he explored her body.

And there were no angry words. There was no sense of fear. No sense that the world was crashing around them and they had to hurry and make the most of the moment or it would slip away.

It just felt…it just felt right. He felt right.

She pushed his shirt up over his head, and gloried in the sight of his muscles in the sunlight.

"Alaina," he growled against her neck, then he bit her.

She yelped, arching against him.

"Too much?" He was breathing hard, his voice rough.

"I thought I had to take what you gave me," she said, rolling her hips against his.

He growled low, deep in his throat. "It's not fun unless everyone's having fun," he said.

"Can't you tell I'm having fun?" she asked, taking his hand and moving it down beneath her skirt, between her legs, where he could feel that her underwear was already damp.

He pressed his forehead to hers, and growled again, making her tremble beneath his gaze. He stroked her, pushing his fingers beneath that fabric and finding out just how wet she was.

He kissed down her neck, his teeth scraping along her collarbone, his hands moving to her hips, calloused palms sliding up her soft skin as he pushed that dress up and over her head, off of her body.

So she was just wearing a pink bra, and matching underwear, and she was gratified by the expression on his face. By how much he liked it.

He moved his hand over her body, and paused right there at her stomach, which was beginning to get rounder.

"Perfect," he said. "You're perfect."

The rest of their clothes came off with ease, their bodies tangling together, and when he slid home, she nearly wept. Because this was what she had been waiting for. This was what she had waited for, really, because she hadn't experienced anything that was like this. This was really the real thing. Intimacy.

The thing she hadn't been looking for at all, but that she needed all the same. It was what created magic in the pages of those books that she read. It was the source of the spark.

It wasn't just bodies moving together, moving within another. It was the connection of souls.

And she had never understood that. Not really.

But she did now. In this moment. But he came from inside.

And it spilled all over the outside. Made it hot. Made it everything.

The desire that roared through her was like a wild beast, and Gus wasn't gentle. His thrusts were intense, pushing her hips down into the hard ground, bracing her like that, making her take the full impact of him into her.

And she wanted it. Everything. All that he was. The rough and the untamed. Because it was what called to her.

Wasn't that what he'd said about her? That he liked

her passion? That he liked all the things that she was? And what a gift, because everyone else usually saw it as her being a whole lot of extra.

But Gus had always admired it. And that thing in him that made other people afraid? She wanted it. She could take it. With ease.

Just maybe she was made for him.

And that feeling was like being overcome by an emotion so deep she didn't think there were words for it. Only groanings in her spirit that filled her with an ache so deep she could scarcely breathe.

When her climax came over her it was like a shower of glory, wave after wave of pleasure, and she kissed him, dragged him down with her, felt him shatter beneath her hands, within her, as he roared out his own release.

"Gus," she whispered against his mouth, and that mountain shook as she held him.

He lay back on the blanket, and she looked at him, fully naked in the sun. Examined the places where the flames had licked over his body, and where they hadn't. And she didn't find one part of him better looking than another. It was all part of who he was. And she liked all of it.

"I promise you, I didn't bring you up here for that," he said, looking up at her.

"It's okay if you did."

"Oh, I intended to have that happen. I just figured we'd wait till there was a bed."

"I don't need a bed. I just need you."

She meant it, but as soon as the words came out of

her mouth she felt a little bit vulnerable. Gus wanted her, but that didn't necessarily mean anything deeper than that. Hell, she didn't know if she wanted it to mean anything deeper than that, because they had to keep their heads and figure out how to make all this right and good for the child that they were going to raise together. Figure out how to make this work long-term, when neither she nor Gus had any experience with any such thing.

It made her want to hide. Conceal all those raw feelings.

But they were right out in the open, and she was naked, and when it came right down to it, she didn't really know how to hide.

But he did. And she could sense that he was doing it now. And she wanted to break through that wall; she just didn't know how. And anyway, right now the idea scared her.

Because of what he might do.

If she pushed him...

She wasn't afraid of him physically, but emotionally... Yeah, that was scary.

"Right. Well."

"I just like you a lot," she said.

And he laughed. "You know, I don't think anyone's ever said that to me."

That made her stomach go hollow. He might be laughing, but she didn't find it amusing at all.

"Well, then they're mean."

"You're something else."

"I try. Or, maybe I don't. My family is not exactly known for its restraint. I can't claim to be unique among

my sisters. Though, they expressed their strong person-
alities in slightly different ways."

"Definitely a different experience than growing up
at the McCloud house, which was all testosterone."

And they sat there with the reality of that. That her
house had been entirely feminine, especially after her
dad had left, and he had lost his mother, and had ended
up with all men.

"Do you suppose that's what drove my dad away?
All those girls?"

"I suspect that your dad's own issues drove him away."

And he said nothing for a long moment. And she
didn't want to say anything about his mother, because
she knew full well why she had left. Because of his father. Because he'd been dangerous and frightening, and
it was difficult to blame any woman for leaving him.
Except she left her sons, and that was the thing that
Alaina would never understand. She'd left Gus. And
then he'd been burned. And that…that just about destroyed her. She wondered if it destroyed him too. And
knew that she couldn't ask that. Because she could feel
the walls.

He was so good at pretending there weren't any. But
she knew that there were. Because when he told her the
story of what had happened to him, and confessed that
he never told it, she'd known. Because it became clear
the more time she spent with him, that every bit of his
lay-it-all-out-there kind of demeanor wasn't strictly the
truth.

And she wondered how much more he had hidden
down in there.

But also knew that if she pushed him now he would push back. And it wouldn't be any fun for her.

"What kind of baby names do you like?" she asked, elbowing him and reaching into the picnic basket and grabbing a carrot stick. She crunched it. It was not a chip. And she was a little bit sad about that, but she appreciated that Violet was trying to be healthy. It was just that Alaina didn't much care for that one way or the other.

"I don't...think that I should be responsible for naming another human being."

"Why not?"

"I have never thought about it in my entire life."

"Oh, I did. I had baby names written down in my diary from the time I was fourteen."

"You said you didn't even know if you wanted kids."

"Well, no, I didn't, but I really liked to kind of dream about that future. That perfect one. That would have kids and a husband and all of that. And I may have cut out a picture of a wedding dress or ten too and put them in the journal."

"Wow."

"You didn't have a diary, Gus?"

"No," he said, and she reached down into the picnic basket, took out another carrot, and he stole it, popping it into his mouth.

"That's disappointing. I was hoping that we might trade some secrets."

"Sorry. I never had anything I much wanted to write down."

"Oh."

And then she just felt a little bit sad.

And she realized that she had never written about her dad leaving. She'd never really written about her life, just her hopes for later.

"I guess I didn't really like keeping record of the bad things either. I was really close to my dad," she said. "More than my mom. I thought I was more like him. I thought we understood each other. And he used to laugh and joke with me and he made me feel safe. And one day he was gone. And he's never been back. It's like he turned into a whole other person. Or maybe I did. And I could never understand... I could never understand what I did. Because it seemed like I had to have done something." And for some reason the words were coming now in great rushing torrents, and she was telling him things that she had never even let fully form inside of herself. All these uncomfortable feelings that she pushed to the side whenever possible. All these things that she never wanted to think about or talk about or spend one moment longer than she had to with.

"He wasn't a distant father. He was a *good* father," she whispered, the words scratchy. "And then he was just gone. How does it happen like that? How can someone just change like that?"

An unsolvable problem. The one that had started it all. Had made her afraid. To care, to feel bad—because how could you ever know if you'd feel right again?

"Because people are messed up," Gus said. "And they have demons that are difficult to see. And I'm not excusing them. Any man that can leave his kids like that... He doesn't deserve any excusing. Okay?"

"Yeah. I know."

"I'm just saying, I don't think it was you. Whatever it was, it was him. He was the one that couldn't keep his promises or handle his life. He was the one."

She really hoped that he would share. About his mother. Instead, he stood up, and started collecting his clothes.

And she slowly put her own on.

They packed all their things up, and put them back in the truck. And right when Gus got in the truck, just before he closed the door he said, "My mom used to bring us here for picnics."

And he didn't say anything more, but she felt like he had handed her a piece of his heart, no explanation, just that simple and that deep.

There was so much in Gus that he couldn't say. And she realized right then that what she wanted more than anything was to be the one that he said them to.

Somehow. Someday. That was what she wanted.

CHAPTER FIFTEEN

IT WAS TOWN hall day, and Gus couldn't really focus on his presentation, because he was obsessing about his wife. An easy thing to do, when she was blowing his mind multiple times every night. He hadn't had this much sex in…ever. Because he was so selective, because of the way he did things, and because of…

Because he didn't like to give himself what he wanted. Not too often. But hell, he'd dropped that completely with her. He was getting exactly what he wanted all night long. For the last three nights. And he was feeling pretty damn good about it.

After the picnic, they'd gone to their separate rooms, and then last night, they'd ended up making love on the couch, before going their separate ways. It suited him. That little bit of distance and time to clear his head.

Because damn…

She was something else, that woman. A firecracker that was too hot to handle.

But he had to get his head on straight, and think about the meeting. Not that he was up against any opposition. It should be pretty straightforward. It was just any time you had to come forward and ask for a bigger share of the community money, he felt you needed to be certain of what you were asking for.

Transparency was a huge part of what made all this work.

Transparency...

The word stuck in his chest. Well. Transparency when it came to professional things was different than personal things.

Alaina wouldn't like any transparency in him.

He went downstairs and there was Alaina, dressed in another one of those pretty summer dresses, her arms laden with baskets.

"What are you doing?"

He went over to her and snatched her burden off of her arms.

"I wanted to bring a few of the extra flavors of preserves with me."

"You don't need to carry all that," he said.

"Don't start treating me like I'm fragile. You know, pregnant women can keep doing most of the same things they did before unless there are extreme circumstances."

"Well, I don't know anything about pregnant women. How do you?"

"The internet," she said, sniffing.

He shrugged. "Okay. That...seems reasonable."

She laughed. "Of course, I did a whole bunch of mad reading right when I found out. That's how I knew about the one cup of coffee."

"Fine then. How about it's not for your health, it's just the point of having a husband."

She grinned up at him happily, and he...just stopped.

Everything in him stopped. Had anyone ever looked at him like that?

Not in his memory.

Well. It was different, but there had been a time when… when he'd figured that he had that kind of safe space. When he figured that there was someone who cared a lot about him. A respite from the danger in the house.

His mom.

Army men and broken promises.

Shit. This whole impending-parenthood thing was really getting under his skin.

Making him think too much about the past.

He probably shouldn't have taken her up to that picnic spot. He hadn't been up there in…years. But that was where his mom would take them all sometimes. For an outing, she'd said, but he had the feeling it was mostly just to get away from their dad.

She'd left them.

And that was hitting him harder and harder these days.

He knew that had to do with the baby. Watching the way that Alaina was embracing motherhood, even though it was unexpected. And his own convictions about how the kid needed stability.

"We should go early," Alaina said. "Because my sisters will have everything to set up."

"Sure," he said.

He was not one who ever went early to the town hall. Mostly because he was never part of the refreshments. The Sullivans tended to host because they had a barn most suited to housing that many people. And while they traded around who provided all the food, they tended to do a lot of it. As did the women in the Garrett household these days.

The Kings were reliable for barbecue. And the Mc-Clouds tended to contribute…store-bought things.

It was strange, because he'd spent any number of years rejecting domesticity of any kind, and now his house was a hive of it.

And it was making him want to give some things back. And he didn't know how to do them.

But he agreed to go early with her, and they got into the truck, where he unburdened himself of the baskets, and took the quick drive over to Sullivan's Point.

It hit him then, that the women fluttering around in the field by the barn were his sisters-in-law. It hit him that the family had expanded. It was just the strangest damn thing. Because there had been separation in all this. Compartments where he had kept everything, and now the lines were starting to blur. He was trying to sleep with Alaina, and not be… Whatever that could become. But she was his wife. And it was harder and harder to pretend she wasn't his wife for real. There was all this space inside of him. Distance that he was working to maintain. For obvious reasons. Reasons that were obvious to him, anyway. And it just…seemed a little bit shaded here.

"Hey," Fia said, waving as they both got out of the truck, him taking the baskets again.

"Hey," Alaina said happily, skipping ahead of him, and he walked slowly to the proceedings.

Fia took the baskets off his arm and set them on the

table. "How's it going, Angus?" she asked. She looked at him speculatively.

"Going good, thanks."

Fia was much closer in age to him than Alaina, and consequently, he had known her in a different context for longer. Particularly when they had taken up the charge to reform the ranches. And she was as skeptical of him as it came, he could see.

Alaina was happily chatting to her other sisters, Rory, who was bookish and difficult to know, and pint-size Quinn, who always wore flirty, feminine dresses, but seemed ready to punch someone in the face if need be at the drop of a hat.

They all had different shades of red hair. And all of them were pretty.

But Alaina was the only one that had ever made him feel sucker punched. She was the only one that had ever gotten to him like that.

But then, she was the only woman in all the world that had ever gotten to him like that, and as inconvenient as it was, he couldn't deny it was the truth.

"I trust you're treating my sister well."

"I like to think so."

"She seems happy," Fia said. "Thank you. And I'm sorry that I was mean to you when all of this first went down."

"Hey, I might've been mean to you too."

"No, really, Gus. Rory and Quinn and I were not... It's not fair. I'm sorry. You don't deserve any of the rumors that go around about you. I mean, I know you let them off, but it isn't fair. You never once acted like your dad…"

"Hey," he said, his chest turning to granite. "Don't go absolving me of everything, Fia. I'm not a nice guy. I let everybody talk about me because I don't give a damn. But I do give a damn about your sister. So."

"As declarations go, that's not terribly romantic."

"Yeah, she tells me I'm not romantic. And I'm not. But I won't hurt her." Fia deserved that truth. He liked her, respected her, always had.

"I know you won't," Fia said. And she looked like she was thinking about whether or not to say something, and he could see the moment she decided to go ahead with it. "You care about her, don't you? I think that's what I didn't realize. That you care about her. A lot."

"I do," he said. "I sure as hell do."

"She's been hurt so badly. By our parents…" And she looked at him even harder. "But you know that too."

"Yeah. I do."

"Good then. Don't hurt her."

"I just told you I wouldn't."

"I meant her *heart*, Gus."

And it was on the tip of his tongue to say he didn't think Alaina's heart was tangled up in him like that. But for some reason he decided not to. Maybe because he didn't want to expose them. Because what was happening between them was private. Because it felt sacred, which was a damn strange thing to think about the best, dirtiest sex he'd ever had. But, it was a fact.

"Are you grilling my husband?" Alaina asked, crossing the space and moving over to grab his arm, then his hand.

And everything in him lit up like a power grid. She held his hand. Just casually, standing beside him like she belonged there.

"Yeah," Fia said. "I am. But he's a big guy. He can handle it." Then Fia patted him on the shoulder, and he felt... buffeted. By all these women.

Just a lot of women all of a sudden.

"I want to take my sisters into Copper Ridge to go to the thrift stores." She looked up at him.

"Oh. Okay. What does that have to do with me?"

"I'll be spending your money. And bringing things into your house." And she got up on her tiptoes and kissed him on the cheek, and right then he would've given her any damn thing she asked for.

"Fine with me. I don't have to go, right?"

"No," she said. "In fact, you weren't invited. It's a sister shopping trip."

"Far be it for me to interfere. When is this happening?"

"I don't know. When are you free, Fia?"

"For a Copper Ridge day? I can make myself free. It's been too long since I've driven out to the ocean."

"All right then," Gus said. "Do what you must."

"Can I borrow a truck and trailer in a couple of days?" she asked, smiling sweetly.

"Shit, woman, how much stuff are you going to buy?"

"Your house is empty," she said.

It wasn't entirely, and there were rooms that hadn't been disturbed since his childhood, and he decided not to think on that.

"Fine. Fine."

And pretty soon after that everyone else started filtering in for the meeting. He shook hands with the Kings, and exchanged brief words. Only Landry lingered for a minute to make conversation, and he had to wonder if he was doing it just to loiter in the vicinity of Fia, who was doing her best to keep her distance from him. As always.

He knew that Alaina—and everyone else—thought that Fia and Landry had had an ill-fated love affair. Gus didn't think so. Of course, he didn't know what else would explain the behavior, but he just didn't think that was it. One thing about being distant from people was that you watched them. And he'd seen quite a few love affairs come and go among staff on the ranch. It just didn't look like that in the end. There was something more like…embarrassment that seemed to come off of Fia, and something else. But it wasn't his business. Even if Fia was…borderline family now.

He got to speak first at the meeting, standing up and outlining the increased financial demands that they were running into. The need for new electrical in all the buildings, and how that had really run up the tab, and the cost of various permits, which was adding up faster than he'd anticipated. Plus the certifications. "But we already have people signing up. And I think it's going to make a big difference." He read some of the stories, including the newly adopted autistic boy, a child who had seen his mother killed by his father and had lost his voice. So many tragic stories coming in, and far too relatable to Gus in many ways.

And when he was finished, he knew he had everybody pretty well on the hook. Well, maybe not Denver, who was sitting back with his arms crossed. But it was always hard to tell with him.

Next up it was Fia's turn to talk. "The renovation of the barn is going well, but we have to have a road put in. I need to negotiate with Levi Granger. And we need to come to terms on the cost arrangements. But I have a feeling the burden is going to fall largely to us." She named a sum of money that was actually more than what Gus had just asked for.

"Time-out," Landry said. "Levi Granger? And his anti–Four Corners ranching collective?"

"His collective has nothing to do with it," said Fia, her outrage at him daring to address her obvious. "And anyway it isn't inherently anti-us."

"It is, but even if it weren't, this is overextending the community pot."

"Excuse me?" Fia said, her eyes burning bright.

"With what the McClouds are up to, and what you Sullivans are up to, we're spending left, right and center."

"Both are ventures we stand to profit from," Fia said.

"I understand that," Landry said, standing up and taking the floor. "But the budget is what it is. We have an agreed-upon amount for the year."

"Oh, that's bullshit, Landry," Fia said, like she had forgotten she was in front of anybody. "What does it matter if we spend more now, or spend more next year? It's arbitrary."

"Finances are not arbitrary."

"Look who's a fucking accountant all of a sudden," she said.

"Just a second," Gus said, standing up. "It doesn't have to be like this. We can figure something out."

"I'm going to convince him to split the cost," Quinn said, standing up, her strawberry-colored hair bouncing with the moment. "I've got a plan, and I intend to bring the community into this. We'll have a meeting about the farm store and projected impact and then I plan to get Levi—"

Landry lifted a shoulder. "What would be in it for him?"

"A lot," Quinn said. "In fact—"

"If I were you I'd save the sales pitch for Levi Granger, Ms. Sullivan," Landry said.

And that earned him a glare from Fia so steely Gus thought there might be an actual explosion.

"The profit margins are not going to be terribly high and…"

"You should let us have some of your pastureland," Landry said.

"Landry King, I swear to God…"

"Well, you should figure out how to make your land more profitable," Landry said. "Because like you said, the profit margins on this venture aren't going to be very high. We accept the fact that you have to hire more outside work than the rest of us do."

"You're an asshole," Fia said.

"Okay," Gus said, lifting his hands, unsure how he became the unofficial peacemaker here. "Let's just back it up. Why don't we go away, we'll call a special meeting, we'll figure out a compromise. If I look at what money McCloud has specifically, then…"

"I don't want your charity, Angus," Fia said.

"And I don't want your attitude, Fia," he said.

Everyone present in the barn was watching the exchange. They didn't often have disagreements, but then, they weren't often all trying to make moves toward different ventures all at once. And they agreed to put a pin in it, went over other ranch business and by the time it was done, Gus was thankful that extra kegs of beer had been brought around to this particular meeting.

Some of the tension from the earlier moment faded when they went outside, the bonfire already high and burning bright, various members of the ranch setting up to play live music, and brisket being served onto plates.

The evening was cool, the October air crisp, and the fire illuminated everything in a glow. Someone handed him a solo cup full of beer, and he took it, right when the music started to kick up high.

Fia was sitting off by herself looking angry, and Gus scanned the crowd for his wife.

"Hey," he said, when he found her standing with Rory and Quinn. "You pissed off at me?"

"It's not your fault. I'm not even mad at the Kings. The thing is, Landry's not wrong. There's only the money there is. And we are going to have to solve the rest of the problem."

"Well. How nice for you to be levelheaded about it."

"Levelheaded isn't in Fia's wheelhouse."

"Numbers are an immovable object," Rory said. "It's why I prefer books."

"We'll figure it out," he said.

"Oh, I know we will," Quinn said. "If I have to dig the road from our barn to Levi's to the highway with nothing but my fists and determination, then I will."

"Somehow unsurprised by that."

One of the hands started singing a country song Gus knew well, his bass voice doing a decent job of imitating the singer. And Alaina's eyes brightened, and she took his hand. "Dance with me."

"Dance with you?"

"Yes."

"I don't dance."

"Please dance with me."

And she grinned at him, and it was irresistible in a way nothing else ever had been. In his life. The song lyrics asked, "Would you go with me?"

And he realized that he couldn't deny her.

"All right," he said.

And he felt like an idiot, even though most everybody got out there and danced, but she spun around, illuminated by the firelight, and when she smiled at him, he thought his chest might burst open.

He held her close and then twirled her, and the joy that radiated from her was catching.

And he had a moment of wondering if all the stuff in him was catching too, which concerned him a little bit, because Alaina didn't deserve to catch any of the bullshit inside of him.

And when she came back to him, there was part of the song that asked, "Would it be okay if I didn't know the way?"

And he didn't know the way, he realized that.

And he wanted her. He wanted this.

And just now he wanted to embrace it. Not have any of the walls up, not have any of his defenses in place. Because he just wanted this moment.

And she laughed, and he felt himself do it in response. Until he was spinning right along with her, grinning, and not caring that it stretched his scar tissue all to hell.

To smile that wide.

He so rarely had a reason to, but tonight he had her. Like a spark in his arms, and he never wanted to let her go.

And they danced until the fire died down, and the evening quieted.

Then they got back into his truck, and she was still singing along with every song they danced to.

"You don't even like country music," he said.

"I think I do now," she responded, smiling up at him.

He cleared his throat, and decided he was going to go ahead and follow his next impulse, because his impulses had taken him to some pretty decent places tonight.

"Why don't you sleep in my room tonight?"

"Okay."

And when they went up to bed, she was that same spark she'd been by the fire. And it took a long time for the two of them to cool. And when they did, they fell asleep holding each other. And in the morning she was still there.

CHAPTER SIXTEEN

"WE'RE ALL GOING dancing tonight," Hunter said.

Gus didn't look up from the stall he was mucking. "Good for you."

"Don't you think that maybe you should take your wife dancing?"

And he couldn't help but think about the night that he had picked Alaina up from Smokey's Tavern. Yeah, he couldn't help but think about that.

She'd been out dancing with other men. But never with him. He didn't go down to the tavern. And maybe that needed to change.

Except he hated the idea of changing at all.

Because everything is so great?

"I just danced with her the other night," he said.

"Dancing with her at town hall is hardly the same as taking her out, Gus."

Gus grunted. "Who is *we all*?"

"Everybody. Elsie. Me. Lachlan, so probably Charity, and Brody will be there scamming on beautiful women, and I think Tag even convinced Nelly to come out and dance."

"Well, that is really something," he said.

"Bring your wife."

He made a dismissive noise in the back of his throat. "She already married me. I don't have to keep on wooing her."

"What exactly do you think is going to keep her happy, Gus? That ranch house that she's had to do all the fixing in, and your dick? Because while I appreciate the confidence…"

"She hasn't complained," Gus said, his tone flat.

"I'm sure she hasn't. But, eventually, it might become a problem if you never want to do anything with her. If you never want to go out, you never want to…"

"So concerned about my business."

"Yeah, you were concerned about mine. If I recall correctly."

"Rightly so. Elsie Garrett is a sweet girl."

Hunter gave him a hard look. "Alaina Sullivan is a sweet girl. And you're not a sweet guy."

"*She* thinks I am," he said.

And Hunter just stared at him for a minute.

"What?" Gus asked.

"Hell. You better keep her happy. Because you're not going to find a woman like that just anywhere. A woman who thinks you're sweet."

That stuck in a strange place in his chest. And he didn't know what made him okay with talking to Hunter right now. Maybe it was because Hunter had a woman. A woman who happened to be Alaina's friend.

It made him feel like Hunter might…get it. He let out a breath, long and slow.

"I don't want another one anyway."

And he realized that he'd admitted something he hadn't even fully admitted to himself.

He didn't.

He hadn't wanted another woman for a long damn time. And the whole thing about how he was just going to find another woman to have sex with if he felt like it was...a lie. Had been from the beginning. Because he didn't want another woman. Ever since that moment down at the lake when she'd been eighteen, he hadn't.

Ever since Alaina Sullivan had turned his life inside out with her smile. Ever since he'd seen her—really seen her—and everything he'd thought about the world had been taken apart piece by piece.

"Then you better figure out how to keep her."

"I didn't think I was in any danger of losing her."

"You aren't. Now. Because seems to me that right now you two are head over heels in lust, and that will carry you for a while. But eventually you hit up against that wall."

That pissed him off. Even more that he wanted his brother to keep talking as much as he wanted him to stop because the idea of losing Alaina was completely unendurable. "What wall would that be?"

"The wall of your extensive issues, my guy."

There was no denying that was a thing.

"And somehow me taking her dancing is going to help with that?"

"You learning to live a little is going to help with it. You can't... You're so separate all the time, Gus. Find a way to be part of something. So that she can be part of things. Because otherwise..."

That he understood. He had no intention of isolating Alaina. No intention of keeping her separate. That wasn't what he wanted for her at all.

She was too beautiful for that. Too perfect. And if that was all she was going to get from him, then…he would be better off letting her go.

"Fine. Point taken. What time is dancing happening?"

"Heading out at eight," Hunter said. "See you there."

He took his phone out of his pocket and texted Alaina. Dancing tonight?

A few minutes later she responded. Okay.

He was surprised by how satisfying that was.

He had a date. With his wife.

SHE DIDN'T KNOW what to wear. How silly was that? She remembered when Elsie had borrowed some stuff so they could go out and try to pick up guys. She didn't need to pick up a guy. She had a guy. And she was the one that had flirty dresses. It was just that it… She wore them in front of Gus all the time and she wanted something special. Because they were going out together. Because she was proud to be on his arm. He never did that. Never went to Smokey's with everyone else. But he wanted to go with her.

She found what she thought was the sexiest dress she had, and critically eyed her growing baby bump. Her chest had filled out a little bit more, along with the belly, so it seemed to add a little bit of balance. And anyway, Gus certainly hadn't complained. She put makeup on, fluffing her hair and eyeing herself critically. And then when she went downstairs, Gus was standing there, wearing black jeans, a black T-shirt and a black cowboy hat, and every bad boy fantasy she'd never known she had roared to life inside of her. He looked dangerous.

He looked wonderful.

"Well, don't you look amazing."

"Me?" he asked, looking incredulous.

He was looking at her like she was special, and it made her whole chest feel like it was burning bright.

"Yeah," she said. "You. You know...you are an incredibly handsome man."

"Now, don't go lying to me," he said, crossing the space and extending his hand.

She took it, and he began to lead her out of the living room.

"I'm not lying."

"Okay," he said slowly, "sexy I've heard. But not handsome. They are not the same thing."

"You are, Gus."

"I'm not fishing for compliments. I'm just saying."

And she really wished that she could make him understand. How she saw things differently now. The way she saw him differently now. How her concept of beauty felt different now.

They walked out of the house and to his truck, and he opened the door for her. She stretched up on her toes and kissed his cheek. "Handsome."

"Get in the car, mite."

She obeyed, that old nickname mingling with the new way they were together sending sparks all up inside of her.

It was a short drive off the ranch and down to Smokey's

Tavern, and she had a strange sensation crawl up her spine. Because she hadn't been here since the night she had hooked up with Travis. But it wasn't really him that she remembered. Not now. What she remembered was Gus being there. What she remembered was him being there for her. The way that he always was.

"It's crowded tonight," she said.

"And how," he said.

He parked, on the edge of the lot, half the tires on the gravel, because there was no room. Inside was packed. Loud, full of honky-tonk music and people drinking beer. Dancing and flirting.

She'd found the scene exciting just a few months ago. Had seen it as her window into being taken seriously in town as a grown-up.

And it was funny, because it wasn't the scene that interested her now. It was just being with him.

"There's everybody," he said. He gestured to the corner, and there was Hunter and Elsie, his brothers, Nelly, Charity.

"Wow. Everybody really is here."

She hadn't been here with Elsie since that night she had been here pining over Hunter.

What a funny memory.

What a strange thing to feel like you were living an entirely different life than the one you'd been living only a few months ago.

"Can I get you something?" Gus asked as he steered her over to the tables where everyone was sitting.

"Diet Coke?"

"Sure thing."

She took a seat next to Elsie, leaving an empty space next to her for Gus.

"Wow. Gus is actually at Smokey's. It's a minor miracle," Elsie said.

"No kidding," Brody added. "Gus hasn't come out with us since... If he ever has?"

"Oh. Well," Alaina said. "He asked me if I wanted to come tonight."

"Damn," Lachlan said. "I had no idea how good marriage would be for him."

"Here's your soda," Gus said, coming back to the table with a beer in his hand, and her drink in the other.

"Thank you."

"No problem."

And she looked around the table, and saw the couples touching each other casually, and she wanted to do the same with Gus. But so often she felt like he was a big, skittish horse. And if she put her hand on him wrong he might jump. Might spook.

So she put her hands on her cup, and swirled her straw.

It was a funny thing, to sit around this table, with people who were family now. By marriage. Even Elsie was her family by marriage.

And she tried to draw comfort from that, even as she felt the slight bit of distance between herself and Gus.

He had brought her out, so there was no point being churlish about it.

"I want you to finish telling me about Hunter," Elsie said, brushing Hunter's hair back from his face in a casual gesture that made Alaina's stomach dip.

"Oh, sure," Brody said, grinning wickedly. "But he's the baby. So, you know he has issues."

"Hey," Hunter said. "At least being the baby is *something*."

Brody snorted. "Unremarkable?"

"You're a dick," Lachlan said.

"Yeah. But you knew that."

"How about you?" Lach said to Brody. "Third oldest isn't a thing."

"But being the almost-baby is?" Brody shot back.

Their eyes drifted to Gus. "What?" Gus asked.

"As the oldest brother, since you're here for story time, did you want to spill some tea on your *baby* brother," Brody asked.

"What the fuck does that mean?" Gus asked.

"It's a thing the kids say," Lachlan said.

"You need to stop dating girls who don't know the theme song to *Fresh Prince of Bel-Air*," Gus said.

Lachlan laughed. "Oh, Gus. I don't date."

"I don't know. Hunter was the same kind of trouble as all of you. You were…all kind of little assholes, now that you mention it."

"You'll be a wonderful father, Gus," Brody said, his tone dry.

"I'm just being honest," Gus said.

"Do you have any specific stories about Hunter?" Elsie asked.

"Why?" Gus said.

"Because," Elsie said, "Hunter has always seemed wizened and older to me. But of course he doesn't to you."

"She's looking for stories for the wedding. Which irritates the hell out of me," Hunter said.

"Yeah. But you can't do anything about it," she said, smiling sweetly.

"Maybe not," Hunter said.

"No. But I do remember when you were a little brat," Brody said. "So I can malign you with firsthand knowledge."

"Don't worry, Elsie," Tag said, grinning. "I owe Hunter for the best man speech he gave at my wedding. So, don't you worry. We'll show up with the goods."

"I trust you," Elsie said.

"This is a spectacle," Gus said. "That's why you should just get hitched with a couple days' notice. That way nobody has time to give any speeches."

"Oh, are you going to tell us how it is now, Gus?" Brody asked.

"I always tell you how it is. Because I'm the oldest."

"Yeah. You try," Lachlan said.

"You ought to listen," Gus said. "Because I'm smart."

"You know," Hunter said. "A good point has been made here. Angus didn't have a proper wedding. Where we could all plan to make speeches. So maybe we should tell his beautiful bride stories now."

The brothers laughed, and raised their bottles of beer. And Alaina leaned in. "Oh, please do," she said.

"Well, there was the time our cat had kittens up in the hayloft. And had them all wedged in a place where no one could get to them. And he was concerned that the little mites were going to have problems."

It was a funny choice of word. *Mites*. She knew that

Gus had probably called them that, which confirmed for her that he thought of her as a little angry kitten.

It made her stomach dip.

"Anyway, he went on a cat-rescuing mission," Brody said. "And you have never seen a person scratched all that much to hell, trying to get those little critters out of that tight spot they were wedged in."

"Yeah, that was probably his first set of scars," Lachlan said.

"Well, what was I supposed to do?" Gus asked. "It was hot up there. Way too hot for them."

"Gus is a softy," Tag said.

Gus glared.

Alaina thought of when he had plucked her out of the pond, and really, just thought of the two of them. Everything she'd seen of him.

"That's Gus," Lachlan said, his face suddenly flat. "Saving anything and everything."

She shifted, feeling somewhat uncomfortable. Because she knew that was true. He had saved her. And it was Lachlan that he'd saved from their father, and she looked at Lachlan closely, wondering if he would mention that. Wondering if he would bring that up.

He looked at Gus, but he didn't say anything. And it made her wonder how much of it was that they had an agreement not to talk about those things.

"Gus used to read us stories," Hunter said. "And he always did all the voices."

She looked over at Gus, who was glaring down into his beer bottle.

"Yeah," Brody said. "We made a tent. Up in our

room. And we'd read really late. He'd put a flashlight on his face and make it really scary."

"I admire your restraint in not finishing that joke," Gus said, tipping his beer bottle up for a long drink.

"Oh, there was no real restraint involved," Brody said. "It was *before*."

Gus just stared straight ahead. "I know."

And she couldn't quite pin down the tension coming off of Gus just then. But it passed quickly, as he took control of the situation. "All right. So you remember when I rescued the kittens from the hayloft. But do you remember the time that I rescued Tag from the roof?"

And then he went on to tell the whole story of Tag getting stuck up on the roof when he was eight or so, with the ladder kicked down to the ground with no one realizing, leaving Tag stranded for hours. It ended with Gus finding him exhausted and crying, resituating the ladder and carrying Tag down like he was a sack of potatoes.

By the end of the story, everyone was laughing. Even Gus.

Right then the music kicked up, and Hunter stood, extending his hand to Elsie. "Come on. Let's dance."

"All right," Elsie said, taking his hand and bounding up behind him. Tag and Nelly got up along with them, and Lachlan did too, but Charity didn't follow. He went and grabbed a pretty redhead who was standing in the corner, and Brody followed suit, picking up a brunette.

That left Alaina, Gus and Charity sitting in proximity to each other.

Charity forced a smile, then looked away. Alaina

didn't really know Charity. She was Lachlan's best friend and she didn't socialize with everyone else on the ranch much. She hadn't gone to school with them; she'd been homeschooled as far as Alaina knew.

Alaina could never quite figure her and Lachlan out. Charity was wearing a floral dress with a turtleneck underneath, her blond hair held back with a big headband. She looked almost comedically demure. And Lachlan was in no way demure.

"So," Alaina said. "You're…a veterinarian?"

Charity blinked her wide pale blue eyes. "Yes. Didn't we just do that checkup together?"

"Well, yes," Alaina said. "But this is awkward. And I'm making clumsy conversation."

Charity laughed at that. "Right. And you…"

"Help with the horses. That's all really."

"You do a damn fine job at it," Gus said, and Alaina practically flushed with her pleasure at being praised.

"Yeah, I'm having a lot of fun helping out. It's really great. The whole gardening thing at Sullivans' wasn't really my thing."

Feeling bad for Charity, she scanned the room. Maybe there was a guy that would ask her to dance.

Of course, Alaina's own husband hadn't asked her to dance. But she felt like it was pretty poor form of Lachlan to bring his friend out and then leave her sitting there without a partner.

Then a man came over to the table, a cowboy probably somewhere around Alaina's age. A rancher from a surrounding area or one of the ranch hands from somewhere else, she assumed. He approached her, a smile on his face. "Care to dance, miss?"

And she looked over at Gus, who looked instantly furious.

"Sorry," Alaina said. "I'm here with my husband."

He jumped back. "Sorry. I couldn't tell…who was with who."

Because of course Charity was on the other side of Gus with the same amount of distance between him and her that was between the two of them. He didn't touch her casually the way that his brothers did with their wives. So how would this guy know?

"In that case," the guy said, "do *you* want to?"

Charity's expression went incredibly bland. And she could tell that the other woman was waffling between her desire to not sit there and be in this awkward situation, and her offense over being the man's second choice.

"Why not," she said, standing. Alaina couldn't help but notice her white socks.

Alaina kept her eyes on them, watching as Charity struggled to get into a rhythm with the guy.

"Oh no," Alaina said.

Then she looked over at Gus, who was still scowling.

"So what the hell is up with that?" he asked.

"What?"

"Men are all over you all the time. Even though you're pregnant. And married to me."

She narrowed her eyes, genuinely irritated with him. "I'm hot, Gus," she bit out. "I don't know what to tell you."

"I'm not saying you aren't pretty. Obviously, you're

pretty. It's just...you seem to attract a lot of attention for someone sitting right next to her husband."

"You aren't dancing with me. And you aren't even sitting closer to me than you were to Charity. Sure, we have rings on, but we don't look like we're together."

He looked slightly stricken by that. "Really?"

"Yes. Really. Gus, this is a meat market. People come here to get meat. Whatever the hell that all means. But it's a metaphor for sex. At home what we have is passionate. But you certainly don't show it out here. Look at the way that Elsie and Hunter are. And Tag and Nelly. They act like a couple. It radiates off of them. We're just...two people who happen to be married who also sleep together. It's different. And it looks different." She sighed. "We look more like Lachlan and Charity."

She tried not to sound hurt by it. She tried not to *be* hurt about it. Because it wasn't personal. She knew it.

It was just how Gus was. Soft, yes, but underneath a wall of granite. Showing it wasn't easy for him.

She had been really excited that he wanted to take her out. But he was just still Gus. Even here. And they hadn't...they hadn't crossed whatever bridge that was. That changed things from bed partners who happened to live together to...to a couple.

It was being here and seeing this that made her realize how they were different from the others, and that she didn't want to be.

She wanted more. She wanted to know more about the Gus that rescued kittens, and read to his brothers and rescued her. She wanted to get down to that man that clearly had a softness inside of him. That obviously felt things very deeply. But she didn't know how, and he certainly wasn't giving her a map.

"Fuck it," he said. "Dance with me."

Alaina was staring at him like he'd just sworn in a church. "What?"

"As declarations go, that is not the most romantic one."

"I'm not trying to be romantic. I'm trying to give you what you want."

"What do *you* want, Gus?"

"For men to stop thinking you're available. So if it takes dancing and whatever else, then I'll do it."

"You don't want to dance with me."

"I feel *silly.*"

"We danced at the bonfire."

"Yeah. We did. But that wasn't the bar."

"Why does it make a difference?"

"Because. I'm... Look at Four Corners—it's one thing. But look at me. *Look at me.* It is actually absurd that you're with me. You are so beautiful. And young, and you're not an asshole. And I am..."

"I'm here with you. Shouldn't that be enough?"

He looked at her and he knew he had to decide. To let go of the baggage holding him down to the chair, and to let her be enough.

"All right," he said. "Let's dance."

And he felt ridiculous, having said all of that, but it was true. It was true. She was beautiful, and she was bright like the sun. And he was just Gus. And everyone here knew it.

But she was his. And everyone ought to know that too. That was what it came down to.

So he took her hand and led her out to the dance floor. And of course as soon as they got there, the music went slow. But she leaned on his chest like there was nowhere else she would rather be, and he wrapped his arm around her, his chin resting on the top of her head.

"Thank you," she said.

"For what?"

"Understanding that I needed this."

And he didn't know if he actually understood. It was just that it had felt like the right thing to do, and he was jealous, and he was kind of a mess. So he'd done it because he didn't want any more men rolling up on her. So he'd done it because it was better than sitting there and watching someone else have her.

He didn't know if it was because he understood.

But right then, part of him wanted to.

And he realized he was going to have to change more of himself than he had anticipated. Because the thing was… Hunter had a point.

He had married a young girl with a lot of expectations about what her life was going to be, and the fact that he was an eighty-year-old man in his soul didn't mean that she was. He let her out of his sight for five seconds and she had men all over her. It wasn't about trusting her; it was just about…wanting the world to know that she was his.

He adjusted his head, looked down at her and tilted her chin up. "You're beautiful. But more than that. You're mine."

She fluttered her eyes, looking up at him through her lashes. "Am I?"

"Yes. Mine."

"Well, then you're mine. I hope you know that. I hope you know I've felt that way for a while."

"Good."

And suddenly he wondered if he needed to take her on a honeymoon. If he needed to do things a little more traditional. Because the fact was…she wasn't wrong. He had spent all this time acting like they were one thing during the day and another at night. They slept together, but he had married her and didn't really treat her like a wife.

Did he need to buy her flowers? Take her away to fancy dinners? He knew how to take her to thrift stores and buy her frying pans. He wasn't sure that was romance. He didn't really know how to do romance.

He'd taken her on that picnic because he felt compelled to, but he didn't know if that was romance either.

"What's up, Gus?"

"Just trying to figure out what the hell to do with you."

Because suddenly all the taking care felt inadequate. And what he wanted felt like lots of different things he couldn't quite figure out how to join up.

"You have me," she said.

Yeah. He did. For now. And he didn't really have much deeper trust in the universe than that.

It had never given him a reason to.

And looking at her…

Hell, she was either the reason, or she was a bait and switch.

And he didn't know how to figure out which.

CHAPTER SEVENTEEN

THE NEXT DAY, Gus had promised to take her out on a ride with some of the horses they were preparing for therapy.

The air was starting to get a little bit cooler, but Alaina didn't mind it. It gave her an excuse to swaddle herself in warmer sweaters. It was one thing to wear a little dress for the unseasonably warm fall days, and to wear one out, but they certainly wouldn't be cutting it today, which had plunged them into a different season altogether.

So she was dressed for the weather, and feeling cute, with her hair in a braid and a wide-brimmed hat on her head.

She hoped that Gus thought she looked cute. He had been up and out before her today. And she couldn't help but think back to last night. To what had happened on their date. He had been extremely put out by the fact that men were flirting with her. And then weird about the dancing. And she didn't quite know why.

She also knew that he didn't want to tell her. Just like he probably wouldn't want to go into detail about reading stories to his brothers.

Oh well. They were married. And like she'd said last

night, the problem was that they were still acting like two separate people, rather than a couple.

There had to be some kind of melding. She'd become certain of that last night.

And it was more than just sex.

More than just friendship.

She was looking for something deeper. And she didn't even really have the words for it.

She walked down toward the barn, and started to jog, a little surprised when she felt an unexpected tension in her bladder.

She put her hand low on her stomach. Was that the baby? Added weight?

She hadn't expected that.

She grimaced, supposing she had to accept these changes. And that she would need maternity clothes.

The idea made her feel depressed.

She had *just* been so excited about clothes.

But the idea of getting pants with a big stretchy panel did not appeal.

When she got down to the barn, Gus was already standing outside, with two horses tacked up and ready to go.

"Ready?"

"Yes," she said, mounting the horse swiftly, easily, and immediately feeling a little more herself.

Maybe it was the crisp air, or the leaves beginning to turn. Maybe it was that her outfit went so well with all those things. Or maybe it was just being with him.

Either way, it was an instant mood boost.

"Not long now," she said.

"No. Mid-November. It's all coming together."

"It's amazing. Really. What you've put together here."

"It's not just me."

"Well, maybe it isn't just you. But, I have a feeling it has a lot to do with you. A lot to do with who you are."

"You give me a little bit too much credit, Alaina."

"Or maybe you don't give yourself enough. I heard what your brother said. About how you read to them. And rescuing kittens."

"You already knew I rescued cute kittens," he said. "Didn't you, mite?"

"If you mean me..."

"I do."

She pretended to scowl, but she didn't mean it. It pleased her. The way he'd confirmed the link between the two. It made her feel connected to him.

She urged her horse forward, loving the way the golden light flooded the trail. It made everything look rich. Deep. This shaded glow all around. And when she looked at Gus, he was all gold too. It was likely no one ever had called him an angel. Not with a craggy face like that, and a big burly build that made him look more mountain than man. But in that moment, he felt a bit like her angel. A guardian one, with a big sword of fire, but an angel nonetheless.

But when his lips curved, it all went wicked, and that place between her legs started to ache.

Good grief. Never had anyone put her through so many emotions in such a small space of time with so few words. With just the tip of his mouth. But Gus McCloud had a hold on her like no one else ever had.

"I'm not a kitten," she said.

"But I bet you'd like it if I scratched you behind the ears."

An arrow of arousal shot straight through the center of her thighs. "Not fair," she said.

"What's not fair?" he asked, his expression comedically innocent—he was nothing of the kind.

"You're being dirty."

"Yeah. But you like that. I figured that one out. The rest... A little bit less so."

"I think you have me pretty figured out," she said. "You took me out last night."

"And I made the wrong decision with the dancing."

"I would have sat with you at that table and I would've been happy. Just to be with you. I was glad that we danced. But we didn't have to."

"That's awfully forgiving of you."

"You know, it's funny, Gus, I didn't really spend a lot of time fantasizing about getting married. I'm finding out what I want a little more every day."

And what she didn't say was that she was also learning she didn't want just a husband. She wanted him. *He* was the thing. He was what she wanted, not a generic husband. Not a generic marriage.

But him.

And that meant it was easy—or at least easier—to deal with things when they weren't some kind of romantic ideal.

And she might ache a little bit to experience the casual touching and other things that she saw Elsie getting to have.

But Elsie didn't have Gus. So at the end of the day, Alaina couldn't be jealous of her.

Gus was the important part. The nonnegotiable. Whether he realized that or not.

"Well, I'm working on it. I definitely never thought I'd be anyone's husband."

Something in his face went hard.

"What?"

"I never thought I'd be anyone's husband, because I never hated anyone more than my dad. I never thought I'd be anyone's dad for that same reason."

"And now?"

"My job is to figure out how to be anything but him."

"You're not him. You know that."

He looked at her, but she couldn't dissect the expression, and he didn't say anything to help her translate it.

"Cat rescuer. Read to your brothers…"

And his face got really shuttered then. "I'm glad that they remember that in a happy way. But… I'm just glad they have good memories."

She wondered if Gus had any. What was good for him growing up. What had made him happy.

"What are your good memories?" she asked.

"It doesn't matter."

The picnic. That place.

His good memories were his mother. But he didn't like to talk about it. He skirted around the edges of it. Talking about how he didn't cook. Taking her to that place.

But he never went there. Not really. And this was part

of her changing. Part of her growing. Pushing into the hard things. Because it was also part of them being...more.

"What was she like, Gus? Your mom."

"Beaten down. Beaten down so hard she had to go. That's it."

"That's all?"

"All that matters. Because in the end she left. She let Hunter blame himself. Hunter... Hunter really thought that it was him that sent her away. Because that little boy thought he had to tell his mama that she could go so that she'd be safe. And he carried that all those years. Hunter deserved better than that. But at the same time... I don't think the blame lies at her doorstep. It's *his*. I told you. I hate my father. Because he robbed us of everything that was any good in this world, including our mother."

"She never read to you...? She never...?"

"Look. It's just... It's a closed subject. That's all."

"Why?"

"Because some shit should stay in the past. I mean, what about you?"

"What about me?"

"Do you have good memories with your parents?"

"Yeah. I do," Alaina said. "And that's what makes them disappointing me suck so much. That's what makes not having them around so difficult. I did have good memories with them. I thought... I thought my dad and I had the special relationship. But then he went away. He went away and he...he doesn't see me anymore. He hasn't since I was twelve years old. And you know for a while you can let that shit go. You can excuse it. And you try. Because you love them still. That's the messy part, isn't it? That you still love them."

"I don't."

"Your mother or your father?"

"Both."

It was a final word. One that didn't invite any other questions, any other comments. One that spoke definitively about his feelings.

"Well. That must be hard too."

He shrugged. "There's nothing hard about it. It just is."

"Well. If you say so."

"I'm not making up stories. She left us. Left us with nothing. Maybe she had to, but I don't *owe* her anything. And as for him… I hate him."

"What are you doing with it?" she asked.

She felt like she was holding her breath. Trying to find the right words. The right method of pushing. She didn't want to push him away; she wanted to push him to her. She just wasn't sure she had the right balance.

"What do you mean?"

"What are you doing with all that hate. Does it serve you? Does it give you anything? Does it bring you any kind of joy?"

"Hell no. It doesn't do a damn thing for me. Except remind me. Remind me of what he was. And sometimes…sometimes I like to hang on to that. But you know, it's a little redundant. Because I can just look at my face and see. No. The problem is… He succeeded in what he did to me. He killed something in me all right."

"Gus…"

"No. It's true. Do you know how long I spent in bandages? Recovering. Dealing with infections. It is an ugly thing to try and get well from. It messes with your head, and you have way too much time to think. And way more pain than could ever be felt all at once. So you just feel it all the time. For years to come. Because what else is there? What else is there but the pain, and the particular kind of isolation it gave you."

His words were so honest, so full of pain. They transferred the pain to her. She could see it, that what his father had done to him had created a legacy of pain he'd carried with him every day since.

"I'm so sorry, Gus."

"I know. The sorry doesn't change it. Any more than my anger changes it. That's just the thing. None of it changes a damn thing."

"You read stories to your brothers. And you were there for them. You protected Lachlan from your father's fists. Maybe it doesn't mean anything to you. Maybe it feels futile to you, but I bet you changed an awful lot for them."

"That's the only hope I have," he said. "If I have any at all."

"And what about for us? Do you have any particular hope for the two of us?"

"I just like to do more good than I do bad," he said.

The sun was golden and the air was perfect, but that list of joy that she'd felt earlier was muted now. Because he was so…

Scarred.

And it wasn't the scars on his face that truly concerned her.

It was the ones on his soul. And it was the one place he seemed bound and determined to not let her reach.

So she brought her horse up beside his, and put her hands on his face. Because those scars, those physical ones, he let her touch those. And so she would. So she would.

"You don't have to do anything. Just be you. That guy that rescues kittens. And everything will be just fine."

She said it for herself as much as for him. And she tried—she really did try—to believe it.

And even as she did, the feelings in her heart seemed to swell to the point of bursting.

She cared about this man so much. And she honestly didn't know if he cared about her...

Or if he still saw just a kitten that needed to be saved from drowning.

CHAPTER EIGHTEEN

It was go-shopping-in-Copper Ridge day, and Alaina was thrilled to pieces, and had co-opted Elsie to come along on their caravan. Her sisters were in a separate car, and she and Elsie were in the truck, pulling the trailer.

"I hope we find good stuff," Alaina said.

"There is nothing worse than a thwarted shopping spree," Elsie said.

"You don't shop, Elsie," Alaina said.

"Well, maybe not so much. But sometimes I need a new horse blanket, and nothing makes me madder than when I can't find a horse blanket when I've already decided I'm going to spend up big on one."

"I didn't know you had terribly specific horse blanket needs."

"Sometimes one does," Elsie said sagely.

And Alaina knew better than to argue with that.

The drive was a nice one, and they kept the conversation light, and Alaina was somewhat relieved. Every time she was with Elsie and things felt normal, she felt relieved. And she was glad that even though she'd been hurt momentarily over the thing with Hunter, she had not let it blow up their friendship. Because here she was, standing on the other side of it and knowing that being with Hunter would've been wrong. Very wrong. And…

"Okay," Alaina said. "This might be awkward. But I just wanted to say that I'm really glad that you ended up with Hunter and not me. I mean, I wouldn't have ended up with Hunter. But if I'd been with him… Look, your relationship with him aside, and obviously how that would've made your life not awesome… I am certain me being with his brother is something Gus wouldn't have been able to get over."

She could feel Elsie looking at her speculatively. "Sorry, I'm not following."

"Well, I did a rash and dumbass thing, because I was sitting in my life feeling uncomfortable, and trying to do something to shake it up. And I homed in on Hunter for that. And I am just really glad that it didn't work out. I'm glad that nothing happened. I'm glad that nothing came of it. I think it was always supposed to be Gus. I'm not sure if I'd be with him if the whole disaster with Travis hadn't pushed us. As much as it felt like a mistake, I think I needed everything to happen exactly like it did."

"Oh. So, you *really* have feelings for Gus."

"Yes. I'm not sure if I'm rewriting history or…or what. But he's special. And he always has been. And I keep thinking back on all those moments. All the sweet things he did for me, and how I was blind to it. I want to believe that I always felt something for him. That I wasn't so shallow that I didn't see him just because he was scarred." Tears gathered at the corners of her eyes.

"I think he's beautiful, Elsie. And he's not second best, and he's not just the guy that swooped in to rescue me. I…" The word that she felt expanded in her chest and bubbled up, but she didn't want to say it. Not now. She didn't even really want to think it; she just wanted to let it be there. Building on itself. While she got accustomed to the feeling, and what she was going to do about it.

"It's okay if you didn't," Elsie said. "It doesn't make you a bad person, just because you didn't realize."

"I just feel like I was really stupid. And I didn't actually know what I wanted. Or know what was important. Or know myself at all. I didn't understand what attraction was. Because what he and I have… It's not like anything else. Kissing him isn't like kissing anyone else. Or even… Wanting to kiss him isn't even like kissing someone else. It's that I can't stay away from him. I don't want to. And I want to feel closer to him, and nothing ever feels like enough. I want everything. And I… You know, I've been feeling really good, and really confident, and suddenly I'm realizing how stupid I was, and it hurts. And I don't mean… It's not about making a mistake with Travis. I'm not being down on myself about that. It's about not understanding what I wanted. And it's making me question everything. Everything about myself. Because I was so certain, Elsie, I always have been. Because any moment of uncertainty has been so uncomfortable I couldn't handle it. So I always made a decision. I always tried to figure it out. What if I've been figuring things out in the wrong direction all this time?"

This was why she avoided these things. Caring and

sharing and pushing. Because when she stayed in her own little bubble, she could pretend her certainty could power through it all. But not now, not with this.

She worried.

That no matter how much she cared it could all go away.

"Everything you do isn't wrong," Elsie said. "It's also just part of finding out who you are. Alaina, I wasn't any smarter about this kind of thing than you were. I didn't know I wanted Hunter. I spent most of my life teasing and tormenting him trying to get a little shred of his attention and thinking that it was because he annoyed me. Realizing that I was attracted to him just about did me in. I thought I knew everything there was to know about everything. Especially myself. I wanted Travis because he felt easy and manageable. But I didn't *think* that was why. I thought I knew what I wanted. Because I had never…been with anybody. How are you supposed to know what you want when you've never done it?"

Alaina laughed. "I guess that's true. I thought… I thought sex just wasn't really all that great."

"It's supposed to be," Elsie said.

"I know that now." She sighed. "He's really difficult. I mean, he's not. I love being around him. Even when he's a hardheaded mess. It's just that there's so much that I don't know about him. I can't get it. I don't know if he'll ever let me."

"Falling in love is really hard, Alaina. Because you bring all of that stuff that you don't know and it butts up against all of the things that he doesn't know. And then there's the things you're both afraid of. I almost messed everything up with Hunter because I was so scared."

Elsie had gone and said it, even if Alaina couldn't bring herself to say the word. Couldn't bring herself to talk about love.

Love.

What was love, anyway?

What was it except this brilliant unfolding of all that they could be over time? Years of him proving that her comfort and care mattered. Protection. Being there. Commitment. Kissing. Touching. Talking.

The idea scared her to death.

But she didn't know what else it could be.

"Whatever I thought I wanted," Alaina said. "I just want this now. I'm so excited about everything going on at McCloud's Landing. And very probably my sisters think I'm a Benedict Arnold, considering how the funding is clashing with the farm store. But…this is the kind of work I want to do. And I love having the ranch to go to every day. And the horses to work with every day. And then I leave and I go back to the house, and I make dinner for him. And he comes home…"

"You are much more domestic than I am," Elsie said. "Hunter has to fend for himself. Or we scrounge around together, or eat at Sawyer's."

"Well, I like having someone to cook for. Take care of. I guess I'm a little bit more traditional than I thought. It makes me feel settled. I've never felt settled. I've always felt like I was about to go off half-cocked and cause an explosion. I guess I almost did. But Gus was there to…to protect me. From myself, if nothing else.

But I don't know if I can protect them from him. Does that make sense?"

"Knowing Gus, yes. Because he's a great guy. He really is. But… I do see what you mean. About all of it. About how he's hard to know."

"Impossible."

"Well, he's letting you do whatever you want to with the house?"

"And I will take that freedom."

They pulled into the tiny town of Copper Ridge just then, a picturesque town with white-and-cranberry-colored buildings, some redbrick, and Victorian charm, backed by the gray Pacific Ocean. It was windy already, and there was a salty bite in the air. She was grateful that she had brought a pretty heavy sweater, because while it was a decently warm October during the day just a couple hours inland, it was twenty degrees colder here by the water.

"On to the first antique store," Quinn said, getting out of the little car that the Sullivan sisters had all driven over and spreading her arms wide.

They made their way to the first store—the Wagon Wheel—and picked through a series of antiques.

"What is this?" Rory picked up a figure of a rotund man with powder blue pants and a matching jacket who was tipping a cowboy hat and winking.

"That is so strange," Quinn said frowning.

"He looks like his name should be Big Hoss," Fia said.

"That's it. Big Hoss!"

"But what *is it*?" Alaina asked.

Just then, the cowboy hat tipped right off his head, and Quinn laughed. "Oh. He is a...decanter of some sort. If you want to put your wine in a cowboy."

"Oh, I am so angry that I have to buy that," Alaina said. "Because it goes with Gus's dumb sugar shaker."

"This is amazing," Rory said. "Please tell me that Big Hoss will be the official decanter of all alcohol at further town hall meetings."

"I swear it," Alaina said.

But at the mention of the town hall Fia started to look a little bit aggro.

"Are you still mad about that?" Elsie asked.

"Of course I am," Fia said. "Preference being given to the McClouds' overpriced project—no offense, Alaina—is really obnoxious. But also, it isn't that they can't just reorganize the budget. Trim things next year. And it isn't Landry King's business."

"I think actually the budget is technically Landry's business," Quinn said pragmatically.

"I don't need sense from you," she said to her sister. "I need blind fury."

"Sorry. Now that your needs are made clear I will aim for that."

"Gus is willing to rework some things," Alaina said. "But...if you came and saw what they were doing, if you knew..."

"I get the feeling you don't care about the farm store," Fia said.

"It's not that I don't care about the farm store, Fia. It's just that it was never something I wanted to do. I wanted to work with horses, and I never had a vote on that. You decided—and I understand why—but you decided that we would lean into the fruit and vegetable production. To the baking. I get it, but it was never my passion. You systematically farmed out bits and pieces of Sullivan's Point, and… I never said anything. I never said anything because I didn't want to make waves. Because I didn't want to get unpleasant. And frankly, we've lost enough. But even before I married Gus, I was planning on leaving. Because I wanted something for myself. And that was never it."

"I didn't…" Fia looked flustered. "I thought everyone wanted to make those changes."

"You did. So much that no one would ever dare fight with you about it. And you know, you're the one that got in there and did all that extra planning with the Garretts and the Kings and the McClouds. You were the one that spearheaded the new Four Corners with them. It's only fair that you had a bigger vote. It's just that… it wasn't ever what I wanted."

Fia looked well and truly wounded, and Alaina felt terrible. And she wondered how they had gone from joking about Big Hoss to this. But she had to be honest.

"I really didn't know you felt that way."

"That isn't to say that I don't think you should get funding. We have to work something out. It's just… Please don't be mad at Gus about it."

"You're a McCloud," Rory said, shaking her head.

"I'm a Sullivan too," Alaina responded. "I care very much about your goals. I really do. I love you all, and I really never meant to have it be weird. And Gus doesn't want that either."

"I'm sure he doesn't," Fia said. "He is… He's deeply smitten with you," she said.

And that made Alaina's heart jump. "You think so?"

Fia frowned at her, and then took Big Hoss out of Rory's hands. She waved the figure at her. "The way he looks at you is ridiculous."

"He looks at me a certain way?"

"With his tongue hanging out," Quinn said.

Alaina felt herself turning pink, but she was absolutely delighted to hear this.

"Come on. We can't just leave here with a novelty decanter," Rory said. "We have other things to find."

"But tell me more about how Gus looks at me."

Rory was waylaid by a stack of beautiful classic children's books with gold edging on the pages and lovely illustrations. But Elsie, Quinn and Fia all kept walking with her.

"I can just tell. I've known him a long time," Fia said. "I've never seen him look so happy. The way he was dancing with you… He's really happy."

"I hope so," Alaina said. "I really want to make him happy."

"He should make you happy too," Fia said, patting her hand. "Don't forget that."

"He does," Alaina said.

They stopped in front of a midcentury wooden TV cabinet, with big speakers made from a shimmery gold fabric.

"I want this," Alaina said.

"I support you," Quinn said.

Rory came up behind them holding the giant stack

of books. "I'm getting all of them. I will read them to your baby. I'm going to be the best aunt. Because I'm going to have the best books."

Alaina rolled her eyes. "I have the best books."

"You're not going to share those with your child," Rory said.

"Well, eventually," Alaina said. "They're good reading."

"The sex scenes in them are very unrealistic," Rory said, sniffing.

Quinn and Elsie exchanged a glance. "They aren't, Rory," Alaina said. "I'm here to tell you."

Rory blinked. "You can't tell me that Gus…"

"Oh yes," Alaina said. And she smiled smugly. While she was enjoying this. "Crashing waves. Thunderstorms. Whole wildfires. At least three times a night."

Fia looked aggrieved. "You are my younger sister, and I consider him kind of a friend, so I would rather we cease with the conversation."

"You should be happy for me," Alaina said, grinning.

"Super happy for you," Fia said. "Super happy."

"And not at all jealous?" Quinn asked Fia, smiling sweetly.

"If I felt like it, I could hook up with a cowboy," Fia said, turning around and tapping her finger on her younger sister's nose. "I just don't feel like it."

"Then don't sound so salty," Quinn said.

"I'm *not* salty," Fia said.

"You and Landry would…" And then Elsie shut her mouth very quickly because Fia rounded on her like an outraged cat.

"Take my name and his out of your mouth," Fia said. "I do not have a thing for Landry King. *I never did.* This has to stop."

"The *tennnnsion*, though," Alaina said.

Fia looked at Rory, as if demanding she pick her side.

"Sorry," Rory said. "I agree."

"I didn't ask," Fia said. "I didn't ask. Buy your dumb TV cabinet."

By the time they left the store they had the TV cabinet, the decanter, the books, several floral teacups, and a rocking chair that Alaina was intent on putting in the nursery.

They stopped in at a little seasonal decor store run by a woman named Rebecca, and Alaina bought quite a few polished knickknacks, because she was feeling the need in her bones. Then they went to a specialty food store and it didn't take her long to strike up a conversation with the owner of that store, and realize that she was Violet Garrett's aunt by marriage. The whole area was in fact small, and you were pretty likely to run into people you had connections to no matter where you went.

They were referred to the bakery that Violet used to work at, which was run by her stepmother, and when they walked in, there was a pretty woman with red hair behind the counter, and Alaina was certain that there were almost never this many redheads in one shop in town all at once.

Once Fia explained the Four Corners connection, Allison started plying them with free baked goods.

"So you've all known my son-in-law since he was in diapers," she said.

"Yes indeed," Fia said. She was fairly close in age to Wolf Garrett. "He's a good guy."

"He is," Allison agreed. "Though, I'm a little bit jealous you get to see them more often than we do. But it's not a terribly long drive."

They chatted to her for a while as they ate glorious pieces of pie. Then continued on in their shopping hunt, on a tip from Allison, who told them to drive to a new space on the outskirts of town that had antiques, secondhand furniture that had been upcycled and little booths inside the building where people sold their handmade wares.

Once they were there, Alaina might have gone a little bit overboard. She found the perfect crib, another rocking chair, a new dining table, a new couch and coffee table...

"You know, Gus could be spending this money on not ruining my life instead of on this," Fia remarked.

"I am making my house a home," she said archly.

"Right. Right."

"And he does have money to spend—he's looking into that. Remember?"

Fia grumbled.

At that point, they had pretty much topped out the trailer, but they stopped at the local coffee shop in town for some lunch, and then took the drive back to Four Corners.

There, scrambling and huffing and puffing to unload everything was amusing. And once they got all of the nursery things up the stairs, she turned and looked at the doors, not quite sure what to do.

"Which room?"

She was a little bit embarrassed for them to know that she still had her things in a separate bedroom.

"You know, I'll figure that part out in a bit. Thanks for all your help. You guys can...go back to what you were doing."

"Thanks," Fia said. "Because I actually do have some things to do, since I'm in problem-solving mode."

"Sorry," Alaina said, irritated that she was at odds with her sister over something, but not feeling...not feeling as precarious as she might have in other situations.

Her sisters all left, but Elsie hung back.

"Why didn't you want them here?"

"Oh, it's...it's dumb."

"Why is it dumb?"

Elsie knew. That was the thing. She knew the Mc-Clouds, and all their pain. She was Alaina's best friend, but even deeper, she loved Hunter, and she knew his pain. So in that way she knew something about Gus.

"It's just that I didn't know which room to make the nursery. And... I'm thinking maybe it should be this room across from the master bedroom. But it's my room."

"Oh."

"I just didn't want them to know that Gus and I didn't share a room. I mean, we've been sharing a bed. But we didn't really talk about consolidating that. And sometimes I think he still wants his space."

"Well," she said. "He can get over it."

"I need to talk to him first."

"What about this room?"

It was a room she hadn't been in. But they walked down the hall, all the way to the back of the house and pushed open the door. The room was dim and stacked with boxes, and she looked around. She opened the first box, and saw that it had some comic books. Water damaged, but in okay condition. There was another box that had some toys. Little ones. Army men and planes.

"This one," Alaina whispered.

"Then let's get to work," Elsie said.

WHEN GUS WALKED in the door he didn't even recognize the place. It was full of shit. Shit he'd never seen. Ever. And he had no idea where it had come from.

Oh right. The shopping day. There was…a weird TV cabinet, sitting against the back wall, that had a bunch of fall decor placed on the top of it. And he couldn't deny that it looked cool; he just had no idea why there were now two TVs in the room. And one not even where anyone was sitting, like it was a damn decoration.

Decorations.

There were decorations.

It made him want to crawl out of his skin, and he didn't even quite know why.

"Gus," Alaina said, bounding down the stairs, her hair bouncing. And his heart leaped up into his throat as she basically flew across the room and threw herself into his arms, kissing him until he couldn't think about how many TVs were in the room. Until he couldn't think about anything.

"You've been busy," he said.

"Yes. And I forgot to cook dinner. But we still have a bunch of leftovers."

His stomach growled, but he ignored it. Because she was happy. And hell, he didn't contribute to the cooking, so he couldn't complain. He was going to have to learn how to do that.

He'd get around to it.

"I want to show you something," she said.

"I think I'm looking at it," he said, gesturing around the room.

"No," she said. "I did something. I'm really happy with it. I hope that you are too."

She led him up the stairs, and down the hall, and his heart started to feel heavy. Like it hurt when it hit up against the front of his chest. "Alaina…"

"I got the nursery started. I know we don't know yet if it's a boy or girl. But I found all your stuff."

She flung the door open, and a wave of nausea hit him.

What a fucking weird thing. To feel like he was dying just looking at this room. Just standing there.

"Alaina," he said, looking around at the space. At the little toys up on the shelves, and the tattered rug at the center of the floor, and he couldn't remember the place ever looking this organized before. The comic books. The comic books were there.

And instantly, he was back in a place he did not want to be. Huddled in a little tent he and his brothers had made in here, with the flashlight on, with him reading out loud to them while there was screaming going on downstairs. Crashing and violence.

Just trying to keep it so they didn't hear.

And then he saw the army men.

That unopened box.

He'd told himself he wouldn't open it till she came back.

"I didn't tell you that you could get this stuff out."

"I know," she said. "But you didn't say that I couldn't… Gus, it was all in here and… I didn't want to make the nursery my bedroom without talking to you, because we haven't talked about whether or not we're going to share a room, and I didn't want to get into your space. Because I knew that you might not like that. But there was this room, and I thought that…"

"You thought you would drag out stuff from my horrible childhood. And put our baby in the room that I spent months in while I recovered from just about getting burned alive." Just standing in here made him feel claustrophobic. "There's rooms I don't go into here. There's stuff I don't do. There is…"

"Gus…"

"You should have fucking asked," he said. "This isn't your playground. I gave you plenty of freedom, but I don't understand why you didn't talk to me about this."

He was losing it. Losing his temper—he could feel it rising up inside of him, and he…he hated himself right then. He really did.

"I'm sorry," she said, in a voice that was overly calm and soothing. Like he was a rabid animal and she was afraid of being savaged.

"It's not enough," he said. "I didn't say that you could do this."

And she just stood there, staring up at him. Then she reached out and patted him. She patted him on the shoulder like he was a puppy dog, and not like he was a man standing there about to lose it. "You don't need to come in here for now. I think it's a good place for a nursery. Unless you want to share rooms."

"You want to share a room with me?" he asked. *"Look at me."*

"You're having an emotional reaction to something that is emotional for you. I didn't realize that it would be. I'm sorry about that. But we have the space we have, so we're going to have to make some decisions. But we don't need to do it now. I was excited…"

"Well, I'm not excited."

She flinched, and he could tell that he'd hurt her, and he didn't know why he'd said that. Because it had been to hurt her, and that was a dick move.

"It's okay," she said. "It is. You can…you can say what you need to."

"I hate it," he said. And then he turned and walked out of the room.

And slammed the door. He slammed it, like an angry teenager.

He waited for her to yell. Waited for her to dissolve. To recoil. To tell him that he was horrible. Because he deserved it. Because she was getting too familiar, and he was getting too comfortable. And there it was. All up there. Little boxes of trauma that she'd unpacked like they were just toys. And they weren't just *fucking toys*, and they never could be. Just like that could never just be a childhood room.

It couldn't be a *nursery*.

For his kid.

Dammit all, what had he been thinking?

It could never be that simple. How could it be? How the fuck could it be? It would always be that place he'd been trapped in for months on end, with no mother to come check on him and his attempted murderer stalking around the house not taking care of him. His brothers having to see him as an invalid, while the whole story stuck in his throat, something that he could never share. It was always going to be this mess. All of it. Always. And he had…

He had let himself think that it wouldn't be. He had let himself think that it was going to be okay. He had let himself think that… The dancing at the bonfire was enough to erase all the shit he'd been through. But then, that was the story of his life. Because he could dance in front of a bonfire, he thought—on some level flames didn't bother him. But they were always there. The truth of it was always there. And what it had turned him into.

And she should recognize that. She should be afraid of him. She should let it push her away.

She walked past him, resolute, her chin in the air, and started pulling things out of the fridge.

"Why don't you ever get mad at me?" he asked.

"Oh, I'm mad at you. I'm just doing my best to recognize that it comes from a place of pain."

"Maybe you should fight with me," he said.

"I've fought with you, Gus, it's not actually that fun.

Last time I cried, and you left me there weeping. So…
forgive me for skipping it this time."

"Fight back," he shouted.

Because he was angry, but he'd never be the man be-
rating a woman while she just stood there and took it.

"This *is* me fighting back. Because you don't like
it," she sniffed, opening up the fridge and taking out a
beer bottle, and putting it in front of him.

"I don't want beer," he said.

"Oh, stop it," she said, grabbing the bottle opener and
popping the top up. "You want beer. You want someone to call you out because you're being an asshole, so
you're digging in. I'm sorry that hurts you. I wish that
you would share with me. Share with me why it's hard,
Gus, don't just get mad at me. Because I didn't make
your life hell. I didn't make this house hell. We don't
have to live here. You don't have to live here." She just
stopped and stared at him. "Why do you? Why did you
live here all this time, and never go in those rooms, and
save all that stuff that you never want to see, and only
eat frozen pizza and never learn how to feed yourself.
Why are you punishing yourself?"

The words hit him in strange and uncomfortable
places, and at the moment he just didn't like her very
much. Didn't like being with her. All the things that
had felt great an hour ago no longer did. And that passionate vibe of hers was just suddenly a pain in the ass,
and not inspiring in the least.

"Gus McCloud," she said. "You are so happy to let
everyone think you're a martyr, but it's not even that.

You're punishing yourself. And I don't get it. You've never been anything but good to me, to everyone…"

"I'm not good, Alaina. I'm not. I'm not good."

"Where is the evidence of that?"

"I'm a monster," he said. "I'm not any different than my father, I'm not…"

"Why? Because of genetics? Is our kid screwed because Travis sucks? Is he going to be like Travis, in spite of what *you* teach him?"

"So convinced we're going to have a son?"

"Well, what if? Is he doomed because of blood?"

"No. No, the kid is not doomed because of blood. Not any more than my brothers are doomed because they're related to my dad. I'm not that much of a superstitious idiot. But I know myself. I know myself and… You don't know."

"Then tell me. I have been trying to beat down all those walls that you keep up around yourself for all this time, and you don't want to let me in. You'll sleep with me, but you won't tell me. What is it? What is the thing that makes you pull away?"

"I didn't kill my dad, Alaina. But I wanted to."

"I understand that, Gus. I know that things…"

"You don't know. You don't know. I beat him up."

"Yes. But that's understandable. You had to get rid of him and…"

"I made him beg for his life. And I enjoyed it. All that same fear he used to have spilling out of us, I relished getting out of him. I told him that if he didn't beg me that I'd kill him."

She stopped. Frozen. And she did look a little horrified. And for just one moment, that was almost satisfying. That he had successfully managed to surprise her about who he was.

"I don't think I'm violent because I'm his son. I think I'm violent because I've been violent. And it isn't just the act of it, it's the enjoyment of it. Because until you've felt what it's like to let anger be the only thing in you, to let it be the only thing that drives you, to let it be everything you are, to let it blot out everything… While you relish causing someone else's pain… You don't know how terrifying you really are. I know not everyone has the capacity for that inside of them. But I do. I have to be careful. I have to be really careful."

"You've never hurt someone innocent," Alaina said.

"No," he said. "I don't get close to people."

"Gus, I just don't think that…"

"I didn't ask what you thought. That's the thing. I did not ask what you thought. I'm just telling you why. I hate my dad. More than I hate anyone or anything in this whole world. I hate him. My biggest regret about my interaction with him is that I didn't kill him. That I let him walk away. That I let him live. And that's also the thing in me that comes from him, and I have to live with that. So I don't let people close. You still want to have dinner with me? Knowing what I am?"

And with the most stubborn look on her face he'd ever seen, she opened up a Tupperware container and wordlessly scooped a big heaping pile of spaghetti onto a plate, then went to the microwave and started heating it up. Then she sat down beside him, closer than was strictly necessary, her arm touching his. "Might as well serve yourself," she said.

He growled, got some pot roast and put it on a plate, then heated it up, and distanced his chair slightly from hers.

They ate in silence, and then he went upstairs to take a shower.

And then suddenly she opened the door. Naked. And got inside with him.

"What the hell are you doing?"

"You're my husband," she said. "Did you think you telling me something about yourself was going to... make me run away?"

He did. He had. She was supposed to be afraid of him. Other people were. And they didn't even know the whole story. Didn't even know the whole truth of what a hot mess he was. His siblings didn't know. Hell. He never wanted them to know. Just how much of their dad he was. Because they'd never be able to look at him the same way again. Or maybe...maybe they would. Maybe they'd be like her, and pretend they understood because his dad was awful. But they didn't know what it felt like. To understand him. To understand that feeling that blotted out rational thought, that blotted out humanity, and put you in a position where you thought you could go that far.

They didn't know what it was like to know that lived inside of you. He did. He knew what it was like. He didn't want anyone understanding it. He sure as hell didn't. And he didn't want her in here now, not when he needed distance. Not when he needed to get a grip.

"I'm not running," she said. "Unless it's to you."

She pressed her breasts up against his chest and he groaned. He didn't have defenses against her. None. She shot them down, every time he put one up. Like it was nothing.

And it made him feel like maybe it wasn't her that needed protecting.

"For someone who hates all that anger inside of him, you sure get angry a lot." She stroked his face, looking up at him.

He grunted. "Well, that's kind of the issue. It just happens."

"Or maybe you actually do like it. Maybe it does something for you."

"That should worry you."

"I'm sorry," she said, not sounding sorry at all. "I'm not afraid of you."

He growled, backed her up against the tiled wall.

"Is this when I get to see the beast?" she asked.

He grabbed hold of her thigh and lifted her leg up off the ground, hitching it up over his hip. "Maybe."

"Good. I don't want there to be any girls out there who have gotten something from you that I haven't. All those girls, all those girls you took to bed, and you thought of me. You better give me as good as you gave them."

He was so hard it was physically painful, and he should pull away from her. He should walk away from this. Because he was on some kind of edge, and it was too foreign for him to even know what edge it was. But she was looking at him like that, the vixen, and she was wet and slick, all over, and he wanted her. Wanted to do exactly what she was asking for.

He was never with women who knew him. He didn't expose himself. He kept things compartmentalized. But this was Alaina, who he had known her entire life. They were married. They were going to have this baby together. And there would be no walking away the next day.

The consequences for opening himself up and pouring everything into her was...

But he couldn't say no. He couldn't turn her away. And yeah, it had been a shitty thing. To think of her while he was with other women. To use them to satisfy a fantasy that he didn't think he would ever get to fulfill. He had her now. He had her. And that felt dangerous. But it was also irresistible.

And he was weak. He had spent so much time trying to rebuild himself after all the bullshit. And here he was, recognizing a fundamental crack in his foundation. One shaped like her. So deep that it could break all of him. He reached behind, grabbing hold of her wet hair and wrapping it around his fist, tugging, pulling her hair back and exposing her throat. Then he leaned in and kissed her right there, and scraped his teeth along her sensitive skin.

"Gus," she said. Like she always did.

His name. His name on her lips, and not anyone else's. She wasn't thinking of anyone else. She was thinking of him. He took his free hand, pressed his thumb against her lower lip and parted her mouth for him. "Look at me," he commanded. And she opened her eyes. "Say my name again."

"Gus," she said.

"Good."

And this was everything. This moment. Where she gave him exactly what he demanded, exactly what he needed. Where he got to be in control.

Perfection, everything he needed lining up together. Her, and all that need to be in charge.

Because he had spent a hell of a lot of years with no control over his life, and it gave him a thrill to have it in the bedroom.

And there was nothing he wanted more than her.

And suddenly, what he needed… He needed…

"On your knees," he said.

And she obeyed, while he relaxed his hold on her hair, letting her go, down to the floor slowly. "You know what I want," he said.

She nodded, looking up at him with those beautiful eyes. Alaina's eyes.

"I've never done this before," she whispered.

Because it had been about her, every time till now.

And he had to brace himself against the wall, because that damn near knocked him off his feet. She wrapped her delicate hand around his hardened length, then leaned in and tasted him. And damn but it was perfect, and so was she. And as she continued to explore him, growing bolder with each stroke of her tongue over him, everything in his mind went blank. There was nothing, nothing but his need for her. His need for this.

When she took him in deep, his growl was almost enough to rattle the walls.

He rocked his hips forward in time with her movements. Then he grabbed her hair again, and lifted her up to her feet. "Not like that. I'm not done with you yet."

He shut the shower off and picked her up, carrying her, soaking wet out of the shower and into the bedroom. He moved his hands all over her curves, slick and perfect, then he turned her in his arms, setting her down on the bed on her hands and knees. He positioned himself behind her, testing the entrance to her body with the head of his arousal.

"You ready?"

"Yes," she moaned, curling her fingers into the blanket. He pushed himself into her, and she arched against him, and he grabbed her hips as he slammed home. And he lost himself. Completely. But he never lost her. The indent of her waist, the flare of her hip, that curly red hair. The sounds that she made, the arch in her spine. It was Alaina, and there was no losing that.

The way she said his name. Over and over again, and it was the only thing that kept him from forgetting who he was altogether. And for a moment he wished he could. For a moment he wished she wouldn't speak his name at all. So that she could be her, and he could be anyone else. The kind of man who hadn't experienced everything he had. The kind of man who hadn't been broken once a long time ago.

The kind of man who hadn't spent the last twenty years duct-taping himself back together and doing a pretty shitty job of it.

But he was here. And he had her. So he supposed the rest didn't matter all that much. Or at least right now it couldn't. Because all he wanted was her. All he wanted was her.

He held her hips tight, pumped into her until he couldn't think at all.

Until it was nothing but feeling, fire and need, and he knew what fire felt like. He really did. And he didn't use it lightly here. Because she was scorching him, from the inside out, and he knew that he would never be the same. Because you never were. Not when you'd been burned alive.

And Alaina Sullivan had the power to do just that.

McCloud.

Alaina McCloud.

And it was that reminder. That reminder that she was his, that was what sent him over the edge. On a growl, he spilled himself inside of her, and thank God he felt her go over the edge with him, her internal muscles pulsing around his hardened length. And she was perfect. It was perfect. Everything, in that moment.

He brought her up against him, held her to his body, let her feel the way that his heart beat rage, how hard he had to breathe to catch up, all because of her.

"I knew it was you the whole time," he said.

And she made a little whimpering sound, wiggling against him.

And it hurt so much, and he didn't know why. Why something this good cut so deep. And suddenly he was just tired. Because it was the fight they'd had earlier, or tried to have. And the one they'd had the other day after the ultrasound. And the ultrasound itself. Hell, the wedding. The engagement. Finding her on her hands and knees throwing up at the town hall. Picking her up from the bar that night, knowing that something had happened. The first time he'd ever been attracted to her. And all the years before. Exhausting as hell.

And he wanted to relax, wanted to sleep. Wanted to just hold on to her and breathe for a minute, but he didn't know how to do that.

Because sometimes everything seemed fine, and the night was still, and there wasn't a fight, and the next morning someone was just gone, and they never came back.

And when you thought things couldn't get worse, you were usually wrong. That's what he had learned.

That's what he had learned well.

So no matter how good it felt, no matter how tired he was, he knew he couldn't drop that wall. He knew he couldn't relax.

"I've got some work yet to do," he said, knowing his voice sounded rough.

"It's dark out," she said.

"I know. I know. But… I gotta find a way to make it so we can pay for our portion of this. I don't want your sisters to not get what they need."

"Look, Fia might just have to wait. She might. That isn't your fault. That's just the reality of the situation."

"I bet that she won't see it that way."

"Well, that's too bad. She and I have a difference of opinion on this. In that I think the work you're doing on the ranch needs to take priority. I stand with you on this."

"Thank you."

"So. Whatever work you're doing… I'm going to go with you."

His chest went tight, and he looked at her, all bright eyes staring up at him. "Alaina…"

"What?" A smile tugged at the corner of her lips. "Do you have to admit now that you were trying to avoid me?"

"I…" He shook his head.

"You do that. We get closer and you pull away. And you got mad, and you tried to push me away. Gus… I'm really sorry that I messed up. With the room. I didn't know that there was stuff. I didn't know that…"

"Come on," he said. "Get dressed. Come with me. We'll get out the ranch financials and have a look. This is your place too."

And she looked so delighted by that, it made something in his chest hard. And then she got out of bed and put his T-shirt on, which barely came to the top of her thighs, and when she turned around he could still see the little crease right where her thighs met her ass. And if this was getting dressed to her, then he wholeheartedly approved. He put his jeans on, and didn't bother with a shirt, and he could feel her staring at him, and he'd be lying if he said he didn't like that too.

They went down to the new kitchen table, one of the many new things she had gotten, and he got out the ledgers for the ranch. "We just need to see what we can afford. That doesn't go into the general pot. I'd like to not have a fight with your sisters, actually."

She stared at him, her eyes luminous. And then she leaned across the table, putting her hand over his, and kissed him on the mouth. He closed his eyes and reveled in it. Luxuriated in the moment. How many moments like this had he ever had in his life? Quiet calm and a connection with another person?

"Gus," she said. "I love you."

CHAPTER NINETEEN

SHE HADN'T MEANT to say that. On the heels of this crazy fight they'd just had, right after they'd made love, and he'd tried to pull away from her again. But something had to change. And she'd realized that when they were trapped in that storm of Gus's own making.

They got closer, he retreated and she let him. She never did anything to change it. To push them to a new place.

And she wanted to change that. Needed to. So someone had to take the first step. To change what they were. To change what they did.

"Alaina... You don't have to say that."

"It's true. I do. I've fallen in love with you over these last weeks. And I wish... I wish I could say that I always did. I always cared for you. My mom said something to me... I talked to my mom. She said something to me about the fact that we had a special connection. And I think that is true. I wanted to believe that I always felt something. But I didn't. I had to change. I had to grow up. I had to figure out what was really important."

It was uncomfortable, this. To put herself out there, to admit all of these things. All of these feelings. But if she didn't admit it, then what? And what was the point of it? The point of any of it, or the lesson there? If she didn't grow, if they didn't change…why were they doing this? That was what she kept coming back to.

He just sat there, staring straight ahead, his jaw set like granite, his eyes unreadable.

And for a minute, she thought this might be it. She thought she might've pushed him away completely. Because wasn't that how it kept on going? Advance, retreat. She moved forward and he moved back, and that was the way it had been.

"You love me?"

The question was asked softly, but intensely.

"Yes," she said. "And before you ask, I didn't fancy myself in love with Travis, not even a little bit."

"I wasn't going to ask," he said.

"Well, I just want to make it clear."

"It isn't a thing for me. That guy. I don't think about him. I don't care about him. He doesn't matter."

That made her feel good. It was hardly a declaration, but it was something. And she would take that. Yeah, she would damn well take it.

"Do you want to know what it means to me? That I love you."

He leaned back in his chair, his palms flat on the table. And she could see that he desperately did want to hear it. But that he was also guarding himself against it.

It was the strangest thing, to be able to feel the wall that he put up between them. Like a physical thing, even though he was sitting there. She just had to hope her love made it over the wall.

"It means I'm committed to this. To us. And means

I want to sleep in your room every night. It means that you make my heart flutter when I look at you. And even just when I think about you. It means that I can't imagine another man touching me. And I can't imagine a different future. Not now. I ache with it. With what I feel for you. With my regret over all the things I didn't know before. About myself, about you. About the world.

"I had this idea that there was no space for me, and… I didn't even know what kind of space I wanted. How can you know what you want when you don't know yourself?"

"That sounds like some kind of new age stuff."

"It's not. If you sit down in the quiet and you listen to your heart, you know what it tells you. But I never wanted to sit down in the quiet. Because I was afraid of it. And I just don't feel as afraid now."

"Alaina, I… I'm going to tell you something, and you're going to think it makes me a bastard. And it does. But there's not a whole lot I can do about it, and I'm going to give it to you honestly. I *like* that you love me. But I can't give it back."

His words were like a sword being driven straight through her chest. And she knew that he wasn't going to explain, not in the depth that she wanted him to. She loved him. He had changed her. Fundamentally. What she thought about herself, what she wanted. What she wanted for her life. And he wanted to keep that wall up. She was welcome to continue to lob her love over to the other side, but he wasn't going to open the gates.

But she wanted him. She wanted this life. She wanted to have this baby with him. And it would be okay. Because he was Gus. It would be okay because he had always been there, and he would continue to be.

She could handle this.

At least he was being honest. At least he wasn't pretending. Hadn't her dad pretended with her mom for years? Hadn't he pretended to be faithful, to be a husband who was invested in her and in the kids, only to just flake out one day?

"Okay," she said.

"That's it?"

"Gus, when are you going to get it into your head that you're not going to drive me away? I'm not afraid of you, and you can stop growling every five seconds and trying to make it so that I will be. I'm not weak. I love you. So… I can handle that. I can handle you."

And it felt a little bit sad. To say those words to him. *I can handle you.* When what she wanted was so much more. *Maybe it will change…*

That was dangerous. But she would rather have dangerous with him than be safe without him, and whatever that said about her… It didn't matter.

"I want to be a husband and wife. Not this… We married each other for convenience and are sleeping together sometimes, and they're two separate things. You and me. The same bed. The same room. And you can hold my hand when we go to family things, and maybe I'll sit on your lap the way that Nelly sits on Tag's lap."

His jaw went firm.

"You don't hate that," she said.

"No," he said.

And that made her smile a little bit, because things

weren't as grim as he was acting. Not if he actually wanted those things.

It didn't really matter what he gave. That was the thing. Because it was everything he was. That was what she told herself. He was a good man. And he deserved this. He deserved for someone to love him.

"I really do love you," she said.

And he growled, pulling her forward and kissing her. Kissing her and kissing her like they hadn't just made with an intensity so bright it had threatened to burn down the house. Consume them both in a fire that wouldn't end.

That might not leave scars on the outside, but had definitely left her changed inside.

She decided to take this. To take this intensity from him. Because it might be all she got.

Because she might never hear the whole story of those books that he'd read to his brothers, or why those old toys hurt so much.

So she would have to take what she could get.

Because she would rather have some of him than none of him at all.

SHE LOVED HIM. She *fucking loved him*. He had been sitting with that ever since last night. And it was… Well, it was something he was pretty damn thrilled with, he had to admit.

She loved him. How long had it been since another person had loved him?

And she did. Alaina. His pretty Alaina. So beautiful and perfect and everything. Alaina.

He needed her to change that room, though. And she was welcome to move in with him.

He probably should do it himself. Get rid of all that shit in there, actually set all that childhood stuff on fire. He'd thought about it before. It seemed poetic. His own dad had tried to get rid of him with fire, why not sort out all those bad memories the same way?

Eventually. Eventually, he would. And in the meantime, he would just focus on…on having her. Alaina McCloud.

She had stayed with him all night last night. And he'd woken up with her in his arms. His favorite thing to do.

And there was no reason to have all their things separated.

"My sister wants to know if you'll come help out at the farm store," Alaina said.

"What?"

"Fia called. She was wondering if we could come by and help do a little bit of labor on the farm store. She figures the more that we can all do, the more money that it'll save. And she figured since you're the reason she's not getting all of her money…"

"Sweat equity?"

"Yes. But she said she would make you a pie."

"Well. I guess I can't really turn that down."

"You could. But it would be churlish. Especially considering you were trying to figure out ways to cut corners here. Maybe you'll be able to meet in the middle."

"Maybe."

"Actually, I know you can meet in the middle. If both of you try."

"I thought you were on my team," he said.

"I am," she said. "I love you, remember?"

And he took that and held it to his heart like the greedy SOB he was.

"Yeah. For some reason."

They finished out the rest of the day, and at evening, headed on over to Sullivan's Point, where he endeavored not to grumble about the fact that he was going to be doing more work. Considering he'd already done what felt like enough work for the day. But she'd asked him to. Then hell, she'd said she loved him, so he figured he ought to show up when she needed him to.

When he got to the farm store, he was surprised to see not just the Sullivan sisters, but a couple of Garretts as well.

Wolf and Sawyer were there, along with Evelyn and Violet.

"Hey," he said.

"Hey," Sawyer returned.

He hadn't talked to Sawyer this much in years. It was strange, the way Alaina had changed everything. He had noticed the changes to the house. He had noticed her being in his bed. But slowly, she was changing the way he interacted with the people around him, and that was perhaps the most surprising thing of all.

And he felt… He didn't really know what to call it. Something lighter in his chest.

He would've said that he didn't want to connect with anyone. But she didn't make it feel so hard.

Maybe it was watching her do it. Maybe it was just

wanting to make her smile. But it didn't seem like a chore. Or a task.

"What's the objective?"

"Getting the wood paneling up on the wall," Sawyer said. "We can do it real quick if we all pitch in."

"Sounds a good plan."

And they went to work, putting up the panels, swinging hammers, and he felt…pride. To be doing this in front of her. To be building something for her family. Giving her something. He protected her all this time, but he wasn't entirely sure he'd ever given her anything.

But her family mattered to her, and she had pledged her allegiance to him anyway. Which made him work just a little bit faster.

CHAPTER TWENTY

"DAD CALLED."

Alaina looked at Fia. "Oh."

"Yeah. I guess he heard that you were expecting."

"But he didn't call me," Alaina said.

"No. He didn't. He called me, because he figured…"

"What? You're not any nicer to him than I am."

"No. I'm not. Sometimes I think he calls me for that reason. To get a little bit of a scolding. Because I don't know. Maybe it makes him feel like he's reflected and changed a little bit. I probably shouldn't give it to him. It's probably too satisfying."

Fia picked up a nail gun and pressed it against one of the wood panels, firing it in in one shot.

"I've pretty much given up," Alaina said. "On Dad ever… On him ever having a relationship with me again."

"I know," Fia said. "I'm just going to be mad forever that that's the case."

"Mom is excited."

"I know," Fia said.

"You don't have to protect me from this," Alaina said. "It is what it is. You didn't cause it, and there's nothing you can do to fix it."

"Maybe not. But I have to carry all of the issues

from it, don't I? Don't we all. I just… Alaina, I've been thinking a lot about what you said. About how this wasn't your dream. About how you had to go out and get something for yourself. And I feel like this whole thing with Travis…"

Travis. How funny. He had been the catalyst of this whole thing. And he just didn't matter anymore.

She just didn't think of him anymore.

"I feel responsible for it. All of it. I feel like I did something, and I should've just… I should've listened to you more. But I get so caught up in my own thing. And trying to prove that I can fix this. In trying to prove that I can save it. But I don't need Dad, and I don't need to sell it the way that Mom thought. And I don't remember, that you were so young when all of that happened. I don't remember that you're probably hurting and missing things and… I feel it is my fault. That you went and got pregnant, and now you… feel like you have to be married to Gus and…"

"I love Gus," she said, feeling her face get hot when she said it.

And Fia just gaped at her. "You…you love Gus?"

"Yes. I do. I love him. He is the most wonderful man that I could ever have asked to be with. And you don't need to bear responsibility for anything that I chose to do. We've all got issues. You haven't gone and gotten yourself pregnant, have you?"

Fia laughed, a hollow sound. "No. But then, like you said, we all have our issues. I just don't think that I could… I don't trust anyone."

"In what way?"

"How do you trust them to stay? Because it's easy to remember Dad the way that he is now. Such a flake. And so disinterested. But he wasn't. And that's what scares me. How can you have a guy who seems one way, and then he turns into something totally different? It haunts me. And I can't let it go. I don't think I ever could."

"Well, Gus is… He's Gus. I mean, he takes care of me, he…"

"Does he love you?"

"He hasn't said it," Alaina said.

She felt a little bit irritated at herself for exposing Gus like that. And she would not go a step further and tell Fia they had talked about it, and that he'd outright said he couldn't. Fia wouldn't understand. She'd judge Gus too harshly, in ways he didn't deserve.

"Why hasn't he?"

"Fia. If you think that we have daddy issues…"

"I know his dad was abusive."

"His dad *burned* him, Fia."

And she thought back to all that rage that he had expressed the night she'd said she loved him. All that pain. The lengths that his father had driven him to. The violence.

She felt so bad for him. He was a man who had been pushed into an impossible situation.

How was he supposed to handle things? How was he supposed to feel about anything?

"He could say it," Alaina said. "He could say it and not mean it. Just make me feel better. But he hasn't done that. And he's always been there for me."

"Don't take on my stuff," she said. "That's not what I'm trying to get you to do. I'm not... I'm not suggesting that you shouldn't trust Gus. It's just... It would scare me. It all scares me. For you. I worry. And I just... I don't want you to be with someone who doesn't love you back. And I definitely don't want to feel like I pushed you there."

"It's okay," Alaina said. "He deserves for someone to love him. Difficult and crusty and whatever else he is, he deserves it."

"What about what you deserve?" Fia said.

And her words stopped Alaina cold.

Because she didn't see what that had to do with anything.

She needed to be there for Gus. She needed to care for him. And she got plenty out of it. He had given her so much. And loving somebody didn't... It didn't cost. It wasn't a transaction. She just did because he was wonderful and because he was Gus.

"Don't worry about me," she said. "I'm happy."

"You're getting absolutely everything out of this that you want?"

And she couldn't say yes. She couldn't look Fia in the eye and lie to her like that. Even though she wanted to. She wanted to say yes, because she wanted to believe it. Because she wanted to be able to tell herself that she was getting what she wanted.

Yeah. She really wished that were true.

"Not everything. But some people don't get everything, do they? I mean...we don't get to have our parents be normal people. We get to have what they'll give.

I can't go back and make a different decision about... well...this," she said, putting her hand on her stomach. "And Gus was there for me and..."

"Is he a compromise?"

"No. He's everything I've ever wanted."

"Except in love with you. I know you, Alaina. You like romance novels. And you want that for yourself."

"But I don't get to have it."

"Says who?"

"If Gus won't love me, then I don't get it. Because no one else will do."

"Maybe you should ask him for more."

"But I offered him this for nothing."

"That's great. It was a free trial. Having a bright, wonderful, perfect woman in love with you for a while. With no expectation. Now maybe you need to set one."

Her sister patted her on the hand, and Alaina didn't quite know what to do with any of it. And it was something she couldn't get out of her head, the whole way home. Something she couldn't let go of, when she and Gus went back to the house that night.

And it wasn't about the words, actually. It was about the distance she could feel, and the things that he held back from her. Like the issue with the bedroom, and the other things he decided were closed doors.

It was that she thought the more she felt for him, the more she became aware of the wall in him, the more she felt lonely even when she was with him, 'that she could feel the distance between them even when they were sitting right next to each other.

WHEN THEY GOT home from the evening of working at the farm store, Gus was beat.

He went into the kitchen, conscious of the fact that he had a hitch in his back, opened the door and took a beer out. Then he leaned against the refrigerator door, opened up the bottle and took a long drag on it.

He didn't know where Alaina was, but frankly he could use a little bit of distance.

He was feeling…tired. Old.

He was feeling like he was on the edge of some things falling apart and he couldn't even say why. Because she loved him.

And that was perfect.

He was going to be a father.

His throat felt tight.

And somehow, everything felt like boxes, stacked up inside his soul, precarious, on the edge of collapsing.

"Hi."

He looked up and saw her standing in the doorway, wearing a white nightie that barely grazed the tops of her thighs.

"Shit," he said, nearly choking on his beer as he set it down quickly on the counter.

And he would've said that he was hoping she'd gone to bed. That he didn't have the energy for all of this. That he wanted the distance. But she was here. Standing right there looking like an angel, and he wasn't going to be able to deny that.

He denied himself for so long. On so many levels. And now she was right here. And she wanted him. And he'd done a pretty weak-ass job of denying his need for her—that had to be said.

He wasn't going to start doing a better job now.

"I thought you might like a bath," she said.

Her voice was husky and seductive. And she was everything.

"With you?"

"Naturally."

"Great."

He left the beer, followed her out of the kitchen and up the stairs. Her hair was a bright red waterfall, that robe such a glaringly innocent white. But his thoughts were anything but innocent. Anything but pure.

She looked over her shoulder as she ducked into the bathroom, and it was enough to send him straight to his knees.

She had the bath filled up with water, and it had bubbles.

And Gus McCloud had never taken a bubble bath in his entire life. But he sure as hell was about to.

He started to pull his clothes off, and she stared at him. Like she was hungry for him. And the kick of lust that went through him was more than he could bear. She untied the belt on the robe, and let it fall away from her beautiful curves. Her stomach was showing more.

Evidence of what was to come. The baby.

"We need to get our rooms moved," he said.

Because it triggered that thought.

One of the few coherent thoughts he was able to have while staring at her in all her glory.

"I'm looking forward to sharing with you."

"Whatever new stuff you want to get for the baby. You can get it." Right now she could have anything she wanted. Anything. He'd sell off half his horses and get her anything she asked for.

"Thank you," she said. "But we don't need to plan anything right now."

She took his hand and led him to the tub, and he got in, and she slipped in behind him, moving her hands down over his chest. And he groaned. He leaned back against her, her breasts pillowing his head, her core hot at his back.

And she started to rub his shoulders.

And he couldn't remember the last time anyone had just touched him. Casually. With this kind of care.

It was sexual. But there was something more to it.

The kind of sweetness and softness he'd never experienced before.

"Thank you so much for helping with my family today. That was really wonderful."

"It was important to you."

"I like watching you work," she said, moving her hands down his stomach, coming maddeningly close to that part that was stiff and hard for her. But she just barely grazed him, and he groaned.

"This is kind of a silly question," she said. "But why did you stay? Why do you love this place? Because I know it's hard for you. I know being here is difficult. I know that the room is difficult."

He stiffened. He didn't really want to have this conversation; he just wanted her to keep on touching him. He didn't want to do this talking thing.

"Alaina…"

"No. I need to say this. I'm tired of feeling like there's distance between us. I miss being as close to you as another person can be, without you being inside of me. I'm not going to judge you. I'm not going to use it against you. But who do you share with, Gus? You take care of everyone else. Who takes care of you?"

And something lodged tight in his throat, and he couldn't breathe past it. Couldn't think past it.

"I don't need anyone to take care of me."

"You do. You do, though. I know you, Gus. And you are a giant wound. You care so much about so many things, but you don't know how to let yourself have them. You keep everything at a distance. But it's more than you ever let on. Because you take care of this land, and I want to know why. I want to know why you're so hell-bent on turning this place that was the site of so much pain for you into something good."

"Because what's the point if it's all just ash, Alaina? What's the point? Something good has to come from it. It is the only thing that I have. On this godforsaken planet, this ranch is the only thing that I have. And I can take it and I can make it into something different. I can take it and I can make it into something better. But I shouldn't have to start from scratch just because my dad was a dangerous asshole. And I shouldn't have to start from scratch just because my mother left. I got to take what I have and do something with it. Is that a good enough reason for you?"

"It's a good reason," she said.

His heart was pounding, and he didn't know why it

was hitting him like this. Why it was all hitting him this hard. It didn't actually make sense. Her line of questioning about the ranch was simple, and included things he'd talked about before. His desire to make a difference. His desire to do something better… It didn't make sense that any of it would bother him so much.

"My sister said something to me tonight. About not being certain about how you felt about me. And how that would scare her. Because of how our dad left. But I know you're not going to leave, Gus. I do know that. Because look at you. You stayed. All this time. Even though stuff is awful. Even though things here were a nightmare for you. Even though that room… Even though it houses so many demons for you. You've stayed. And so I know you're never going to leave. But one thing I also know about you, Gus McCloud, is that you are very good at being in the same room, and sharing the same air, and not really being there. And I want more of you."

He growled, turning over quickly, pinning her against the wall of the bathtub. "How can I be more here? How could you have more of me?" He flexed his hips forward, let her feel how hard he was. "How can you have more of me than this?"

"I don't know," she said. "It's just something I feel. That distance between us sometimes. Like you're holding things back. Like you're holding yourself back."

"Because I am," he said. "I already told you. I… I have tendencies that are like my father. And I have to police myself for…"

"No. That's not it."

"You don't know," he said, his voice rocky.

"I do know. I do. Because you are the man that rescues kittens and me. Because you are the man who read to your brothers."

That pushed his mind back there, and he didn't want to go there. He was angry now, that they had ever mentioned that to her. That they had ever brought it up.

"And I'm this man now," he said, putting her hand up on his face, dragging it down the side of his scarred neck, to his chest. "And this is what you get."

"I love you," she said.

It hit hard. Like a lightning strike. Right there at the center of his chest.

"What does that mean?" he asked.

"What?"

"Loving me. My mom loved me too."

Shit. He despised that. That weak-sounding phrase that had come out of his mouth. The way that his voice shook. He despised it.

He despised himself. Why did he care? Why the fuck did he care what a woman who had abandoned him all those years ago had said?

Why did it matter?

Someday I'll come back for you.

Well, she hadn't. Because she didn't love him. Not really. Or maybe she knew. Maybe she knew all along that he was finally like his father. Maybe she knew all along about the fire. And she didn't want a scarred, damaged kid slowing down her new life.

He didn't blame himself. Not like Hunter.

But he knew he wasn't enough. He knew he wasn't enough to bring her back.

Take care of them. Keep reading to them.

I'll come back for you.

And she'd handed him a new package of army men like that would fix it. All those fucking army men.

But she hadn't come back, and he'd never opened them because he wouldn't accept it. The parting gift that was meant to…to what? Assuage her guilt?

No. He hadn't taken them. Not really. They'd been a reminder, nothing more.

Why were they still there? Why had he kept them?

"It means that I am willing to turn myself inside out for you. Gus, I didn't know what love was until this. I never even really thought about it. Because in my house… Yeah, I guess I had the same problem you do. What does it all mean? Because my dad left. Because no matter how much my mom loved us she still got so lost in her own pain that she couldn't be there for us.

"Except I look around at my sisters, and I look at this land, and I see love. I think that's why you're still here. Because you love your brothers, and you love this land, and you believe that we can put more in it than just the blood that is soaked into the ground over all these years. It's love. I want you to love me at least as much as you love this ranch, and I want you to love our baby the same way. Our baby, Gus. Because you're the one that's here. That's what makes a father. You're going to be the father because you're here. Because of love. But it has to be love, Gus. It has to be."

"I can't do it," he said, his voice choked off.

"Gus, why not?"

"Because it doesn't mean anything. Because people leave you anyway. Because they leave you to burn. Because they leave you to burn."

"Gus…"

"And they never come back, and maybe it's because… Maybe it's because she knew. Maybe because she knew what I was, maybe it's because she knew what had happened to me, maybe it's because… Just because it wasn't strong enough. But I don't want it. Not anymore."

"But you took my love easily enough."

He growled, rolling his hips forward, and then he kissed her, with all the pent-up ferocity in his body. None of it made sense. And he felt like everything was caving in. Over him, around him. Alaina was the only person that loved him. Alaina was the only person, and he didn't know how to be worthy of that. He didn't know how to give her what she was asking for. All he knew was this. So he kissed her.

He kissed her to try to drown out the feeling of total vulnerability that made him like an open wound, scrubbed with salt and left there to die.

He hated himself. More than he ever had. Because she was right there. She was right there and he didn't know how to reach across that space. That space that he had cultivated out of a sense of need. The desire to not be his father. The desire to never hurt anyone.

Or is it just that you don't want to ever be hurt…

He growled, held her face between his hands and

kissed her. "Fuck me," he said, reversing their positions so that she was over him. "Do it."

"Gus," she whispered.

"This is all I understand," he said. "So you show me. Make me feel something."

He felt something. He felt plenty. Echoing, raw, empty pain. And he didn't have any walls anymore. He didn't have any defenses.

Because memories were barreling in on him. Things he didn't want to remember. Things he'd never wanted to remember.

It's too bad you're not dead. But you are an ugly son of a bitch now.

Yeah. That had landed. When he'd been recovering in that room. With those army men still in their package.

Waiting for her to come for him. Waiting. But she left him. She left him to die.

And he was the last line of defense. Just him. And who was there for him? No one. She was right about that. No one.

No one was there for him.

He lifted her, and impaled her, thrusting up inside of her, watching as she took him. All of him.

Watching as she gave herself up to this pleasure, even though they were both lost in pain.

And this pain was his fault. She gave to him. And gave to him.

She said that she loved him.

And the problem was his.

Formed so long ago.

And maybe he couldn't do this. *But you need her. You need her.*

And he lost himself in her. In the warmth of the water, the slickness of her skin. The way that her body rippled around his as she came closer and closer to her release.

He moved his hands over her curves, up to cup her breasts.

And he kept his eyes on her face. Beautiful and wild and his.

His.

His.

And when the storm was over she collapsed against him, and moved her hands over his face. His body. "I love you."

And he felt an undeniable sense of sadness that moved through him. Like he'd lost her.

And he didn't know why he felt that. Didn't know why that certainty pervaded his soul. He chose not to acknowledge it. Instead, he picked her up from the tub, brought her into his room and laid her down beside him.

He wrapped her in a blanket, but he didn't hold her.

And he lay there for a long time. For a long damn time.

He couldn't sleep.

GUS WENT WITH her to do shopping in Tolowa. It was a long drive, and he hadn't seemed particularly happy about it, but he had also agreed that it was appropriate enough for him to be involved in choosing all of the nursery things.

They were going with all new, since he had been so aggravated by the bedroom she'd set up. She hadn't gone back in there, and neither had he. They just left it.

So they went to Target, and they picked up a full range of nursery items. To go with the antique furniture that she'd already gotten down in Copper Ridge.

Blankets and curtains and rugs, adorable little lamps. Arts and other little trinkets that made her smile.

Maybe she shouldn't have gone overboard since they didn't know the gender of the baby yet, but she had gone with mostly white and cream, with moons and stars and other fairly gender-neutral items. Gus was stoic, but then he had been since that night in the tub. He'd been very distant. They had cleared out her room, and she had moved into his. He did not hold her at night.

She said that she loved him, and nothing changed. He seemed to accept it. He even seemed to like it. But something had happened that night. When she had tried to get underneath his shield. He hadn't liked it. And he was punishing her for it. Maybe not on purpose. But he was.

He deserved to be loved. What she'd said to Fia was true.

He deserved this.

He took her out for a hamburger. "You need to learn how to cook," she said again.

"You keep offering."

"Tonight. Tonight I'm going to teach you how to make pizza. How about that?"

"All right by me."

"Great then."

They went to the grocery store, and she still didn't think she would ever get used to seeing Gus with a grocery cart.

Because however much more he seemed like a mortal man to her now, he was still far too big and sexy to be doing something as mundane as going through a grocery store. But it made her heart feel tender. And maybe she just had to accept that these were the things that she would have. That big strong Gus McCloud would go to the grocery store with her. That he would buy nursery items with her. That he would learn to make a pizza with her. Maybe that was the thing. Maybe it was just all about adjusting what she wanted.

Maybe that was it.

They picked up all the pizza supplies, and began the drive back.

She put the groceries away while he took the larger items up to the nursery. And she started unpacking all of it and arranging it.

She felt genuine excitement when she looked around the nursery. More than excitement. A deep well of love like she'd never known. And she wondered if it would be a little boy or a little girl. The Sullivans were all girls. It would be interesting to see a boy. Her heart clenched when she wondered if a boy child would look like her father. But she imagined that was something she would just have to deal with.

She carried the genetics of a person who made decisions she didn't like.

Gus had to live with that.

She would love this child. And she would teach them

to do different. To be different. Gus and the way he loved the land, the way that he cared about doing the right thing. His commitments… He would instill those things in their child.

And she would…

Something in her heart faltered just then.

When she tried to think what she would teach this child.

Well, she was headstrong. She cared a lot about things. She loved. Very fiercely. She would love them, the way that she loved Gus. And she would teach them…

How will you show them what they deserve?

This growth hurt so damn bad. Because she knew now that she had to demand more. That she couldn't hide, or run or deflect.

It wasn't who she was anymore.

She swallowed hard, pushing that thought away as she went downstairs. "The cooking lessons are starting," she said.

They went into the kitchen, and Gus pushed his sleeves up, pushed his cowboy hat back. "Okay. Where do we begin?"

She smiled, trying to push her doubts away. Trying to push her issues away. But it was strange how that completed nursery had filled her mind with images of not just having a baby, but of what kind of mother she would be.

And she thought more about what Fia had said. Worry that she would be abandoned. Worry about the kinds of things that hurt and concerned her.

She didn't worry that Gus would abandon her. She didn't.

She didn't worry about being like their mother.

Although she had to wonder. What it would be like to have this one-sided love with Gus for years on end.

What it might do to her over time. And what kind of mother it might turn her into. What kind of person.

"First let's start with the crust," she said.

She got out a recipe and mixing bowls, and pretty soon both she and Gus were covered in flour.

"I'm thinking it's going to be a remake of the pancake fiasco," he said.

"Maybe we should've started with hamburgers."

"You just had one for lunch."

"I can't get enough of them."

He had his hands in the mixing bowl, moving the ball of dough around, and she reached hers and put them over his. He went still. His movements going stiff.

"What?"

"Nothing."

"Why did you pull away?"

"It's not a big deal." Except that she could see in his eyes that it was. And this was what it was going to be like always. Because this was what it was like when you were all in and the person with you wasn't. When they were holding back a part of themselves.

And she knew that Gus had been hurt. Worse than she had been. She'd had pain in her life. But she was young, and she'd had opportunity to recover from some of these things. In a gentler way. She hadn't settled into them like he had.

"Gus," she said. "I just wish that you would tell me."

"This is a pizza lesson. Not a cross-examination on feelings."

"All right then. Knead the pizza dough," she said.

She moved away from him, and turned around, looking out the window at McClouds'.

And then she looked back at him. His broad shoulders, his lean waist. His utterly perfect male beauty. She loved him. She loved him so much. And she believed in her heart that he deserved to be loved.

And a broken cry escaped her lips.

Because she deserved to be loved too. And she had been holding herself back from that. From that reality. From that truth.

She understood what had damaged him. She knew that it was more complicated than just his father's abuse and his mother's abandonment. But she tasted shades of it and she understood how it could affect what she felt about herself.

She had convinced herself, not in so many words, that she could take less. She hadn't dreamed about a husband and children, because she had been taught that she couldn't trust in those things. And shouldn't want them.

She had gone after Travis because he was easy. She liked Hunter because he was impossible.

She had cared about Gus in a deep, real way since she was young enough that it wasn't sexual. But she had cared for him. And she had never let herself get closer than that because of the fear of rejection. And now here she was. And she realized he wouldn't reject her. But he would keep taking. And it would do them both a disservice. That wall would stay up unless she challenged him to knock it down. He would pull away and pull away and pull away and she would draw closer and closer and closer. And they would do that dance forever. And what would she tell their child? About what they deserved. If she could not admit that she deserved to be loved. She deserved it. More than just protection. She deserved it even though she had made a mistake. She deserved to be loved fully and completely.

She didn't know if there was a man out there that she could ever have that with, not the way she did with Gus. She was actually pretty sure there wasn't.

She had wanted him to protect her because she wanted to be with him. And she would be another person who walked away from him. And that killed her. But staying with him just might kill her too. And she would be dragging her child right into it.

"Gus," she said. "I want you to love me."

The air around them went still, and his whole body went straight. "What?"

"I've said that I loved you a bunch of times. I mean it. I keep saying it, and nothing changes. That isn't what I want. I want you to love."

"I already told you that I…"

"I know that you did. But I'm sorry. It's not enough."

"It's not enough? Alaina, this was never part of our deal."

"No, I know. But it was never part of the deal for me to fall in love with you either. But I did. I have."

"You can't take it from me," he said, walking across

the space, his voice intense. "You can't offer me this, and then take it away from me."

"I'm not. I didn't. I'm not taking it away from you. I love you. I love you, but I need you to love me."

"You will not leave me," he said. "You can't fucking leave me."

"I don't want to leave you, Gus. I want you to love me. I want you to…to deal with whatever that thing is inside of you that is keeping you from doing it. Because if I don't demand that you do it, you're never going to be able to give me what I want. You're never going to be able to give our child what they deserve. And I won't be able to be a good example. I won't be able to be a good mother. And I want… I want nothing more than to try to get comfortable with this. I want to stay with you. I want this to be enough. I want to have sex with you every night and sleep with you, and stay with you. I want your body, and I want your hands on me. And I want to live with you. But I want your heart and I want your soul, and if I don't demand it…then neither of us will get everything we deserve. Because one-sided love doesn't lead anywhere."

"I need you," he said, his voice sounding broken. "Alaina, I need you. You can't just be there for me, and then not be."

"Then love me. Love me enough to do whatever you need to do to…"

"What if it's all bullshit? What if there's nothing more than this? What if there's nothing more? Then how can you say that you really love me if you can't take me exactly like I am? How?"

Tears started to pour down her face as he said exactly what she felt in her heart. How could she leave, how could she profess to love him and not take him with all of his flaws?

Because it was selling him short.

"Because it's not love if you can have more and we take half. Because it's not love if I let you stay there bleeding. What is love? Loving someone enough to reset the bone, isn't it? Even if it hurts. It doesn't help anyone to let you stay broken if I know that you could be whole."

"You don't know that I can be."

"I know you're not violent. Whatever you say about that…whatever you did to your dad, I know that's not who you are."

"It is."

"Fine then," she said. "It is. But it doesn't scare me. Stop holding back."

"It's not that."

"What is it?"

"I can't do this," he said. "I can't do it. Just go. Leave, Alaina. If you can't take what I'm giving you, then you need to just go. Because it's… I can't give you more than this. I can't be more than I am."

"Bullshit," she said. "You would just have to risk something, and you're not willing to do it."

"You don't get to tell me what I feel."

"But you don't get to set the limits on us."

"What are you going to do? You're just going to leave? Go back to Sullivan's Point. Divorce me? You're going to be just like everyone. You're just gonna leave me. You can leave me, and you never really loved me because if somebody loves you they won't leave."

"Gus…"

"No. It's fine. I'm used to it. That's how it is. She left me too. It's never really love."

"You listen to me, Gus McCloud. And you listen good. I'm not leaving you. I will be at Sullivan's Point, and you'll know exactly where I am. And when you're ready, you can come and get me. And I will go with you. When you're ready. I'm not leaving you with a madman. Well, no one except you. And you are going to have to sort out what you want. You're going to have to sort out what it all means. I can't do it for you. Because you won't let me. I would be happy to sit with you and picture your broken childhood piece by piece. But you don't want me to do it. And I can't keep reaching out only to have you push me away. But I'm not her. You'll know where to find me."

"You told me you wouldn't leave me," he said.

"I thought that was the kindest thing," she said. "But I see it now. I see us. Falling into the same pattern over and over. I have to break the pattern."

"You promised me."

She felt like she was dying. "I think…separation, distance, is what we need. Otherwise after this, we'll have sex, and then it will all be okay for a while. Until I get too close to your wounds again, and we'll go on like that. On and on."

"You're just the same as everyone else."

He was angry and hurt, and hell, so was she. "No," she said. "I'm not leaving you to burn. I'm trying to get you out. I said I didn't need you to love me back because I didn't know better. I do now. I need it, but even more, you need it."

"You're just going to leave me with a nursery and a half-made pizza and…"

"Unless I'm leaving you with a broken heart, the rest of it doesn't matter."

She felt sick to her stomach, and with shaking hands, still covered in flour, she walked into the living room. She looked around at all of it. Everything that she had done to try to build a life with him. And all she could see was her marks layered over his.

Because they had never really become one. She wanted it. Maybe he even thought he did too. But there was one final piece that was missing. The one thing that could complete the picture, and he wasn't willing to do the work to get there.

She had to go. For herself. For him. For the baby.

Maybe he would come after her.

Her chest gave a giant twist. And she had to take a sharp breath to keep herself standing. To keep herself from collapsing.

And she walked out of the house, her heart pounding a sickening rhythm in her head.

And she got into her truck, and drove toward Sullivan's Point. And she waited. To see headlights behind her. To see Gus coming after her.

Because Gus… Gus had always been there for her. Until she'd asked for this.

She had to just make the drive. She couldn't fall apart. Not now.

It took five minutes to get to Sullivan's Point, and each one of them felt interminable.

Finally, she arrived, and she got out of the truck, practically falling out and running to the farmhouse.

It was Fia that answered the door.

"Alaina…"

"I left," she said.

And then she dissolved into heartrending tears. And she didn't think she would ever be whole again.

CHAPTER TWENTY-ONE

GUS WAS STILL trying to figure out what the hell had happened. He was standing in his kitchen, with his hands in a bowl, covered in flour.

She had asked for him to love her. She had asked for him to love her.

And he couldn't do it.

He couldn't do it.

He put his hand on his chest. There was a sharp pain there, and it felt like a heart attack. Maybe it was a heart attack.

That would figure. He couldn't access his damn emotions so his heart was going to give out on him. Like it was forcing him to involve it.

It doesn't need to force you, you jackass.

What the hell was this? And what did any of it matter? What did it fix?

Why couldn't she just accept what they had?

Why...?

Because you feel it. You know it's there. You know it's there. You hold her at arm's length.

Well, what was the other choice? To just... To admit how much he needed her? He couldn't do that. That was insanity. He couldn't be…needy and in pain, he couldn't be weak.

He could never be that idiotic boy lying in a bed at thirteen, clutching unopened army men, comfort he wished he could take while he lay there burned all to hell, still convinced that his mother was going to come back for him.

He had wanted… All he had wanted was for somebody to love him enough to protect him.

That was all he had wanted. And it wasn't there. It didn't exist.

He stormed up the stairs and kicked the door open to his childhood room. All this bullshit that Alaina had gotten out of the boxes and set up. All this bullshit.

He growled, and he swept his hand across one of the shelves, flinging all the toys there onto the floor.

They had never meant anything. Parting gifts. Shit that she had left them with. That wasn't them.

And he had loved her. And what had that gotten him? He had loved her, and she had left him to die.

And who had been there for him? He gathered up his siblings and read to them while those fights raged on downstairs, so they couldn't hear. So they didn't know the things that he knew for as long as he could possibly protect them. And then what? She'd left, and all the violence had spilled over onto them. And he had tried. He'd tried. And he had loved everybody enough to put himself in between them. To be lit on fire. But who the hell had loved him enough?

Who the hell had ever loved him enough to protect him?

And he took that box of unopened army men, and he

crushed it in his hands. The packaging splitting on the sides, tearing open. "Fuck all of this," he said, throwing it to the ground and stomping it beneath his boot. "Fuck it all," he said.

He shouldn't have a kid. He shouldn't have a wife. He should just have nothing.

Nothing at all. Because this rage and the sense of unfairness that lived inside of him was destructive. And he didn't know how to make other things bigger than this.

Didn't know how to change.

And he looked at that bed in the corner. Where he'd spent those months trying to recover. Dammit all to hell.

The pain was overwhelming. It was just too much.

And he let it close in around him. And he really let himself just wallow in it. And how fucking sorry he felt for himself. And she was gone; she wasn't holding him up anymore. That's what she'd been doing.

She'd been a balm for his soul, and she had covered this pain, and now she left him to bleed out.

And he had to feel this. This unending pain that he had been avoiding all this time. Because hadn't he been through enough?

And who had been there for him?

She was just another person who would let him down... She was just...

She was there. She was there for him.

And it played through his mind like a movie. The joy on her face when he brought her candy. The way that she'd fought him when he pulled her out of the lake.

The way that she looked at him, and smiled and hadn't recoiled at his scars.

How she'd taken rides on his shoulders. And made him feel like maybe he wasn't a monster.

How even when she'd been a teenage brat who was too pretty for his own good, she smiled at him.

How she'd become his most cherished fantasy, because she gave him softness when no one else did.

She's been giving to you.

And there's this whole story about how you take care of her. But look at her.

Look at all she gave to you. She just wants you to love her. And you want to take from her. You want to tell yourself that taking care of her is just as good. That it's the same.

But you aren't giving her what she needs.

Alaina, bright and beautiful, who had brought him back to his humanity. Who had made him want to try. Had made him want to be more than he was. Better.

But in the end he'd fallen short.

She deserved more.

She was right to demand it.

You don't think you should try to become more?

He growled and dropped down to the floor. Down to his knees.

What the hell were you supposed to do when everything just hurt?

How the hell were you supposed to get through it?

He felt like that burn victim he'd been at thirteen. In endless pain, completely unsure how to get past it.

You don't. You just have to heal.

You have to let it heal.

And he knew what he had to do. He knew exactly who he had to talk to.

CHAPTER TWENTY-TWO

"I HATE THIS," Alaina said, the next morning over coffee, with Fia and Rory and Quinn sitting around the table with her.

"You can't live with a man who doesn't love you," Fia said pragmatically.

"No," Quinn and Rory agreed.

"I'm not sure I can live without him either."

And for a moment, everything inside of her hurt so much that she wanted to claw it away in a panic. Wanted to solve it. Right now. Today. She wanted to run back to Gus and tell him that she was sorry. That she didn't mean it. That they could be together. She wanted to go back on all of this. To say that she didn't deserve to ask for more from him, not after everything he'd given, and see if it would be enough, and if he would take her back, and if she could get rid of this unending pain inside of her.

Except...

That wasn't the right thing to do.

That was what she used to do. Panic when it hurt. Turn away from it. Run from it. She had to sit in this. She had to sit in it and see where it would go. Because what was the alternative? Half-healed wounds.

Things that never reached their potential.

She had to trust that Gus was strong. And that so was she. That she could withstand this.

No matter what decision he came to.

"I just love him so much," she said. "And I don't want to be apart from him. But I just think being his crutch for the rest of my life isn't doing either of us any favors."

"Well, your baby will have a passel of the best aunts ever, and we love you. And we support you. And you will never be alone," Fia said.

"I know. I was so afraid of it. And I just kept... The abandonment stuff, it just... It really got to me. But the real reason I married Gus was that I wanted him. I didn't have the language for it, or the maturity to understand it, but it's always been him. I was just afraid of it. Because it was such a deep feeling. We've known each other for so long that it wasn't lust. Not first. It was love first. And it didn't become romantic until the time was right. But it's inside out, and that made it hard to recognize. It was certainty before it was butterflies. But the damn butterflies made everything a whole lot more confusing."

"That's special," Fia said. "I don't think there's very many people that get to experience love that way."

"It's only special if he pulls his head out of his ass," Quinn said.

She sighed. "It isn't that. He is so hurt, and I can't get to the bottom of it. I can't quite get to the why. I want to, but he won't let me. He thinks he's like his dad, but that's not the thing that's hurting him. Not really. I just wonder if he's been lonely for so long he doesn't actually know how not to be."

"If he loves you as much as you love him," Fia said, "he's going to figure it out."

"I just have to be strong enough to let him."

"Good thing you're a Sullivan. As well as a McCloud. I think there's enough stubbornness between the two of those names to sustain you."

Alaina sighed. "And whatever won't... Well, I have you."

"You do. Always."

"Hunter," Gus said, standing outside his brother's front door at 6:00 a.m. and shouting his name.

He'd knocked already, but his brother hadn't come to the door.

"Hunter," he shouted again.

He heard heavy footsteps, and the door jerked open, his brother still buttoning his pants. "What the hell?"

"Am I interrupting something?"

"Yeah," his brother said, crossing his arms over his chest. "You are."

"Sorry." He pushed his way inside anyway.

"I don't think you understand how sacred morning sex is, Gus. The amount of times I have actually... You're not okay, are you?"

"No," Gus said.

He stood and looked at his younger brother, and felt about a thousand years old.

"What's up?" Hunter asked.

"She asked me to love her. And I don't know how."

The look in Hunter's eyes, the pity, hurt, but he had to stand there and take it because he was pitiable right now and even he had to admit it.

"Well, that's bullshit. You've been loving her for years."

The words just about knocked him flat. "What?"

"You look after her. You protect her. You want her more than you want any other woman. You've been faithful to her. You were there for her when she needed you most. You've been loving her this whole time."

He felt like he'd been shocked by a live wire.

He'd loved her.

All along.

From pulling her out of the pond, to seeing her standing at the lake.

Loved her as a protector.

Loved her as a man.

He hadn't realized.

"Well... *What the fuck?*"

Hunter put his hand on Gus's shoulder. "It isn't that you don't love her. It's that you're just so damn guarded." He patted him twice, and moved away from him again.

"I don't know how not to be."

"Yeah, I know. It's tough. But...here's what I know. What I know, Gus, is that you can't stay safe and be in a relationship. You've gotta put it all out there. You've gotta be willing to be vulnerable. And I think you're close. I think the love part is there. But you're real difficult to pin down, buddy. And it's hard to feel... It's hard to get a read on what you feel. She needs more than that.

She needs more than that, and you can't blame her. She needs feelings, some flowers and all that. And mostly, she needs your heart. Because love's no good if you're just holding it inside of you and not sharing it. Believe me when I tell you, I get it. I get how hard it is. She left us. I blamed myself. You probably blame yourself. Hell, we probably all do. It's probably a roulette wheel of self-loathing. Because it's a vicious cycle. Not wanting to be like Dad, feeling angry at her. It's not simple. But you have to tell her what you want. Then you have to show her. What you feel."

"But what I feel is a damn mess," Gus said.

"So, give her the mess."

"But…"

And he realized that all of this was about never being disappointed again. All of it was about not being vulnerable again.

Because he was still that little boy holding those army men, whether he kicked them off to the side or not. Because he was still damaged. Whether he wanted to admit it or not, because he had once wanted someone to love him so much that they would upend their lives to be with him. He had loved his mother. And she had never come back for him.

"But she didn't leave. You know where she is. You know where Alaina is."

"You're right," Gus said. "I… I need her." Admitting it felt like pushing broken glass into his own chest, and it was stopping short of the truth of it. But those words didn't come easy, and he would be damned if he said them in front of Hunter before he said them to her. "Dammit. I need her and I… It makes me sick. Because…"

"You don't want to be hurt."

"No. And I don't want to tell her… I don't want to tell her." He didn't tell Hunter what. Because if it was that easy to tell the story, he would've done it a long time ago. But somehow, he could see that Hunter knew what he meant. He didn't want to share that deep trauma. The real one. The one that made him feel ruined.

Because Hunter had his own version of that. Much the same way he was sure they all did.

"You have to, though. Because it's the thing that breaks it all loose."

"I'm not sure I want it all loose."

"Well, that's the thing. She sacrificed something. To demand everything of you. And now it's your turn."

And he felt like he'd sacrificed enough in his life. But he realized right then that for Alaina, he had to sacrifice more.

And he would.

"Quick," Gus said. "Tell me how to be romantic."

CHAPTER TWENTY-THREE

SHE WAS WORKING in the garden at Sullivan's Point. And it was an interesting exercise. Considering it was a place she'd said she didn't really want to be. A place she'd said she didn't really want to work.

And here she was.

Working out all kinds of things.

She was happy to be here. With her sisters. And all right, maybe the pulling of weeds wasn't exactly her best life, but it was better than…

Well, better than taking half.

Better than letting Gus settle for half.

Maybe. She wasn't really sure yet. Considering all of the sadness in her body was like a ten-pound weight, constantly settled on her shoulders. And her bladder was being weird. Because there was a baby resting on that. And everything just felt kind of sad and strange and not at all what she wanted.

What a gift, to suddenly know for sure what she wanted. She wanted Gus to love her. She loved Gus.

She didn't have Gus.

How nice for her.

She straightened and wiped her arm across her forehead. And put her hand on her stomach. "I guess it's just you and me, little one. Except, I pretty much bet that no matter what, Gus is going to be your dad. Because he said he would." Her eyes filled with tears. "And one thing I know about him, is that he'll do what he says. That's kind of the thing. He can't say that he loves me because he's afraid of what it means. And what it doesn't mean. And he's a man of his word. So, he takes all that stuff really seriously. Another man might have just said it. To smooth things over. To make me feel better. But not your dad." Her throat went tight. Gus was this baby's dad. She knew that. She was confident in it. Even if the two of them couldn't work anything out…

"I'm not sure that I deserve so much confidence."

She turned around, and looked beyond the fence that was there to keep the deer out, tall—very tall—because they were persistent, and there was Gus. Standing there with his hands in his pockets. He was wearing a tight black T-shirt that showed off his gorgeous physique, his cowboy hat pulled low over his eyes.

The handsomest man she had ever seen.

"Well. The last couple of days have been touch and go," she said. "But I know the content of your character. So whether or not this is going the way I want… I have confidence in that."

"After everything you've been through, to be able to have confidence in me says a lot about you. Not really quite so much about me. I've been… I've been an idiot."

"Keep talking," she said, tears pressing against the back of her eyes, her throat going tight. "Really. Please keep talking."

She walked over to the fence, and he leaned against

it. She curled her fingers around the wire, and he did the same, just that fence between them now.

"I have something for you."

"Oh?"

"Do you want to come out from the garden?"

"I don't know. The fence is designed to keep pests out, Gus, and the jury is out on you."

"That's why you have to come out. I can't come in."

"Wow. Okay. That was charming. I'm annoyed you can still charm me."

She wandered out of the gate, around to where he was. She leaned against one of the long wooden poles and stared at him.

"Just a second."

He reached into the back of his truck and pulled out a heart-shaped box, a small velvet box and a gigantic teddy bear.

"What…the hell is that?"

"Romance."

And she couldn't help it, even with her heart in her throat, she laughed. "Is it?"

"Oh. And these." He reached in and grabbed a bouquet of flowers. Red roses. "Now it's romance."

"I see it now," she said. "Just the chocolates, the bear and the jewelry didn't say it. But now that you've added the roses I understand what's happening."

"Okay, I know it's cheesy. But I wanted to do that. Because we didn't have it. We didn't do romance."

"Gus," she said, moving closer to him, and taking the bear from his arms. "We have had romance. When we bought our sugar shaker. And my thrift store wedding dress. And the frying pan. When we went and got the nursery stuff for the baby. I'm not looking for you to be something that you're not."

"I am. I'm looking to be something that I'm not. Because I'm desperately afraid that what I am…that what I am falls short of what you want to have."

"Gus…"

And he sank to his knees. Down on the ground like she'd been that night at the bonfire, when she'd thrown up and he'd come to get her. To protect her, because he always did.

On the ground like she'd been in the parking lot of Smokey's when he'd taken her home, when he'd been just what she needed even when she hadn't realized what that meant.

He was on his knees now.

And it was her turn.

"I knew she was going to leave," he said. "They didn't fight that night. It was weird. I was ready to read to the boys until… That's why I read to them. We would sit in a tent on the floor in that room, and I would read to them. I would do my damnedest to drown out the sound of their fighting. Of my dad throwing things. And I'm glad that they remember that. As a happy thing. Because it wasn't for me. It was a challenge to keep talking. To try and drown it all out. Because I had to take care of them. I had to. To protect them."

"Oh…"

"One night, she packed everything up. It was quiet in the house, and I went downstairs. She handed me this box of army men."

"Oh," she said again, this time the sound coming out as one of distress, because she hadn't realized.

The army men.

"She said she was gonna come back for me. For us. She left those with me. It was a present. I told her I... loved her. She told me to be strong and take care of them until she got back. And I decided to save the army men for that day."

Her heart squeezed tight. The box wasn't opened.

All these years he'd never opened that box.

"But she never came back. And it was just me. I wanted somebody to come back for me. To protect me. I didn't want to protect everybody. I was scared. I was scared and then...he really did try to kill me. He almost did. And no one did anything about it. No one was coming for me."

Her stomach sank. "Gus, the rest of the adults on this ranch have a lot to answer for. If they had any idea that this was going on..."

"I don't know what anyone knew. Except my mother. My own mother. And I know that she was afraid of him. But I didn't expect... She just let me go ahead and be a sacrifice. And what I wanted more than anything was for her to love me. When you told me that you loved me, Alaina. Finally. Finally, somebody loved me. Because I felt all this time like there was nobody that was there for me. And I just wanted to take it. I didn't want to tell you I loved you. Because the last person I ever said it to was her. And she left. It didn't make any difference."

She crossed the space between them and bent down and wrapped her arms around him. Crushed the flowers and the candy between them, and she didn't care. "I love you," she said.

"And I let myself get really angry, that night in the bathtub. And the night you left. I let myself get really angry. About the fact that no one was there for me. No one was there for me. Except for you, Alaina. It was always you. You were my sunshine before I ever knew why."

She held his face firm in her hands. "I loved you before there were butterflies, Angus McCloud. Before I understood what it was."

"Me too." He swallowed hard, and her stomach lifted. "I did too."

"It's hard to say?"

"Yeah."

"It's okay." And it was. Because she didn't feel that distance between them. Not anymore. The walls weren't there. But Gus was there. With hearts and flowers. He was there, sharing the things that he'd been through.

"I don't think your anger makes you dangerous," she said. "I don't think your passion is wrong. I do think that you let yourself be protected by that anger. Because it lets you tell yourself that maybe you didn't deserve all this."

"That's true," he said. "It was easier to hold people at a distance that way. I'm okay with the whole world being at a distance, Alaina. But not you. Not anymore. You are all I have ever wanted. You have no idea. It ruined my life. Ruined my damn life when I looked at you that day at the lake and saw you as a woman. At least that's what I thought. Now I know it saved me. It saved my life."

As his declarations went, that was a pretty damn good one.

"I love you," she said, kissing him on the mouth.

He just held her.

But she knew.

SHE MOVED BACK in with Gus. And they worked on revamping the place together. Including the old kids' room.

Which they did decide to go ahead and make a nursery. They turned the other room into a guest room, for her mother to stay in when the baby came. It was kind of a tricky bridge to build, but she decided that she would rather build it than not.

That she would rather have a relationship with her mother than hang on to the bad things.

There were a lot of things in Gus's life that would go unresolved. Relationships with his parents. She had the power to fix things with hers. At least, as best as they could be.

She finally called her dad and told him that he was going to be a grandfather. He was actually excited. In that way that he could be. It was never going to be perfect. But she didn't need it to be. Because she wasn't lacking. Not anymore.

She and Gus decided not to find out what the baby was. And they spent a lot of time sitting on the couch with a show playing in the background, talking about the future. And one night, he put his hand on her stomach, and the baby kicked. Right against it.

"The baby knows," she said, smiling up at him. "That you're their daddy."

And something changed in Gus's face. And his eyes went bright. And he just froze for a moment, looking down at her.

"You changed my whole life, do you know that?"

"You changed mine."

He shook his head. "No. You changed everything for me. I never thought that anyone would love me. I never thought… I waited. All those years for my mom to come back. For my love to mean something. You make it mean something. This means something."

He leaned in, and he kissed her. And she could've sworn she felt dampness on her face from his. "I love you," he whispered against her mouth.

The words were rough and scraped raw, heavy, as if he wasn't sure that he could carry them.

"Thank you," she breathed.

He grinned. "I tell you I love you, and you say thank you?"

"Well, I'm about five hundred I-love-yous ahead of you. I don't hold it against you. But I'm just saying."

"I love you," he said again. And pressed her back against the couch. "I love you. I love you."

They didn't get easier with each passing declaration. They seemed harder. Rougher. And she loved him for it. Even more than she already had. Even more than she thought possible.

And it only grew.

Alaina McCloud had always been proud of the way she landed on her feet. But now she was happy to have fallen into his arms.

And she always would be.

EPILOGUE

"IT'S A BOY."

Gus was torn between looking at the tiny, screaming bundle, and his wife, who was sweaty and exhausted from hours of labor.

"A boy," he said, feeling suddenly light-headed.

"You have a son," she said, smiling up at him. And suddenly, these two people were all he could see. All he could see in the whole entire world. Nothing else mattered. Not the things that had hurt him in the past, and not anything they might face in the future. Because they had love. Stronger than anything he'd ever felt before.

"I was thinking," she said. "We can name him Cameron. Cameron McCloud."

"Perfect," he said.

And he didn't mean the name. Though, it was a fine name. But he could've named the kid anything. Because this moment was the best moment of his entire life.

Angus Evander McCloud was an immovable object once his mind was made up. And his mind was made up.

He loved Alaina McCloud. And he loved this child. And he would protect them, care for them, with all that he was.

He had thought for so long that he didn't have feelings. But here they were. Every feeling. More feelings than a man could possibly contain.

He wasn't his father. He was *this* little boy's father. He was Alaina's husband. He wasn't an abandoned son. He was a man with brothers who cared for him. He was a man with a family. And those were the things that mattered.

The only things. From now to forever.

* * * * *

HARLEQUIN
PLUS

Try the best multimedia
subscription service for romance
readers like you!

Read, Watch and Play.

Experience the easiest way to get
the romance content you crave.

Start your **FREE TRIAL** at
www.harlequinplus.com/freetrial.